Autumn Sand

Joe Football

Drop One Publications

Joe Football

ISBN 978-0-9967954-5-6
Library of Congress Catalogue Number 2017942182
Cover design by Pixel Mischief
Edited by All About the Edits
Proofread and Formatted by The Last Step Proofreading

Chapter 1

Favor

I hate parties. No, scratch that. I hate football. Ugh, correction, I hate parties for football. If you grew up in the type of family I did, then you would hate it also. My friends Jana and Cal, however, don't share my skewed opinion on the subject matter.

"Come on, Favor. This will be the most epic party of the year," my overly enthusiastic cheerleader friend, Jana, begs me.

This is a conversation we revisit weekly. I exhale loudly while covering my eyes with my forearm. "Isn't that what you said about *last* week's party?"

"Doll, last week's party was epic. This week's party will be epic-er," Cal pipes up.

"Epic-er? Is that even a word?" I sit up on my bed, rolling my eyes at Cal.

"Well if it isn't, then someone needs to contact Miriam-Webster," he jokes, as he flips through pages of Jana's copy of *Vogue* while sprawled across her bed.

"Guys, you know how I feel about football parties," I explain, yet again.

Jana places her nail polish bottle on her desk, and walks over to me while waving her hands in the air to dry her freshly painted pink nails. Her lips part slightly as she stands in front of me, and her eyes soften. "Favor, I know how much you dislike the reminders, but you really are missing out on so much." She opens her mouth again to speak, but closes it and bites her bottom lip.

A swelling of emotions forms in my throat closing my passageway. Cal places the magazine on the bed and strides over to us. His large brown eyes are teary. Bending slightly, he pulls me into a hug and squeezes gently, the simple action speaking volumes. I choke up some more.

"I love you guys so much," I manage to croak out as I lean deeper into Cal's hug.

"We love you too," Cal mumbles into my hair. He inhales deeply and relaxes his hold. "Damn girl, your hair smells really good." He pulls away and stares at me with a wide grin on his face, before pulling me in to sniff my hair again.

I push him gently and laugh at his antics. Cal is known for breaking a mood when it gets too serious. Like Jana, he hates to see me upset.

Mindful of her nails, Jana carefully loops her arm around my waist. "You really should come with us. No one knows who your family is. Your secret is always safe."

Since I use my mother's maiden name, no one at this school, other than my friends, knows about my family's football dynasty. I often joke with Cal and Jana, calling my parents Mr. and Mrs. Joe Football. My father is Kyne Hollister, the former star quarterback for the National Football League's team, the Charleston Blockers. America's favorite team, known for their over-the-top-pay for their players. Their stadium, right here in South Carolina, has the latest technology for player advancement.

My father is kidded to be the unofficial governor of the state, with his movie star good looks and larger-than-life personality. America wept when he retired from football, while my brother and I celebrated. *Finally*, we foolishly thought, *we get to have our father to ourselves.*

The day he was inducted into the NFL's Hall of Fame, I took it as a personal slight. While the rest of the country celebrated his passing yards and touchdowns, I only saw him being rewarded for missing countless birthday parties, and dance performances. Ha. *How dare they*, I thought, and decided to do a protest of my own, wearing a "Football Sucks" t-shirt, complete with the graphic art of a middle finger. When my mother saw me come down the steps as we were getting ready to leave for the ceremony, she quickly told me to go to my room and stay there. I did so happily, flipping them both the bird, further fueling the drama flame. My brother just stood off to the side and laughed, finding the entire exchange hysterical.

Even though he was retired, my father was frequently brought in by the Blockers as an advisor, until he eventually went on to become a sports analyst for the NFL network. The time my brother and I thought we would get with him became a distant memory. My brother did get to spend more time with our father than I did, only because Dad was training him to be a star quarterback like himself.

"Honestly, I don't understand why you don't like going. They have some really hot guys on the team, and even hotter ones that go to those parties. I, for one, am a living testament to that, since I'm hot and I go," Cal says matter-of-factly, as if everyone knows this.

"Yeah. None of whom are interested in you," I joke.

He places his hands over his heart. "You wound me," Cal mock pouts.

I blow him an air kiss, which he catches and places on his cheek with a smile and a bat of his eyelashes.

"Favor, I swear you're missing out on the whole college experience. You need to come out tonight. If you don't like it, we'll leave." Jana pleads her case once again, hoping to change my mind.

"Guys, seriously. I would prefer just to do some stuff around campus by myself. I'll catch the next party with you."

They both look at me, knowing I'm full of it. Cal crosses his arms over his chest. "No. You're coming with us tonight."

Realizing that my two closest friends will not give in, I throw my hands up in the air in defeat. "Fine."

Jana and Cal jump up and down, high fiving each other, like they just won the lottery. "Finally. Miss Thang is coming out to PAR-TAY." Cal announces.

I roll my eyes heavenward, hoping this night goes by quickly.

****

We arrive at the bonfire for the team, where the air is electric with excitement, and everyone is in a partying mood. Everyone except me. As soon as the three of us get out of my car, Jana is swarmed by members of her cheerleading squad, who immediately drag her towards the kegs. Jana, of course, pulls Cal and me along; no man left behind and all that.

Cal is pumping beer from a keg, when a huge guy in a Cougars t-shirt pukes by his feet. Cal jumps back just in time, and the player just laughs, murmuring an apology as he stumbles off with a couple of girls draped around him.

"Wow that was *epic*," I say dryly to Cal.

He smiles and winks at me. "It's all a part of the experience. Lighten up."

"Yeah, whatever," I call out, as I turn and head towards the coolers on the other side of the bonfire.

"Where ya going?"

"Grabbing a bottled water. I'm the designated, remember." I wave him off and continue my trek towards the coolers.

Images of my mother in tears after receiving the devastating news that my brother, Trevor, had been killed in a car wreck flood my thoughts. It's been three years. He and his best friend were juniors at this very college when he was suddenly taken from us that night. Because of Wayne's drunk driving, I lost my only ally in this world.

That crash took two lives that day. Wayne was arrested for DUI. He did a stint in jail and got out early on probation. He lost his football scholarship, and as a result, his life spiraled out of control. I hear that he is back on campus to finish his degree, and I pray I'll never see him again.

I grab a bottled water from the cooler, glancing at the drunken college students. *God, what am I doing here?* I stomp away from the party goers to get some peace and quiet. Finding a log near the lake, I sit down to drink my water and watch the party from afar.

"Needed a break, huh?" a deep voice says from behind me. I turn my head to see who's talking, and closely-cropped hair and brown eyes stare back at me.

"Yeah, I did. Is that your excuse too?"

"Looks like it," he replies, as he stretches his long muscular legs out from his sitting position on a nearby log.

I look away from him, twisting my bracelet as the sound of different insects hum around us. The weather is humid, and I wipe at the beads of sweat forming on my upper lip. Days like this, my brother and I would run down to the lake and take a dip to cool off. A heavy weight hits my heart, and I swallow down the tennis ball-sized lump in my throat.

"I always see you around campus, but never at the parties."

My head whips around. "Really? Do I know--"

"*Favor.*" I cringe at the sound of Jameson's nasally voice. "Favor, where are you?" My question is instantly forgotten as I look around for a place to hide.

"Umm, isn't that you he's calling for?" the deep voice asks, a hint of amusement in his tone.

"Yeah, seems to be," I whisper as I crouch lower to the ground.

"Not interested in being found?" He fights a chuckle.

"Not really. Well, not by him." I say the last part under my breath.

Effortlessly hoisting himself off the log, he walks over to me and offers his hand. Looking at it, I weigh my options. My mother always said you can tell a lot about a man by his hands.

Well-manicured and no callouses means he is not used to hard work. A man who gets others to do the job, someone who keeps secrets. Calloused and rough means he doesn't mind rolling up his sleeves to get a job done, a man to trust. Decision made, I place my hand in his outstretched one and instantly feel the scratch of the callouses against my skin.

Helping me stand, he places his finger over his mouth. I follow him towards the wooded area near the pond.

"He won't be able to find you here," he says conspiratorially.

My muscles relax as I sigh. "Thanks."

"Why were you hiding from Jameson?"

I shrug. "No reason."

He arches an eyebrow at me. "Word around campus is the two of you are an item."

I look away briefly. Jameson is considered football royalty on campus. He, like his father, came to this college as a backup quarterback. His father transferred to another college after a year to become a starter. Similarly, Jameson took over the starting position after the Cougars' starter had a career-ending injury last season. But Jameson lost the top spot to a newcomer who transferred from Penn State.

Jameson, as hard as he tries, will never really have the talent to be a starter, and his dad hasn't forgiven him. My father, since the loss of my brother, has taken him under his wing.

Even though we are not, and never will be, an item, the rumors persist. There isn't enough room in a relationship for three people. In this case, me, Jameson, and his oversized ego. We are as different as night and day. He loves to flaunt his parents' wealth. I try not to think or talk about mine. He rides off his father's name as being the son of a former NFL quarterback. I enrolled under my mother's maiden name, Fontaine, for the anonymity.

Hairy legs and thighs appear in my peripheral vision. "Umm, what do you think you're doing?"

"I'm going to take a dip in the lake. You can join me if you want," he says as he straightens the band of his boxer briefs.

Decorum dictates that I should look away but before I do, I steal one last longing look at his perfection.

He is tall, lean, and muscular. Most would call it an athletic build. I, however, would say he's built like a god. The moon's rays shine on areas of his chiseled, sweat-glistened body. As if in a trance, my eyes linger on his form longingly.

Lithe for his build, he runs into the lake and starts swimming. I want to strip down and join him, but I'm also hesitant to get too close.

He pops out of the water and calls out to me. "Are you coming or what?" he has a wicked twinkle in his eyes that makes my heart skip a beat.

Against my better judgment for the second time today, I strip out of my clothes, down to just my bra and panties, and step into the lake, swimming up to him. The cool lake water is a nice reprieve from the warm, humid weather. He gives me the brightest smile. "Glad you joined me." His voice becomes slightly husky.

"Well, you left me hanging over there." I try not to get caught up in his penetrating gaze but fail miserably. Feeling my cheeks warm, I look for a distraction. "So why did you walk away from the party?"

"Ehh. I don't know. These parties are starting to bore me." He looks past me, in the direction of the bonfire before bringing his eyes back to mine again. "They all seem to be the same. One drunk fest after another. Sometimes I just need a break from it all. You know what I mean?" His eyes search mine as I take in his words.

I do. I understand exactly what he means. "I guess so."

"Hey guys, looks like the party has moved to the lake," a girl, who is most definitely three sheets to the wind, yells out. We both let out a groan.

"Ahh, guess the gig is up."

"Guess so," I whisper, anxious to find an escape plan and perhaps a few more minutes alone with him.

"Favor, there you are. I've been looking for you," Jameson yells from the edge of the lake, while stripping out of his clothes. In just his boxers, he swims over to me and the sex god on a stick. The lake is starting to get more and more crowded with partygoers at this point.

"Hey, I see my friends over there...see you around." He swims off before I can respond. My eyes follow the ripples of water behind him as he swims further away.

"What were you doing out here with him?" Jameson lectures as he reaches me.

The hairs on the back of my neck rise, and I don't bother turning to face him. "None of your business."

I can only imagine what his facial expression looks like right now. "Stay away from him."

At his words, I turn to look at a glaring Jameson. "Oh? Why?" I bite out.

"Because..."

"Because is not an answer." I lift my finger and jab it into his chest. "Let me remind you one more time. I'm not your girlfriend. It's none of your business what I do or who I do it with."

"Your father--"

I cut him off again. "My father is none of your business either."

My heart beats faster against my chest as I feel my temples throb. I turn around, looking for Jana and Cal. I'm so ready to leave. I spot them and begin swimming in their direction without another word to Jameson. Jana and Cal are with Regan, the muscular god, and a guy with tattoos. The one with the tattoos I recognize as a minor campus celebrity. He's the frontman of a rock band that has a pretty loyal following in this state. State of Mind, I think.

Trying not to once again stare at him, I turn my head slightly towards Jana and Cal. "Guys, I'm leaving." But I just can't help myself, and I peek at him from the corner of my eye. "Are you ready?"

"Already? I feel like we just got here." Cal pushes his bottom lip out playfully.

"You're always such a killjoy, Favor," Regan, the campus wannabe, adds. In our freshman year Regan, Jana, Cal and I were close. Regan and Jana both tried out for the cheerleading squad. Jana got in and Regan did not. Crushed that she didn't make the team, Regan spread some ugly rumors about Jana around campus. Jana chose to give Regan a second chance; I on the other hand have not.

Jana looks at me with unsure eyes. "Uh..." She looks at the two guys, as if she's trying to make the most important decision of her life.

"Let her stay," Regan protests, wrapping her arms around the tattooed guy and tipping her chin at me. "You should stay too."

"I think if she wants to go, everyone needs to respect that," the stranger says with authority while looking at me. His words have an absolute finality to them, leaving no room for anyone to question him.

Regan looks visibly upset by this and turns her attention back to the tattooed guy. He grabs her by the waist and pulls her closer to him as she squeals in delight.

"Come on, Jana, Cal. Let's go. Please."

Cal looks like he wants to argue, but decides against it. The three of us swim back to shore. I dry myself off with my shirt, and my breath catches when I look up, seeing the stranger still watching me with almost a hint of amusement in his eyes.

Chapter 2

Brice

I stare at her and her friends as she swims back to shore. As the starting quarterback for the team, I always get attention from girls. Favor, on the other hand, is the exception to the rule. A rule I hope to break soon. My freshman year, I tried to ask her out on a date, but she cut me off quicker than a hangnail. So, I always look at her from afar. I've labeled her my golden unicorn. My mythical creature that's so far out of reach.

"Hey, man. Let's grab some chicks and go," my best friend Egon says, with a girl already in his arms.

"Heeey." I think her name is Regan whines.

"Sorry babe. I meant he should grab a chick and let's go." He smiles down at her. She leaps up and wraps her long legs around his waist, kissing him.

My best friend Egon is the frontman for an up-and-coming band called State of Mind. The group is mostly locally known, but they are gaining some traction with their fan base. They have also been slated to play a few halftime shows at our home football games. I wouldn't be surprised if he and his band get a record deal before we graduate college in two more years. When we were kids, Egon always dreamed of being in a band, and now his dream is finally here.

He has a certain celebrity status around campus, which makes him an instant chick magnet. Also, girls dig the ink on his body. I can't tell you how many times he's gotten laid because of it. At one time, I considered getting tatted up simply for that reason alone. But I can't complain. I get my fair share of the ladies, most of which are one-night stands. Now and then, I might go for a second, but never a third. Girls get caught up with emotions and shit. Can't have that. Favor Fontaine, on the other hand, is a woman I could get into a relationship with. She's beautiful, smart, doesn't do the party thing, and she seems to be about her business.

"Hey. You think the rumors are true?" I ask Egon.

"Huh? What rumors?" he replies, with Regan dangling from his arm.

"Is Favor dating Jameson?" I try not to look like a creeper as I watch her dry off.

He places Regan back on her feet and looks in the direction that I'm staring. "Man, you still chasing that?"

"I'm one of her closest friends you know," Regan chimes in.

I cross my arms over my chest. "Is that so?" I play along.

"Yeah. And she's with Jameson, for sure," she slurs slightly.

"Is that so?" I say again, wishing she would disappear.

"Yep." She giggles as Egon picks her up and kisses her.

"Bro, come on. Let's eighty-six this party. Find yourself a bedwarmer and let's go."

"Nah. I'm not in the mood. But you're right, let's get out of here," I say as I watch Favor and her friends drive off in the distance.

"You sure you don't want to pick out a sweet piece of ass?" Egon goads.

"I'm good, bro. Seriously." Girls make it too easy for me. There isn't any more chase now that I'm the starting quarterback for the team. I'm, for lack of a better word...bored.

"Mind if I bring this one back to our room?" Egon tips his head towards Regan.

I look at her and shrug. "What do I care?" I don't know why he would want to hook up with this girl at all. She's known around campus as a bottom feeder.

"If you want, I'll do you both." The smile that, a second ago was all for Egon, is now aimed in my direction.

Oh hell NO. She thinks I'm dipping in after my best friend? Egon and I have always considered ourselves to be brothers, but that's toeing a line. "Ehh, nah. I'm good," I say, giving my best friend a 'what the fuck' look.

She tips her chin down and frowns. Egon looks at her with disgust, but I know him; he doesn't feel like throwing this fish back into the ocean to find another. This is an easy piece of ass, most likely a one and done for him.

"Brice and I don't exactly like to share, if you know what I mean."

"Oh." Her chin touches her chest bone. "I was just joking anyway."

"Riiiight," I turn around and swim to shore, the two of them following behind me.

After drying off, I drive us back to our dorm.

Once inside of our room, the two of them waste no time in getting it on. After an hour, I'm ready to tape her mouth shut. I hate chicks who put on the theatrics in bed like they are in a goddamn porno. I know I'm good in bed, but damn, baby...really? They go at it until the sun comes up. Figures it would be my luck that Egon would pick tonight to be the *Energizer* bunny.

When silence finally settles in our room, I'm able to drift off to sleep with dreams of Favor screaming out my name. Yeah, that's more the way I like it.

Chapter 3

Favor

I've had a grueling day of classes, and I expect it to become even more exhausting with my trig class to finish up my long day. As I walk past the math building, I see Jameson holding court as usual in the front. I glance at Regan, who is pleading with Tattoo Guy about something. I duck my head in laughter and rush by them. Poor girl, she'll just never learn.

Taking my seat in the back of the class, I power up my tablet, and quickly go over last week's class notes, just in case I'm called to answer a question. A couple of my classmates say hello to me, and I wave, without looking up or breaking concentration.

Professor Todd's presence is announced by his squeaky shoes and a clang of the metal door. Placing his briefcase and folders on his desk, he begins to write on the board without a word. He is notorious for giving surprise quizzes, and the class all breathes a collective sigh of relief as we read the notes he has written.

The creaky sound of the unoiled door reverberates throughout the classroom, and all eyes focus on a newcomer, who walks towards the professor. My eyes bulge at the sight of the person who took my beloved brother from me. I feel as if I'm having an out-of-body experience as they have their brief conversation, before he turns to find a vacant seat. Hushed whispers from those who recognize him echo in the room, and those that do not, try to get a better look at who's causing the commotion.

It's Wayne. He doesn't see me in the back because I have scrunched down in my chair, so low I can barely see over the person's head in front of me. Wayne takes a seat somewhere in the middle of the room, and I try not to lose my lunch. I haven't set eyes on him since before he killed my brother.

My mouth feels like cotton, and I desperately try to remember how to breathe again. Memories of my last conversation with my brother go through my head. I was supposed to visit him on campus, and we were finalizing the details of my trip. We ended our conversation with our typical teasing, him calling me 'Favor Fav' and me calling him 'Terror Trev', neither of us knowing that would be the last time we would speak again. Otherwise, I would've told him I loved him in place of my playful joke.

Someone next to me places a stack of handouts on my desk, causing me to jump, knocking my tablet and sending the papers flying across the floor. All eyes turn to look at me, but only one pair makes the hairs on the back of my neck stand on end.

A few of my classmates seated near me help to retrieve the papers as I mumble out an apology and my thanks. With shaky hands, I put right the papers and pass them on to the next student. I refuse to look up for fear of my eyes settling on him.

I want him to feel the pain he has caused my family and me. He was like a brother to me, and my mother even designated one of the guest rooms as his bedroom. Images of my father the night we received the phone call, running into Wayne's room like a tornado, throwing his things to the ground. Gathering Wayne's belongings, taking long strides past my mother, who was crumpled on the floor in the vestibule, clutching a picture of Trevor to her breast. My father's hopes of erasing Wayne's memory from our house like a discarded sketch only cemented it further. A cloak of mourning enveloped our house and instead of me being able to cry on his shoulders as friends while we grieved my brother, I had to find solace elsewhere. I was utterly alone when Trevor died, and Wayne went to jail. Not having a normal relationship with my parents was only heightened further by Trevor's death. The wailing of my mother from that night still haunts me to this day.

My hour and a half class ticks by slowly as I try desperately not to hear my mother's cries and that blasted ring from the phone that announced my brother's death. As soon as Professor Todd stops the lecture and dismisses us, I am the first one out of my seat to speak to him. I gather my things quickly and rush to the front of the room.

"Umm, excuse me, Professor Todd." I try to speak as quietly as possible as various students walk past me.

"Yes, Favor?" he asks as he packs away some papers in his briefcase, barely giving me a glance over the rim of his glasses.

"Is Wayne Anderson in this class now?" My voice sounds shrill.

Professor Todd gives me a quizzical look. "Yes, he is." He stops what he was doing and gives me his undivided attention. "He used to be a student of mine a few years ago, but had to drop out of school for personal reasons. He is now enrolled back in this school and taking this class." He pushes his glasses up from the tip of his nose. "Is there a problem?"

21

My heart thunders in my chest. "I-I was just curious." I look down at my feet. Eyes. I feel two sets of eyes on me. Professor Todd is still staring at me, and the other set is from someone standing behind me. "Are there any more openings in your other classes?" My words come out mumbled because my chin is tucked into my neck.

His eyes narrow. "Do you know Mr. Wayne Anderson?"

The sound of Wayne's name out loud makes me lift my head quickly. Feeling lightheaded, I reach out my hand to hold his desk for support. I swallow hard and shake my head slowly because telling him the truth is not an option.

"Are you one of the many students at this school who refuses to forgive his past? I'm ashamed of you, Miss Fontaine. You're one of my best and brightest students, and if you're holding an imaginary grudge against this young man for an incident that has nothing to do with you, it is a sad day." Frown lines form around his mouth.

No one knows that my brother was Trevor Hollister, the star quarterback of this college who was killed in a drunken driving accident by his best friend. So, when Professor Todd speaks to me in this way, I flinch and swallow back the tears that threaten to make an appearance.

"I'm sorry to have wasted your time," I mutter and turn to leave.

I look up and see Wayne staring at me from the door, pain in his eyes. His mouth opens, but nothing comes out of it. I brush past him quickly, running through the halls towards the dean of the math department's office to see if I can switch out of this class. Tears stream down my cheeks, blurring my vision. I wipe at my eyes frantically and hit a solid mass. I stumble backward, but large hands grab my arms, steadying me, before gravity takes course.

"Whoa there. Are you okay?"

I grimace. That voice sounds familiar. I look up and see it's the stranger from the bonfire. I quickly look away as my cheeks warm.

"I'm so sorry," I mumble as I glance at the floor.

Still holding onto my arms, he asks uncertainly, "What were you running from?" He looks over my shoulder.

I close my eyes briefly. "My demons, I guess," I answer as truthfully as I can.

He tilts his head, studying me. When I say nothing further, he exhales. "Okay. Are you going inside to see the dean?" I nod, and he smiles. "So am I, actually." He opens the door, "Ladies first," and waits for me to walk through before following behind me.

I ask the dean's secretary if there is availability for the dean to see me now. She rolls her eyes and mutters under her breath as she checks the calendar on the computer.

"What is the meeting for?"

"My class schedule." I shift nervously on my feet, hoping I can pass her interrogation.

"I guess you can, if you are quick." She looks over my shoulder and then back at me again.

I mumble a thank you and take a seat.

I fidget in my chair as Professor Todd's words go through my head, and I try not to notice him staring at me from the chair beside me. The dean finally steps out of his office and smiles at both of us.

"Favor? I'm surprised to see you here. Would you mind if I speak to Brice first?" Brice. *So that's his name.*

"Dean Smith, I'm okay with waiting. You can let Favor go in first," Brice interjects.

Dean Smith perks an eyebrow. "You sure? I don't want to make you late for practice."

Practice? Oh, figures I would be attracted to a football player. I should've guessed it from the beginning, considering I met him at a bonfire thrown for the football team. I was hoping that, by some off chance, he was just a regular student. A well fit, muscular student with the body of a Greek god.

"I'm sure," Brice says, and gives me a kind smile that I return before heading into Dean Smith's office.

"Okay, Favor, have a seat," he says, as he closes the door behind us. Taking a seat, I wring my hands. "What's the problem?"

"I'd like to switch out of my trig class." I rush the words out, for fear that I might start to cry again.

He leans forward in his seat. "Why? Is there a problem with the curriculum?"

"No, sir. I would like to see if I can get an earlier class, perhaps?"

"Favor, you do realize that you are a month into the class already. It would be tough for me to do this for you."

I'm frantic at this point and ready to burst into tears. My shoulders droop, and my head dips down. I search my brain for an excuse to give him. "It's just that, this trig class is at the end of the day, and I feel that I'm way too exhausted by that time. I have a lull in between my morning classes. I can maybe fill it with another class instead, freeing me up for an early afternoon. I can get in much more studying that way."

"Favor, I really would love to do this for you. But all the classes are booked. Your only other option would be independent study if you need to do this. Granted, you won't get the full credit as you are with your current class, but it is something. It is an online course, which doesn't work for everyone, but some thrive on it."

"Sold, I'd love to do that." I place my hands on my knees that are knocking.

He looks at me warily. "Umm, okay. Again, you do understand that this is highly unusual a month into the class?"

"Yes, Dean Smith, I do, but it would be greatly appreciated." I give him my best fake smile.

"Okay, then. I'll have you fill out some paperwork for dropping a class and adding in the independent study class."

"No problem. I can do this on the school's student portal?"

"Yes. I'll email you the link. Please make sure you complete it no later than tomorrow."

"I will," I say as I stand up to leave. "Thanks again, Dean Smith."

He gives me a smile, and I open the door to leave, feeling like my burdens have been lifted. When I walk back into the waiting area, I see Brice. Back straight and eyes forward, I straighten my outfit, and I'm about to walk past him, but he speaks to me. "See you around." I turn around to see his scorching gaze on me. I tingle slightly.

"Brice. I can see you now," Dean Smith calls, breaking the spell Brice has over me. He turns to look at the dean, and I use this as my opportunity to escape. Here I am, running from yet another demon. This time, it is a six-foot-three brown-eyed demon that makes me melt whenever he looks at me.

Outside, I stop to catch my breath. Cal sees me from across the quad and waves at me frantically to wait for him.

"Where are you off to?" Cal asks.

"On my way back to the dorm to study."

He grabs my arm and tugs me in the opposite direction of my dorm. "Oh no, you're not. You're coming with me. Jana has squad practice, and we're going to watch. Also, the Cougars are practicing, so we get to look at some really hot guys in tight pants."

I freeze. The thought of stepping foot in a football stadium sends my stomach into knots. I hated football because it took my mother and father away from me for most of my life.

Now I hate it because it also serves as a reminder of watching my brother play in this stadium. I feel ill at the thought, and pull my arm out of Cal's grasp. "I don't think so. I really need to get back to the dorm."

Cal digs his heels in. "No. You're always studying. Just be a normal college student for once. Please? Keep me company, at least, and support Jana. You never do anything with us, but you call us your closest friends."

Way to lay on the guilt trip. I'm already feeling shitty about the events of my day and now this. But he's right. I don't do the things that they like to do. I guess I *do* suck as a friend. I bite my bottom lip. "Fine, I'll go. But afterward, I do have to do some studying."

Cal gives me a hug, and we link arms, heading to the stadium. Sitting on the bleachers, we watch as the cheerleaders work on some new routines. Jana is amazing with her backflips and jumps. Most of the girls watch her in envy. I'm pretty sure I would've been on the cheerleading squad as well, if my brother were still alive. I was the leader of my high school cheer squad, and my mother had hopes of me joining this squad as well. But after Trevor's death, my heart just wasn't in it anymore. Sometimes I wonder if I ever was really into it. I think I was doing it just to feel a connection to my mother, not realizing at the time that it would never connect us the way I was looking for.

"Jana, you kicked ass out there, girlfriend." Cal beams. I was so caught up in my thoughts I didn't realize practice had finished.

"Yeah, Jana, you looked great out there." And she did. Jana is a natural-born cheerleader. She is always cheering people on in a supportive way with her bubbly personality. Jana has such an infectious laugh that makes anyone smile and feel warm inside.

"Thanks, guys. Favor, thank you for coming out." Jana smiles brightly at me as she wipes her forehead with a towel.

"Well, Cal, wouldn't let me not go. He has pointed out that I'm a horrible friend," I joke.

"Oh, Cal. She isn't a horrible friend. She's perfect." Jana beams.

He rolls his eyes upward. "Oh, go change clothes so we can grab something to eat."

"Okay. Be right back." She jogs off to the lockers.

"Oh, look at that hottie over there." He points to a football player on the field running to catch a ball.

"You can't see his face. How do you know he's hot?"

"His ass is hot. Just look at it. You can bounce a quarter off of it, doll," Cal says, as he leans forward with his elbows on his knees and chin on hands.

I look at the players running various scrimmages plays on the field. I recognize most of them because of my dad and brother. The team looks pretty good out there, and I wonder if Brice is among them. I don't know his number or what position he is on on the team. Jana walks back over to us, fully-showered and changed. She has her hair up in a messy ponytail that is touching her shoulders and a hot pink top with low white waist yoga pants. The colors look great on her.

"Ready?" she asks.

Cal and I grab our things and head down the steps, onto the field. The football team is on break from practice. Some of them spread out across the field to stretch, others get some water, and still others hang around to discuss plays with each other.

The three of us pass some of the players as we figure out where we want to go eat. The group of players we are walking past is talking initially, but when we come near them, they stop, and all eyes are on us. I absentmindedly play with the bracelets that Trevor gave me for my birthday years ago, while wishing we could hide from the stares.

"What are you doing out here on our field, fag," one of the players yells.

"No cocksuckers allowed," another calls out, as the rest of the small group throws more horrendous names towards Cal.

Cal's face turns red, and his eyes begin to water. Jana grabs his arm. "Don't listen to those idiots," she says, loud enough for them to hear her.

"Jana, what ya hanging around him for? I thought I taught you the definition of a real man last week in my bed. If you need another lesson, just come over tonight," one of the players smirks.

"Fuck you, *KEVIN*." Jana yells back.

"We already did. Got the nail marks on my back to prove it," Kevin thunders back.

Jana's bottom lip quivers and her eyes water. I look around and see Jameson just staring, not willing to step in and stop them. *Asshole.* "Jana, Cal, let's just get out of here. These losers are not worth our time." I turn to glower at the players.

"No fags ALLOWED. We don't want you cheering for our team," a few of the team members yell out.

"ENOUGH. Leave them ALONE." Brice's voice booms from behind us. I turn to see him with his helmet in his hand, glaring at his teammates.

"Just having fun," Kevin replies, taking a step forward.

"I don't give a shit. *Leave. Them. Alone.*" Brice spits out angrily, moving the helmet from one hand to the other.

"Or what?" Kevin snarls, clearly prepping for a fight.

Brice drops his helmet to the ground and walks forward, flexing his muscles. "I think you and I both know what'll happen." Brice gets directly in Kevin's face. "Care to test me?"

Kevin' eyes widen, and he takes a step back. "No, Brice. We're good."

"Anyone else got a problem?" Brice looks at his teammates.

Everyone shakes their head and turns to walk away. I place my hand on top of my chest to steady my thundering heartbeat. Jameson just stands, looking at us, as Brice turns around. "You guys okay?"

Jana and Cal look visibly shaken. "Yes, I think so," I say, as I glance at my friends, before my eyes meet his. "Thank you."

"I can't stand asshole behavior like that. It's a total dick move," he replies, taking a few steps closer to me. His brown eyes have a genuine look of concern. "You sure you and your friends are okay?"

"Yeah. I should get them out of here."

"Listen, if you wait, I'll shower and change. Maybe I can come with you?" All the anger that was in him, ready to take on the members of his team a few minutes ago, is gone. He looks kind of bashful, in a cute sort of way.

"Umm, I don't know..." I start, but Cal interrupts me.

"We're going to grab some pizza in town. We'll wait for you in the parking lot," Cal says, as I stare at him, my mouth agape.

"Okay. Let me just tell Coach I'm cutting out. I'll see you guys out there in a minute." Brice jogs off in the direction of his coach.

"What the hell?" I punch Cal in the arm.

He rubs the spot where I hit him. "He has a thing for you, and it is evident to anyone with eyes that you have a thing for him. Give him a chance," Cal defends, all signs of his earlier sadness gone.

"Yeah, he came to our rescue. Something that douchebag Jameson didn't do," Jana adds.

I look over to see Jameson walking towards us. He steps into the circle that Cal, Jana, and I have formed. "What do you want?" My tone is deadpan when I ask him.

"Listen, I'm sorry I didn't say anything. I couldn't. These are my teammates, and we all stick together," he says, while looking down at his feet.

"Well, Brice didn't seem to have a problem with stepping up," Cal throws at him.

Jameson's head pops up as if we slapped him. "Well, Brice always seems to do what Brice wants to do."

"Guess that's why he's the starting quarterback, and you're not," Jana replies with a smile on her lips that doesn't reach her eyes.

"Favor, you understand, don't you? Besides, Cal, you know how some of the members feel. Why would you put yourself in that type of predicament by coming here?"

I jab my finger in Jameson's chest. "How dare you. Don't you put this on Cal as if it's *his* fault. It's those asshole team members of yours. Are you saying you want Cal to hide? Or not be himself? I swear, Jameson, do you hear yourself at all? You sound like a bigger asshole than the rest of them." I storm off towards the exit, with Cal and Jana behind me. Once out in the parking lot, I let out a scream of frustration.

"Forget him, honey." Cal offers me support when it should be the other way around.

I close my eyes and count to ten before responding. "He's already forgotten."

"So, Brice stuck up for us. That was pretty impressive," Jana says brightly. She can always find a rainbow somewhere.

"Yeah, it was. I just met him recently at the bonfire. But I didn't learn his name until earlier today," I say.

"You mean, you had a one on one with Brice at the bonfire?" Cal asked, enthused.

"He helped hide me when Jameson was looking for me."

"Oh. My. GOD. You've been holding out on us, you little minx," Cal yells out while clapping his hands together.

"There was nothing to tell, actually." What was I going to say about that night? I met a really, really hot guy, with a baritone voice that made me want to throw my panties at him and, oh by the way, I didn't get his name? Yeah, that would've gone over well with this group.

"Well, he's sure digging you. I've never seen him look at a girl the way he was looking at you," Jana admits.

"He has quite the reputation as a manwhore around campus. Well, he and his best friend, Egon." Cal places his index finger on his cheek. "I swear, what is with those Philly boys? They are all kinds of sexy. Are they breeding them like that over there?" Cal asks, as he fans himself with his hands in an exaggerated fashion.

Jana nudges me in my side, and I see Brice walking towards us. We abruptly break our conversation and smile at him. He stops and smiles back awkwardly. "What? Do I have something on my shirt?"

"No, but you most definitely have something," Cal says under his breath.

Brice cuts a glance at him, and I quickly say, "Don't mind Cal. He's still in shock from what happened in the stadium." I allow my eyes to roam over Brice's physique, hoping he doesn't notice.

The four of us drive into town for pizza. We order two pies, as it seems Brice can eat one all by himself. However, I can't even eat because I can't stop staring at Brice, all while trying to pretend I'm eating. A couple of girls stop by our table to ask Brice for his autograph and slide him their numbers. Brice takes the numbers and as soon as the girls aren't looking, he tears up the paper. The door chimes as Tattoo Guy walk into the restaurant.

"Brice-o," Tattoo Guy calls out.

Brice turns and smiles brightly. He stands and gives his friend a man hug. "Egon, I'd like you to meet Favor. Favor, this is my best friend, Egon. You already know Jana and Cal, I think."

Egon shakes my hand and flashes his gray eyes at me. "Yeah, I think I've met Jana and Cal once or twice at some parties. You're Regan's friends...right?"

Jana and Cal both nod and say their hellos back. "Sit and join us, bro," Brice says. Egon takes a seat next to us, while watching the waitress in a too-tight skirt walk by. He shakes his head and turns to look at us.

"Wow, so, *the* Favor. Finally, I get to meet the Golden Unicorn," Egon goads. Brice gives him a warning look that Egon ignores.

My eyebrows knit together in confusion. "Golden Unicorn?"

He looks at Brice and then back to me. "Uh, nothing." He clears his throat. "Listen, I can't stay long. I have band practice. Why don't you three come out and watch my band play this Friday? I can get you tickets at Brice's table." Jana and Cal both say yes before I even have a chance to digest what he said. "Great. I'll leave the tickets at the door." He stands and waves bye to us, before heading to the counter to place an order.

We settle our tab and head back to campus. Brice drove, so he parks at mine and Jana's dorm, and walks with us. Jana and Cal walk ahead of us to, I think, give us some privacy. But I don't know what to say to him. He's a football player, and I just can't put myself out there for that type of trouble.

"Would you like to go out sometime?" Brice asks, pulling me away from my thoughts.

"Umm. Well, we are going out, aren't we, on Friday?"

"I meant, just the two of us. I hear it's called a date these days." He smirks at me.

I nibble on my bottom lip while avoiding his eyes. "I can't," I say, as Jana and Cal, who have apparently heard our conversation, spin around and glare at me. *So much for privacy.* I pointedly ignore them.

"Okay. Is it a timing issue?" he persists.

"Umm. No, it's, umm...I don't date football players," I say. Cal and Jana's mouths drop open.

"You don't date football players? Didn't you used to date Jameson?" His head tilts to the side.

"I never dated Jameson." That's the truth. Jameson and I never dated. Our relationship was quite a different thing.

"You never dated Jameson?"

"No, I didn't," I say, with more conviction.

"Okay. So why don't you date football players?" he presses.

"I don't like football," I say honestly.

"I'm not asking you to watch me play. Just out on a date."

"Listen I can't. I'm sorry, but I just can't." I walk past Brice and my friends, and run into the dorm as if my life depended on it. I rush into my room and shut the door, finally able to breathe, knowing I took the coward's way out.

Chapter 4
Brice

Walking through campus, I can't help but replay last night's events. Favor completely freaked out on me and ran away, over me asking her out on a date. I thought I felt the connection we both had, or was that in my head simply because it's something I've wanted for so long.

I even interrupted Egon's band practice last night because I needed to talk about it. When did I turn into a chick? Guys don't discuss how they are feeling, and analyze what another person did or said. But her response threw me. Hell, even her friends were standing with their mouths open.

After Egon spent most of the time teasing me that I had lost my balls somewhere yesterday, he finally said that she must be scared of something. What that something was, though, he didn't know. His response didn't exactly make me feel any better, so I ended up going to the gym to take my frustration out on the treadmill instead.

I make it to the English building and see Jameson talking to a few people. They all stare at him as if he has something important to say. Jameson loves to tell stories of what it was like growing up with a football hero, and he name drops constantly.

The two of us are not, and will never be, the best of buddies, since I took his spot on the team. The team was floundering when he was in the starting spot. Once the coach moved me into the position, we now have a chance at the Championships.

A switch like that could have hurt someone's career, but not Jameson. Jameson has the connections to get him onto any team in the NFL, whereas a schmuck like me has to work extra hard for a spot, even though I have more talent in my pinky finger than Jameson will ever have. I guess the saying is correct that it's all about who you know. I decide to interrupt Jameson and his adoring fans.

"Jameson, what's going on?" I call out as I step into the group that is listening to him most likely bragging about himself.

"Oh, Brice. What's up man?" he says with an unmistakable look of disapproval.

Two girls who, just a moment ago, were hanging on his every word, flock over to me. I smile down at them. "Ladies," I say, pulling out all the charms.

"Hey, Brice," they say in unison.

"So, what are you talking about, Jameson?" I don't care, but I just love to fuck with him, especially right now.

"Oh, Jameson was just telling us about the time when his father's team came over to his house for his birthday party when he was ten," one of the girl's chimes in.

"Is that so?" I say, looking at Jameson as he gives me a look of death.

"Yeah, that is so. Don't you have somewhere you need to be, Brice?"

I do, but damn if I'm going to be the first to leave. "Nope. Got all the time in the world," I gloat and look down at the cute little brunette smiling at me.

Jameson narrows his eyes at me and squares his shoulders. "Well, I have class." He throws the words as if he were throwing fireballs at my head. With one more angry glare and a snarl, he turns to leave.

It looks like I won that round of chicken. "Brice, are you busy later?" the brunette asks me. I look at her, and almost say no, but something holds me back. Thoughts of Favor go through my head and I just can't.

"Sorry, love. I'm busy. But I'll catch you another time, 'kay?" I let her down gently. She gives me a small smile, and I head into the building.

On my way to class, a few of the fellas give me high fives, and girls stare at me. I sit down next to Egon.

"Yo. You see her today?" Egon asks, as a girl turns towards him and gives him a smile. I guess he'l need our room tonight.

"No, I haven't," I groan, wishing that I did see her.

"Well, I did. I overheard her with her friends. They're having lunch in the east cafeteria today at one o'clock. You can thank me later."

We pound it out as a way of thanks. In two hours, I'll set sight on those almond-shaped brown eyes.

****

39

I walk into the cafeteria at one-fifteen to give her enough time to grab her food and take a seat. I mindlessly grab items and toss them onto my tray as my eyes scan the room for her. Finally, my eyes settle on her sitting in a corner with her friends. I pay the cashier and carry my tray in their general direction while trying to give myself a mental pep talk on how to approach her.

"Brice, come and join us," Cal calls out.

"Oh hey, guys. I was supposed to meet up with Egon, but I can hang out with you until he gets here," I lie my ass off, sitting across from Favor. I look at her, and I'm stunned by her beauty. I can get lost in her so easily. "Hey, Favor. How are you today?"

"Hi, Brice," she murmurs, and turns back to Jana to finish her conversation. She's going to make this hard on me.

"So Brice, you and the guys ready for the game next weekend?" Cal asks.

I'm still looking at Favor. "Yeah. As ready as we'll ever be."

"Well, I'm looking forward to a big win from the Cougars," Cal gawks.

"No worries, buddy. We got this in the bag." I was truthful. State U is no competition for the Cougars. We train harder than most other teams.

Favor's face grows pale, and her eyes widen. I open my mouth to ask her if she's okay when Wayne Anderson approaches our table. I've heard stories about him. He used to be on the Cougars team, along with his best friend Trevor Hollister, who was the starting quarterback for the team at the time. One night, the two of them left a party, and Wayne was drunk and driving. He crashed the car into a tree, killing Trevor. From what I hear, Wayne did a little time in jail but got out early for good behavior. I heard the rumors he was back in school again, his football career ruined before it even got a chance.

"Favor. May I talk to you?" Wayne begs.

Wordlessly, Favor stands, her hands trembling as she gathers up her things to leave. *What's going on? What would Wayne have to do with Favor?* As if I'm watching this in slow motion, she dumps her tray and pushes her way out of the crowded cafeteria. Cal and Jana stand to run after her, but I hold my hand up and stand.

"Let me go after her," I plead with them. I want to be there for her, if it's the only thing I could do.

Concern flickers across their face before Cal eventually nods. "Tell her we're here if she needs us."

"Bu-" Jana begins to protest.

"No, he's what she needs."

She bites her bottom lip, mulling over what Cal has said before looking at me and eventually nodding her approval. That's all I need, and I run after her.

"FAVOR. WAIT." I yell, but she is rushing down the pathway outside. I run after her, catching up easily, and grab ahold of her arm, making her stop. "What was that back there?"

She turns around with tears in her eyes and collapses into my chest. I feel as if someone has ripped my heart out and stomped on it in front of me. I hold her to me, hoping I can take her pain away. I stroke her hair and try to soothe her. "It's okay. It'll be fine." And I mean every word of it. Whatever it is that is bothering her, I will make it okay.

"I'm sorry," she sniffs as she pulls away.

"Sorry for what? You didn't do anything wrong."

"I just... I'm just not ready yet. He caught me off guard," she sobs.

"How do you know Wayne Anderson?" I question.

"I can't. I don't want to talk about it." She takes a few steps backward and drags my heart with her.

"Okay. We don't need to talk about it." I hold my hand out to her. For each moment she stares at my outstretched hand, it brings me closer to begging her to take it. The pleading words are at the tip of my tongue when she finally takes my hand, only to drop it when she hears her name.

"Favor." Jameson yells, jogging over to us. His eyes rake over her quickly, assessing the situation. "What the fuck did you do to her?" he growls out, stepping towards me. I place Favor behind me, shielding her.

"I didn't do anything to her, shithead." The anger building in me burns hotter than the sun.

"Why the fuck is she *crying*?" He tries to look around me at Favor, but I block him.

"None of your fucking business." My tone is flat.

"It *is* my business," he snarls, trying to make another attempt to go around me.

"Jameson. Stop. Brice didn't do anything wrong. He was helping me." Favor steps around me.

"Why are you crying?"

"Wayne," is all she says, and what appears to be a knowing look passes between them.

"I told that motherfucker to stay away from you. I'll fucking kill him."

"Leave it alone." She shakes her head.

"Come on, I'll take you back to your dorm," Jameson says to her, holding out his hand.

I stand there, watching and counting the seconds like a goddamn idiot, wondering if she will hesitate to take his hand the way she did with me just moments ago.

Without hesitation, she takes his hand, effectively throwing my heart in my face.

She turns to look at me. "Thank you, Brice." And she goes off with my arch nemesis. *What the fuck just happened?*

Chapter 5
Favor

I wake up the next morning with Jameson's arm draped around me. It feels so wrong to be here with him. I hadn't planned on ending up in bed with him again, but after seeing Wayne, it just happened. It always just happens with us. This has been our MO, ever since my brother's funeral.

Me, so numb after Trevor's death, fell into Jameson's waiting arms. It all started when he offered his shoulder to cry on, and then I gave my virginity to the person who least deserved it. I had always thought my first time would be with a man I loved, not with a man who can only love himself.

I promised myself months ago to get off this hamster wheel, and here I am, right back on it. Still running around, not going anywhere.

I watch his chest rise and fall and wonder to myself, *What am I doing here?* I turn away as my thoughts drift to Brice. He was there for me when he didn't have to be, and I pushed him away. The look in his eyes when I took Jameson's hand hurt me more than I expected.

"You're awake." Long gone is Jana's usual bubbly voice, replaced with disappointment. I'm familiar with that tone since it's often directed at me from my parents. But I have to say, this is the first time Jana has been disappointed in me. She sits cross-legged on her bed, waiting for my response.

I move Jameson's arm gently, so I don't wake him and sit up to face the music. I avert my eyes, my chin dipping to my chest. I search my brain for a response to make this all better, but I come up empty.

"Favor, I love you. You're one of my closest friends in the world."

I grimace at her words, unsure where this is going.

"That's why I'm going to be honest with you. This has got to stop. You're only hurting yourself more each time you sleep with him. He's taking advantage because he knows you're weak. The only thing that binds the two of you is the fact that you hold on to Trevor's death. You refuse to move forward and live a life that *you* deserve. Favor, it's okay that you are alive. Being happy is okay. You have to let yourself heal."

I begin to shake uncontrollably. A moan that started out small turns into a roar. Jana is instantly by my side and holds me in her arms.

"Wh-what happened?" Jameson asks with a start.

"Nothing. Leave." Jana, who is the kindest person I know, pointedly tells him he is not welcome here.

"But I should be here for her."

She lets go of me and stands up with her hands on her hips, glaring at him. "Why? So you can convince her to sleep with you again? You selfish bastard. I told you to leave, and if you don't, I'll get security."

"Favor? Do you want me to go?"

She angles her body so he can't look at me. "I'm speaking to *you*. I live here as well, and I'm telling you that *I* don't want you here."

The bed shifts as Jameson curses under his breath and searches for his clothes on the floor. Silently he gets dressed, and leaves without a word. The close of the door feels like the close on another chapter of my life.

"T-today is the anniversary." An overwhelming rush of emotions comes to the forefront, breaking through my barriers and opening up the floodgates. A feeling, as if I was freefalling toward a rapid approach to the ground, comes over me. *Will I survive?*

Taking me into her arms, Jana strokes my back, healing my soul. "I know, and I'm here for you," she says into my hair, kissing the top of my head. Her tears fall down my forehead, cleansing away my demons.

"I have to be with him today." I've visited my brother's grave every year on the anniversary of his death for three years.

Hugging me tighter she says, "I'll come with you."

My body tenses. Sensing something is wrong, she pulls back and stares at me. "I need to do this on my own."

She contemplates my words before nodding her approval. "Call me if you need me."

Rising, I wipe away the tears. "I will. I promise."

Silently, I gather up my things to take a shower so I can begin my torturous journey. I have a date with my brother.

****

A few hours later, I arrive at the cemetery. The scent of the white lilies that I picked up surrounds the small space of my car. It smells like spring in the midst of death. I stare at my brother's tombstone a few feet ahead. Steeling my nerves, I open the car door and step outside into the Indian summer with the flowers in my hand. Memories of sitting in the church watching his lily-draped casket being carried off by the pallbearers hit me. I stop, so overcome by the memory of that day. I inhale deeply and close my eyes. The smell of freshly cut grass wafts up to my nose, triggering yet another recollection for me, this one a happy one. One of my brother and I running around our backyard. Him chasing me with a garter snake. I tripped and fell on the freshly cut lawn. Grass clippings clung to me, making me look furry and green. I laugh out loud at the memory, and this laugh comes from deep within my soul. A burden I've carried for years feels just a bit lighter in the moment of this laugh. But just as quickly as the burden lightens, guilt settles back in, taking root again. I throw my head back in despair and stare heavenward. The sun's rays beam down on me, cloaking me in its warmth and light. *Is it showing me the path out of the fog of grief?*

My feet feels like lead as I walk towards his grave. My heart is so heavy, and I begin to cry before I even get there. Kneeling down on the dew-covered grass, I see a fresh bouquet of lilies, most likely from my parents, laid in front of the stone. Placing my flowers next to it, I sit cross-legged on the ground, much like the way I used to do when we were kids. Me, sitting on the floor, happily watching him act out parts of a story he was telling me.

"Hey, Terror Trev. Just wanted to be here with you today," I begin, but choke up. A lump forms in my throat, and I try desperately to swallow it back down. My eyes start to blur as warm tears fall down my cheeks. I wipe feverishly at them, wishing I could close the floodgates that have come crashing down around me. I concentrate on my breathing to steady my emotions. *Breathe in, one-two-three, breathe out, one-two-three.* I remain like this until I'm finally able to continue. "I miss you so much, and there isn't a day that goes by that I don't think of you. I miss our talks and how you always knew the right things to say to make me feel better."

I lean my head on the cold stone, wishing it was my brother's shoulder. A shoulder I'd often cried on and sought comfort. "I met a guy, big brother. I like him. I mean, a lot. The problem is, he's the quarterback for the Cougars. I look at him, and I see you, and it makes me miss you more." Pressing my cheek against the stone, I close my eyes and let out a chuckle. "Plus, the fact that I hate football. Am I dramatic? I know you'd say I'm a drama queen."

Happiness fills me as flashes of a memory of my brother teasing me goes through my head when, just as quickly, a darker one replaces it. I'm back in that moment at the cafeteria yesterday when Wayne approached my table. My heart and limbs feel heavy, and breathing seems like I'm getting air through a straw. "Wayne contacted me yesterday. I-I just couldn't handle it. How am I supposed to forgive him? How can I move forward without you?"

I begin to sob into my hands, before leaning my head on the cold stone with my brother's name etched into it. "It's hard, you see. I don't have the strength like you did. You were always my rock. During lunch yesterday, he came to me. I don't understand what he wants from me when he has taken you away. If it is forgiveness he is looking for, I don't think I'm able to give it. Because I don't forgive him. How can I? If I forgave him, I'd feel as if I'm betraying you." I cry harder into the stone. Placing both arms around it, as if I'm hugging my brother, knowing I won't ever feel his embrace again.

"Favor." I hear a voice that I once used to welcome, but have grown to despise.

I whip my head around towards the voice behind me. I see Wayne, or at least a broken version of him. Eyes that were once full of life and mischief are red-rimmed and hollow with sorrow. A posture that would stand tall at his six foot one-inch stature now slouches and gives the appearance of trying to disappear before your eyes. The scar under his eye a constant reminder of the night he made a careless mistake. His dark brown hair hangs loosely around his shoulders, unkempt and oily.

Regret hits me instantly, only to be replaced with anger.

I stand up abruptly, stumbling as I do so. "I – I can't do this." I walk in the direction of my car.

"Favor. Please wait," Wayne calls out to me, his voice raw with emotion.

I stop. My blood runs cold as I turn around to face him. "What?"

"I just wanted to say how sorry I am. I need your family's forgiveness. I loved him like a brother. I miss him every single day," he cries. He looks like a broken man...but I don't care.

"*No.* You don't get off that easy. My brother was cheated. I was cheated. My *family* was cheated, all because you were reckless and careless." I turn around and head towards my car again.

"Please, Favor. I beg you. I'm drowning here," he pleads with me further, but I'm unable to give him what he needs. What about *my* needs? What about what my brother needed that night? This is too much.

"I DON'T CARE." I scream out without a backward glance.

This is too much. Not today, of all days. I can't handle this. I reach my car, but don't have the energy to open the door. Propping my arms on the roof, I lean my head in the crook of my arms and cry. My body shudders with grief, and I feel like a pressure cooker waiting to explode.

"Favor?"

I hold my hand out behind me. "Don't. Just don't."

"Do you need something?"

I spin around in a fury. "My *brother.* Can you bring my *brother* back?"

We stand, staring at each other. If this were a western, it would have looked like we would be drawing guns at noon. He looks away, his Adam's apple moving as he swallows. I take this opportunity to jump in my car. I lock my doors in hopes of locking away the bad memories. *Perhaps I locked them in with me instead?* My trembling hand lifts to press the ignition button while staring out the window, looking at Wayne one last time. He has collapsed to the ground, holding his head in the palm of his hands. For a moment, I debate if I should go to him, but I push that feeling aside and shift the car into gear, driving off.

I drive a few miles, but have to pull to the side of the road. Outside my car, I collapse to the ground, and begin to vomit. My body racks with dry heaves. I gasp for breath and, for a moment, I think I'm going to pass out and die. The fear of death doesn't scare me because I have nothing to live for. I used to, but he is gone now. Lying on the ground next to a pool of my vomit, my eyes slowly drift close.

A bird chirping brings me out of the spell. I open my eyes to see a sparrow standing near me, beckoning me back to reality. With a strength I wasn't aware I had, I stand and dust myself off. The sparrow remains in his perch state, staring at me, giving me his strength just by his mere presence. Holding on to the car door, I give the bird one last look before getting back inside my car. Starting the ignition, I drive off towards the direction I never expected to go; my parents' house. The place that's home in the physical sense, but I've never felt a part of.

An hour later, I'm pulling into my parents' winding driveway. My mother opens the door and stands outside, waiting for me as I walk towards the house.

"Favor? What are you doing here?" Her hazel eyes look at me with a disapproving stare as usual.

The door is open but feels as if it's been slammed in my face. "I need a reason to come?"

"No honey. It's just...well. Favor, I don't know. Everything I ever say to you seems to be wrong, and I never know how to speak to you anymore." My mother nervously pats her grayish black hair, as if a strand would dare be out of place.

Funny, I feel the same way. "I went to Trevor's grave today. I saw the flowers that you and dad left..." My voice trails off, unable to finish the sentence.

"Yes. Your father and I went this morning. I guess if we'd known you'd wanted to go, we would've waited for you," my mother says as she walks towards the kitchen with me following behind. In this moment, it shows the hierarchy of our relationship. She, always ahead, and me trailing.

Standing by the kitchen island, she has the beginnings of a mixture of what looks like will be my brother's favorite chocolate chip cookies.

"I go every year. You know that. He was my brother. Of course, I would go." Unwittingly, my tone went from casual to snarky. The house is warm, yet I feel cold.

She begins mixing the dough, measuring out some vanilla to pour in. Pausing what she's doing, she looks up at me. "I know that he was your brother. He was my son. Your father and I have asked you to join us in the past when we'd go to his grave, but you never wanted to go with us before. You're not the only one who is suffering. You never actually share your plans with your father and I. We pay for your college education, but haven't any idea of what is going on with you." She wipes her hands on her apron.

"You never took an interest in anything I did before. Your only interest was Trevor, never me. It was always him." Here we go. This old argument again. *Why am I here? What was I thinking?*

"How *dare* you. Don't you dare come in this house, on this day of all days, and talk to me like that. I swear, I don't know where we went wrong with you, but we obviously did. If you can't be civil then, you need to leave." My mother pounds her fists on the island. "Not on this day. Leave, please leave." My mom whispers those last words, her head hanging down.

I stare at my mother for long moments, frozen. How long did we last this time before we got into an argument? Five minutes? That has got to be a record for us. I would've given us at least ten minutes, tops. It hurts that today we can't bond as a family who is grieving. I take one last look at my mother, then turn to leave. I am startled to see my father standing in the vestibule, looking at us from afar. His eyes are glassy with unshed tears. He has the appearance of looking through me, though, and not at me. Jutting my chin out, I walk past him and leave my parents' house to head back to campus where I belong.

Chapter 6

Favor

"Come on, Favor, you *gotta* go," Jana complains, for the umpteenth time.

"I don't feel like hanging out tonight. I've had a long week," I groan, as I lay across my bed. Jana and Cal have been nagging me for the past hour, trying to convince me to go out to the club with them. Egon gave us tickets to watch his band play tonight.

"Come on, the hottie Brice will be there. Don't even act like you don't want to see him. The two of you have crazy chemistry," Cal says.

I hadn't seen Brice since earlier this week when he ran after me. I cringe inwardly as I remember that day and how I ended up in bed with Jameson. I would like to see Brice again, actually. "Okay, fine. Give me a minute to change, 'kay?"

"You got it." Jana bounces up and down, clapping her hands.

"Oh no, honey, I'm picking this outfit out for you. You need to look smoking hot tonight." Cal begins rummaging through the closet.

"What for?" I ask, standing behind him.

"Because, girlfriend, Brice will be there, *duh*," he says as he grabs a pair of my designer skin tight jeans that I forgot I had, and a halter top. He thrusts the clothes at me. "Here. Wear this."

I frown at the clothes, especially the too-tight jeans. "I won't be able to breathe in these."

"What do we say, it's better to look good than to feel good. Now hurry up, or we're going to be late." Cal shoos me away.

Dressing quickly, so I don't incur the wrath of Cal, I look in the mirror, and he is right. I do look hot. I allow my hair to flow loosely around my shoulders. No makeup tonight for me, just some lip gloss. "Okay, I'm ready."

"Dayum, girl. You are going to be setting off many fire detectors in that," Cal jokes and whistles at me.

"You got that right. No one will be looking at me because they will all be looking at you," Jana adds, not a hint of jealousy in her voice.

I do a quick spin. "What, this old thing?" I bat my eyes playfully as I look over my shoulder at them.

Cal squeezes my butt. "If I were into girls, I would totally try to score with you tonight."

"My loss," I confess as I grab my car keys.

I drive the forty minutes to the city, just outside our college town. The city isn't large by big city standards, but it is the closest thing we have to civilization. I park across the street from the club, aptly named City Limit. Instantly, a wave of regret for leaving my dorm hits me when I see the line to get inside of the small dingy venue.

"Guys, this line is ridiculous. Let's just go back to the dorm," I plead, borderline whining.

"Uh-uh." Cal links his arm with mine and Jana mirrors on my other side. "We've got tickets in the front. Jana will smooth talk the bouncer."

"Trust me, have I ever let you down?" she giggles as we walk. No, they walk, and drag me with them to the front of the line.

Unhooking her arm from mine, she tosses her blonde hair over her shoulders and strolls to the bouncer with an air of confidence. Watching Jana go into action with the bouncer, who is the size of a sumo wrestler, is like watching an artist paint his greatest achievement. She casually touches the man's chest as she undoubtedly tosses a compliment at him. The man who looked horrendously imposing only moments ago is now a bubble of mush at Jana's fingers. She throws him that winning smile, flashing all thirty-two pearly whites, and he is done for.

She turns around and waves for us to join her. He opens the door for us as we bypass the other ticket holders to get inside.

"What did you say to him?" I ask, as we walk into the dimly-lit room that has clouds of cigarette smoke in the air. I cough a little and pray I don't get lung cancer from second-hand smoke.

"A little of this and a little of dat," she teases. "Oh wait, I think that's our table over there." She stands on her tippy toes and points to a table in front of the stage.

"It can't be. It still has beer bottles on it," I complain. The more I look around this place, the more I think this is not a good idea.

"I think Jana's right. The tickets say front stage." Cal squints at the tickets.

"Yeah, that he wrote on," I scoff, as I wave my hand in front of my face. The smoke is so thick you could cut it with a knife.

Jana drags me behind her, with Cal in tow, to the tables in the front. I don't know how she did it, but she was able to flag down a hostess to clear the table for us. As I take a seat, I'm still mildly confused as to how she was able to spot a hostess in this dark room.

Jana gives the girl our drink orders as I scan the room for Brice, as best I can. But it's hard to see my hands in front of my own face, much less someone a few feet from me. Disappointment hits me, and I briefly wonder if perhaps he isn't going to show up.

Regan somehow miraculously finds our table without an issue. I wonder if she's a nightcrawler with perfect night vision.

She is rockin' a tight black v-neck t-shirt, with "State of Mind" emblazoned on it in studs. Her jean skirt is so short I think, if the poor girl sneezes, it would give everyone a peep show. "I didn't know you guys were coming out tonight," Regan says. In Regan speak, this means, 'you being here will steal my thunder'.

"Well, Egon was kind enough to give us front row seats." I couldn't help but throw that in her face. Catty? Perhaps, but who cares.

Regan's face drops slightly, but she recovers quickly, flipping her long black straight hair. One of the nicer nicknames for her, out of a few, is Pocahontas because of her olive complexion and dark hair that goes down to her butt. "Oh really? He didn't mention it to me. Egon and I are practically a couple." Regan and her daydreams. The word around campus is Egon was done with her after the bonfire party, but she has been chasing after him, begging him to give her the time of day.

I roll my eyes in an exaggerated fashion. "Suuurrre," I reply.

A few people stop off at our table to say hello to me, Jana, and Cal. Some pull up their chairs and sit with us. Before I know it, our party of three has turned into a party of more. This is exactly what I was not in the mood for. I'm starting to get bored when a hand passes in front of me, holding a drink for me to take. I grab the glass and place it on the table without looking to see who gave it to me, or even to say thank you.

"You're looking good, baby," Jameson croons in my ear. I swat at him like he's a fly. *That's what he gets for invading my personal space.*

"Go away," I tell him, holding back a yawn. I hadn't seen or spoken to Jameson since earlier in the week when I stupidly slept with him.

He ignores my comment. "You haven't been returning my phone calls. I'm beginning to feel like you're ignoring me."

I close my eyes. How did I end up in bed with him? I stopped the sexual part of our friendship before the summer. I should've kept it that way. Turning to look at him. "Listen, I think we need to...." Then Brice's voice cuts me off mid-sentence.

"You look beautiful," Brice says to me.

The sound of his deep voice sends me into orbit. "Thanks," I reply, as I swallow hard, trying to steady my nerves.

He takes a seat in front of me. Members of the football team join our table; people instantly stand and give their seats to them. His teammates sit without acknowledgment of the poor schmucks who are now left to stand.

"Jameson," Brice quips. Did I detect a note of hostility?

"Brice," Jameson bites out. *Guess I would be salty too if someone took my spot on the team.*

Brice now has my full attention. I look at him with his brown eyes and dark hair, his loose-fitting jeans hanging ever so nicely on his slim waist. My mother would call the look unkempt. I would say it is swexy. Someone brings him a beer that he gladly accepts. Taking a drink from his glass, he wipes the foam from his upper lip, and I wonder briefly what it would be like to lick it off him. My thoughts are interrupted when Jana asks Brice a question.

"Egon is your best friend, right?"

"Oh yeah. We've been best friends since we were seven years old."

"Wow. That is great," Jana replies in her singsong voice.

"Yeah, it is."

"So, Brice, are you, me, and Egon going to an after-party later?" Regan asks.

Say what?

He looks at her, before turning his attention to me, disregarding her question. "So. I didn't get a chance to ask you since that day. How come you were so upset?"

"Oh, no reason," I respond, praying he doesn't press me further. He stares at me for a moment as if he wants to ask again, but he changes his mind.

Jameson places an arm over my shoulder. I turn and glare at him, and he removes it instantly. I look up to see Brice smiling at me. That smile of his makes me feel warm. Did my heart just flutter?

"Brice? After party or what?" Regan asks again.

"If there is one, I doubt you're invited," he says, without sparing the poor girl a glance.

Her mouth drops open. "What do you mean?"

"I didn't stutter. If there is one, you're not invited," he repeats, this time slower.

Her mouth twists in anger. "I'm his *girlfriend*." She uses the line that she undoubtedly used to get in here with.

"About that. The two of you hooked up once, and that's all. He never returned any of your phone calls or texts after. So, stop going around campus saying you're his girlfriend. It makes you look pathetic, especially when he's still screwing other girls."

Oh, this lad, how he grows on me. I lock up and give him a smile. Regan stands up and throws her drink in his face, storming off, with Jana behind her to console her.

"Looks like you just made a friend," I remark sarcastically.

Some blonde Barbie with perky breasts that I don't think were nature-made wipes Brice's face with a napkin. He gently removes the napkin from her hands and wipes himself off, laughing. God, if only I could be that napkin.

The football team are all whooping and hollering at the whole scene.

"I love new friends. Haven't you heard?" he snickers.

The lights become dimmer in the already dimly-lit room, and the stage is lit up. The band comes on stage, taking their places, and waits for Egon to appear. He comes out moments later in torn, faded jeans, and a State of Mind black form-fitting t-shirt.

"Hel-low City Limit," Egon screams into the mic, and the crowd erupts. "You ready to party?"

Screams of "Yeah." explode from around the crowded room.

Egon plays up to the crowd and steps back, pretending like he couldn't hear us. "I'm going to ask one more time. And when I do, I want you to give me everything you got, just like I'm about to." He signals his bass player. The bass player, whose hair is dyed purple, hits a note. "On my count, when I get to three, you tell me who in this room is ready to party." The bass player plays a chord. "One. Two. Three." The screams from the crowd are so loud I fear my eardrums will burst. "That's what I was waiting for." He adjusts the height of the mic and swivels his hips. Girls behind me scream out his name. He hears them and gives them a wink. "Let's party." he screams, and again, he has the crowd. I'm amazed at his magnetism and how the crowd is with him all the way.

Egon grabs the microphone and starts belting out the beginning of one of their songs acapella, and the mob goes crazy. The band begins to play when he starts the second verse of the song. Egon has a stage presence about him that is undeniable. He rips off his shirt in the middle of the third song, wipes the sweat off his forehead, and throws it to the ladies standing in front of the stage. These girls knock each other over for the shirt that eventually ends up ripped to shreds as they each grab at it.

"They're amazing," I scream out to no one in particular.

Brice leans in close. "Yeah, they are. Egon has been talking about being in a band since we were twelve years old. This is his dream come true."

"And you? Did you always know you wanted to be a football player?" I ask, taking a sip of my water.

He shrugs his shoulders. "I guess so. I was a huge Kyne Hollister fan when I was a kid. Had dreams to be just like him." I try to hide the shock on my face at the mention of my father's name. I should be used to it by now.

Jameson gives him a smirk. "That'll never happen. "

"Never thought I could *play* just like him. I just hope to bring the game as much dignity that he did," Brice responds.

Listening to Brice talk, he sounds so much like my brother in that moment. I begin to get lost in my thoughts when Egon speaks into the microphone.

"This next song is dedicated to two very special people to me. My best friend Brice, who you all know as the Cougars starting quarterback, and my new friend, Favor." Egon begins singing a love song.

All eyes settle on the two of us. Jana and Cal both give me the thumbs up, and I want to melt into the wooden floors. I look up to see Brice gazing at me with a certain look in his eyes. If I had to name it, I would say its hunger. Does he want me as much as I want him? Closing my eyes, I try to shut away the spell he has over me and let the music carry me. Opening my eyes, but still feeling the hypnotic trance that Brice has over me, I see him still staring at me. Instead of being broken out of my trance, he pulls me in deeper. It feels as if everything is happening in slow motion, even when he stands and offers me his hand to take. I stare at his waiting hand and contemplate what would happen if I take it. What would this simple gesture mean? For some reason, it feels like it holds my future and that terrifies me. Jana, who I didn't see stand up and walk behind me, nudges me. The spell of the moment is broken, but not the one he has over me. I take his hand and let him lead me to what I know will feel more like home than the one I've lived in my entire life. Pulling me close, I'm flush against his body and can feel his every movement. Our dance is slow and intimate like the song that Egon is singing.

We let the music move us as we move to it as one. I close my eyes and place my head on his shoulder, taking in his scent of spice and oak. The world is gone, and everyone around us has disappeared at this moment. No one exists but the two of us. The music must've stopped at some point because we begin to hear catcalls directed at us. I try to step back and pull away, but he holds me for a moment longer, and blows out a breath he was holding before releasing me. I step backward, staring into his eyes, still in shock at the hold he has over me.

"Favor?" Jana asks, breaking me out of my trance.

Not wanting to lose eye contact with him, I take a deep breath and then grudgingly turn towards Jana. "Yeah?"

"Regan is pretty drunk. She needs a ride back to campus. Can we go?"

I look back to Brice, who is still standing near me, while various hangers on vy for his attention. He is still staring at me. I shake my head to get the cobwebs out of my brain, and turn back to Jana. "Yeah sure, let's go." She grabs my hand and pulls me in the direction of where she left Regan.

We reach Regan, who is almost passed out at a table as Cal stands over her. Jameson comes up from behind. "Need me to carry her?"

Startled, I turn to him and then nod my head. He lifts her with ease, and we make our way towards the front door.

Jana, Cal, and Regan are settled in the backseat as Jameson closes the car door. He looks at me and frowns.

"Did you have to dance with him?"

"I'm not doing this with you." I cross my hands over my chest, jutting out my chin.

"Everything revolves around you, doesn't it? But what about me? What about us?"

"There was never an 'us', and you know it. I'm sorry if I've led you to believe…"

He throws his hands up in the air. "Forget it." He walks across the street and heads back inside the club.

I walk over to the driver's side and open my door. I see Brice across the street, staring from a distance. My heart drops for a moment as I try to figure out if he was standing there the entire time.

Chapter 7

Brice

Parked in front of Favor's dorm, I've been sitting on top of my car, waiting for her for the past forty minutes. Jana said that Favor went for a run, so I decided to hang out and wait for her. Since that dance we had at the club last week, I know she feels the connection between us. So here I am, waiting and waiting, and waiting some more. A few people pass by who know me, stopping to ask me if I'll be going to tonight's party or not. I'm hoping I can convince Favor to go out with me tonight, so the party option is off the table for now.

Finally, I see Favor walking towards her dorm, sweat glistening on her skin. Hopping off my car hood, I jog over to her.

"Good run?" She jumps, clutching her chest. "Shit, I'm sorry. Didn't mean to startle you." I hold my hands out to steady her.

One hand covering her heart, the other, her forehead, she replies, "Yeah. What are you doing here?"

"Came to see you," I say, putting on my winning smile.

"Me? What for?" She smiles back cautiously.

"Thought maybe you and I could hang out today. After you shower, of course." I pinch my nose jokingly.

She punches me in the arm. "Well, umm, I don't know."

"Okay, you don't have to shower if you don't want." Always did like my women a little dirty.

"Ha-ha. I meant I don't know about hanging out. I don't date football players."

"That includes Jameson?"

"I already told you. I never dated him. We're just friends."

"It sort of didn't look that way outside of City Limit."

"About that. It's not what you think." She bends her head down, her ponytail fanning out across her neck.

"I guess it doesn't matter," I mutter. "Why you don't date football players?"

"It's personal." Her attention appears to be with her sneakers, so I stare down at them too. Hmm, just regular sneakers.

I look back up and cup her chin with my fingers. I want her to feel that night again. I want her to relive that moment with me through my eyes. Her tongue licks out slowly across her lips, and I envy those pink lips.

"Let's not call it a date then. It is two friends hanging out."

She nibbles on her thumbnail. "I don't know." I almost have her.

"Come on. Consider it 'being kind to dumb jocks' day. It's a public service. I hear that by doing this, it will get you into heaven."

She laughs hysterically before saying, "Heaven? Wow. Well, I guess if you put it that way, I don't have a choice. Give me thirty minutes to shower and change." She gives me a playful shove before jogging the rest of the way towards her dorm, but not without first turning to give me another look before going inside.

As soon as the door closes behind her, I do a fist pump in the air like I just won the lottery. But a date with Favor is so much better than a lottery winning; it is life itself for me. I wonder if I have enough time to get her some flowers. I look at my Fitbit Blaze and back at her dorm. She did say thirty minutes but what if she comes out early and I'm not here. Nah, better not risk it. Shit, I should've been better prepared. The first ten minutes, I pace back and forth in front of the building, looking up whenever a student opened the door. Now I know how dogs feel when they wait for their master to come home.

Exactly thirty minutes later, she appears, and I think I'm in love. Not only did she come back on time, because let's face it, chicks say thirty minutes, when really, they mean two hours, but she looks stunning in her jeans and school sweatshirt.

"Okay, I'm in your hands. Where to?" *Hmm, in my hands?* Yeah, I like the sound of that.

"Well, I thought we could go to the coffee shop in town," I say, as she shrugs her shoulders. Closing the passenger door as she settles into her seat, I walk over to the driver's side. We drive through town in amicable silence. Me, partly because I just don't know what to say. I don't want to ruin it and make her ask me to drive her back home. So, I remain silent as I go over in my head some topics we could talk about once inside of the restaurant. Arriving at the coffee shop, we are ushered over to a booth quickly.

"So, were you waiting outside long for me?" she asks.

"Nah. It took as long as it needed," I reply. I would've waited an eternity for her if I had to.

"You are persistent." She smiles, and I feel as if the sun is shining down on me.

"I try. If you would give me a chance, I could show you that I'm a nice guy." I show off a full display of my dimples that usually has chicks falling all over themselves. She gives me a smile and shakes her head slightly.

"I told you, I don't date…"

"Yeah, I know. You don't date football players. But right now, sitting here in this coffee shop, is a man who happens to play football. Football does not define me, or my life. I love the sport, yes, but there is room for one more."

She gives me a look, as if she is searching for a comeback. She shakes her head again at me. "You jumble things up for me."

"Am I cracking the stone wall?" *Please let that be a yes.*

"How about chipping away at it, little by little." She gives me yet another smile, and I feel as if I just scored some points.

We sit and chat about school and various other topics for about two hours. The time flies by so quickly while we talk. One of my teammates walks over to our booth.

"Yo. You think you can give me a lift back to practice?"

I narrow my eyes at him. Is he cra-? And then it hits me what day of the week it is. *Fuck. Practice.* Coach is going to make me do extra drills if I'm late. I look over to Favor, who is staring at the two of us.

"Fav. I'm so sorry. I forgot that I have practice today. Is it okay if we head over to the stadium? I don't think I'll have enough time to drop you off at your dorm and get there on time." I've never in my life forgot practice. This is a first for me.

She averts her eyes, and momentarily, I feel lost without her gaze. "Hey, it's okay. Why don't you go with your friend? I'll find my way back to campus." She reaches for her purse, but I hold out my hand.

"No way." *Please, I don't want this day to end, not like this.* "I'd rather be late to practice than leave you." *I'm willing to suffer the wrath of Coach than disappoint you.* "But seriously, it would be great if you could watch me play a little." Please let her say yes.

She looks at me, then back to my teammate. "Umm. I guess it's okay." She shrugs.

I exhale, offering her my hand to take. Unlike the night at the club, this time she takes my hand without hesitation. I give it a small reassuring squeeze. As if picking up my meaning, she nods her head. The three of us walk outside to my car and hopefully towards a future with her in it.

Parking inside the stadium parking lot, I tell my teammate to go in ahead of me. I want some alone time with Favor. The two of us walk inside of the stadium together.

"Shouldn't you hurry?" she asks as we casually stroll inside.

I pause for a moment. She stops a few steps away from me and walks over. I take her hands into my own. I need to feel her as much as I need to say these words. "Wanted to show you a great spot to sit. Also, I wanted to say thank you. I know you didn't want to come here, but it means a lot to me to have you."

"I-I don't know what to say."

"There's nothing to say. Just let me prove to you that I'm a great guy, wanting a chance with you."

We see some of the team file out onto the field and I know my time is limited. I walk her over to the seats and jog over to the locker rooms to change clothes quickly. Thank goodness I keep extra clothes in my locker, or else I would've been late after all. Back out on the field with my team, we do some quick run-throughs of some plays the coach was working on. This is not going to be a very long practice today. We have a game coming up soon, and Coach doesn't want to work us out too hard.

Distracted from looking over at Favor, one of my teammates tackles me to the ground. The wind is knocked out of me because I wasn't braced for it. I stay on the ground for a while, trying to get my orientation back. Coach and some of my teammates gather around me. I start to sit up, but a feeling of dizziness takes over. Holding my head, I try to shake away the dizzy spell. And that's when I hear it. The sweetest voice coming closer and closer to me.

"Oh, my God. Brice, are you okay?" Favor's concerned voice comes nearer. She pushes past the big players to get to me. For the briefest of moments, I almost decide to lay on the ground longer to receive more sympathy from her.

"Yeah, I'm good. Just got the shit knocked out of me." I start to sit up again, but Favor places her hands on my shoulders.

"I don't think you should move. Just sit here for a while." She kneels next to me.

"Practice is over. Brice, go to the doc and get checked. You took a pretty hard hit," Coach orders. Most of my teammates begin to head to the lockers, while some stay behind to make sure I'm okay.

"Nah. I should be okay. I was distracted when I got tackled." At this point, I could give my teammate who tackled me a handshake. That hit has now chipped away a few more pieces of Favor's wall.

"Safety first. Head over to the doc and give me a full update in the morning," Coach demands.

"I'll take him to the doctor right now," Favor replies, giving me another concerned look.

I place my hands up in surrender. "Alright, I know when I'm outnumbered." I stand up, already feeling better. Coach turns to head towards the offices.

"What are you doing here, Favor?" Jameson asks, stepping in closer to the two of us.

Favor cringes when she hears Jameson's voice. "I came to watch Brice practice."

"Is that so? You have time to watch him practice, but can't seem to find the time to return a phone call or text?" Anger flares in his eyes as his nostrils expand.

Favor pointedly ignores his outburst, turning her back to him. "Come on, let's get you to the doc."

Jameson takes a step towards her, and I instinctively place her behind me. "We got us a problem?" I stare at him, gauging his temperament.

"*Yeah*. Get your fucking hands off my girl," Jameson scowls at me.

"I'm not your girl. Go away, Jameson. Leave me alone." She steps from around me to face him.

"You're dumping me for this loser?" He jerks his thumb towards me. I should take exception to his words but I don't. I did get the girl, after all.

"We were never a couple, so I can't dump you. Please leave me alone, Jameson." She holds her ground against him. He looks at her for a while before walking off the field. She watches his retreating form, then turns to face me. Alone on the field together, I tip her chin up.

"Are you okay?" I ask her.

"Yeah."

"What's this business of him calling you his girl?"

She shakes her head. "I'm not, I swear it. We were always just friends." She looks away when she finishes her sentence.

Something inside tells me there is something more, but I'm afraid to push it and lose her. I decide to file it away and approach it another time.

"How are you feeling?"

"I've taken worse hits than that. I'm all right."

She smiles at me and shakes her head. "I'm sure you have, but we still need to get you to the doctor."

"Sure, but first things first." Stepping in closer, I lift her chin up, and her cheeks turn a nice shade of pink. I want to see if I can deepen that shade. She remains still, her eyes transfixed on my own. I wrap my hands around her tiny waist and bend to kiss her. I move deliberately slow, to give her time to back away if she wants and to my delight, she doesn't. I've waited an eternity to kiss these lips, and finally, we make contact. Closing my eyes, I take in the kiss from the girl I've considered my Golden Unicorn, and wonder, *How the hell did I get so lucky?*

She tastes of cinnamon and maybe vanilla. My new favorite tastes. We begin the kiss slow and easy, but she does something I wasn't expecting. She wraps her hands around my neck and pulls me in deeper. My dick gets hard, and I'm almost positive she feels the effect she has on me. Before I know it, we are pretty much grabbing at each other's clothes in the middle of the field.

Whistles and catcalls come out from across the field. I pull away from her, and we both look over at some of my teammates teasing us. "Shit, didn't realize we had an audience."

"Yeah, looks like they aren't the only audience." She looks in the opposite direction. I turn to see Jameson glaring at us from afar.

Looks like I have an enemy, on and off the field.

Chapter 8

Favor

After the kiss on the football field, I feel like my little world I've built around myself has turned upside down. I felt that kiss down to my core, and I crave it again. But he is a football player, and I don't date football players. *Enough with the damn game already.* My father ignored me for the better part of my childhood because of this damn sport. Every aspect of the game was lived and breathed in my household. I need a break from it. And what does my fool self go and do? Start to have feelings for a damn football player. And not just a regular player, but a star player that the NFL is rumored to start negotiations with, most likely next year. *Ugh, can I be even more stupid or predictable?*

It has been hard being around Brice since that kiss. I swear, I'm changing underwear three times a day because of him. Laundry is getting to be expensive, all because of a kiss that I can't forget and want more of. He has tried to approach the subject with me a few times, but I stick to my usual mantra. I see the question in his eyes, but he refuses to ask. Thank goodness. He still doesn't know that his childhood idol is my father.

I'm surprised Jameson hasn't let that cat out of the bag yet. He's such a cruel person. The night of that kiss, Jameson showed up to my room, demanding answers from me. He wanted to know how could I let Brice kiss me when I wouldn't even let him hold my hand in public. He just can't seem to get it through his thick skull that I'm not interested, nor will I ever be. I know he has been whining about it to my father because he called me. Dad never calls me. Ever. But he called to find out why am I cheating on Jameson, and how could I do that to a good guy like him. He even went as far as to say, 'I thought I raised you better than this'. *He raised me?* A nanny practically raised me. Dad was never home, and when he was, he only had time for my brother. Mom, when she wasn't off doing charity work or planning a party, really couldn't be bothered with me. So, I was always either left to myself or the care of a nanny.

My mother even called under the guise of, when she and my father come up for the dedication ceremony, where would Jameson and I like to have dinner. As if. There is a new wing that will be dedicated in my brother's name. Trevor Hollister Hall, it is to be called. My mother took on the bulk of the fundraising responsibilities to get the wing built in record time. People from all around the football community donated money. And to think it will happen in a just a couple months. I choke up when I think about it. But I'll be damned if my parents are going to force me to be with Jameson. I will not pretend for the dedication ceremony. I absolutely refuse.

Arriving at the English building, I walk past Jameson talking to a group of friends. He looks at me with longing in his eyes, and I ignore him as I walk inside the building. In my English Lit class, I see a usually late Jana already seated. Some of her cheerleader friends are hanging around her, and one of those bitches is in my seat. *Oh hell no.* I walk over and stand right in front of her. She looks up and jumps.

"Oh sorry, Favor. I didn't see you." She stands, and I sit without acknowledging her.

Thank goodness Professor Corey begins class, and the slut brigade goes back to their seats.

Professor Corey hands out the grades for our projects. I don't bother to look at mine because I always get A pluses. Jana stares at her grade and lets out a 'Woo Hoo.' The class cheers her on.

"I assume that means you got a good grade?" I goad.

"Better than good. I got an A minus." She dances in her seat.

"Congratulations."

"I owe it all to you. Thanks for helping me."

"You're the one who put in the hard work."

"So did you. Truly, thank you. We gotta go and celebrate."

"Sounds good," I hedge, waiting to hear her recommendations for celebrating.

"Awesome. My treat, of course. We can get dinner and then go dancing at the club."

"You had me at dinner but lost me at the club."

"I'm not taking no for an answer. I feel like shaking my tail feather." She does a little wiggle in her seat.

"Okay fine. I must love you as a friend."

"I'll text Cal and find out if he wants to join." She takes out her phone and begins a rapidfire texting. "He's down. We're going to par-tay." She is standing and jiggling her butt to a beat that is clearly in her head. Some of the guys in class gaze at her. I can almost see the hearts in their eyes.

Later that night, the three of us go out to eat and head straight to the club. Grabbing a seat at a booth, some friends and members of the cheerleading team head over to us. A round of Bart Simpson shots goes around. I just stick to my usual water. Jana stands and says she is ready to dance so, of course, she grabs Cal and me to head onto the dance floor with her. The floor is wall to wall people, and someone accidentally pushes Cal, who stumbles backward into the football player Brice had words with before, Kevin.

"Oops. Sorry man," Cal says, and turns back to Jana and me.

"Fucking watch where you are going next time, fag," Kevin snaps.

"Dude. I said I was sorry. Someone pushed me, and I stumbled."

"What, if you're not sucking dick, you're unstable on your feet?" Kevin taunts.

Cal's cheeks turn red. I step in front of Cal. "Listen. He apologized. Let it go."

"I don't want no fucking fairy touching me," Kevin yells out, as some people cheer him on.

My body tenses and a burning heat builds within me to the point of boiling over.

"Not a problem. He might catch something," I retort, before I grab Cal, and we head to the middle of the dance floor.

"I can't believe I slept with that idiot," Jana complains.

Neither can I, but honestly, who am I to talk?

"Thanks for defending me."

"Always."

"Listen, let's forget about that asshole and get back to what we came out for. Have fun and party," Jana declares.

We do as ordered and the three of us dance for several hours. I spot Brice sitting with Egon and some friends of theirs. He notices that I've caught him staring and he stands, sauntering his way over to us on the dance floor. Grabbing me and pulling me into his chest, we begin to move to the rhythm of the music. What is it with the two of us and dancing?

"How much longer?" he asks in my ear, so I can hear him over the music.

"Longer?" My tone is uncertain.

"How much longer will you keep denying the attraction we have? You felt it the same way I did when we kissed. I know you feel it now. You wanna take things slow? I can do that. I'm willing to wait. I've been waiting for you for a year, so a little bit more time won't hurt."

Looking up at him, I see the sincerity of his words in his eyes. "Waited for me?"

He places his hand on my cheek. "Yes. I wanted you the first day I saw you a year ago."

"But I didn't know you a year ago." I'm puzzled.

Smiling down at me, he says, "I know. I introduced myself to you at one of the team's bonfire parties. You told me then you don't date football players, and walked away. I've been chasing you ever since."

I'm blushing by his admission. "I'm sorry. I don't remember."

"S'okay. I'm pretty sure I might've come off cocky at that time anyway. I probably deserved it." He has a sheepish grin.

"Hey. Jana is ready to go," Cal interrupts.

"Oh. Okay. We can leave." I sigh heavily.

"Let me go to the bathroom first. Be right back," Cal says, and turns to head to the bathroom.

"Have dinner with me," Brice says.

"What?"

"You know. Dinner. It's usually the last meal of the day. It comes to a couple of hours after lunch. Lunch, by the way, is the second meal of the day, if you were wondering."

"Funny."

"I won't take no for an answer. I've told you before, I just happen to be a guy who plays football. Okay? Nothing more and nothing less."

"Fine. Dinner." I've finally run out of arguments.

"Good. Next week, Friday, work for you?"

I blink rapidly. "A week?"

"Hmm. Don't tell me I'm growing on you." His eyes twinkle.

"Maybe," I admit. Let's face it, I'm disappointed about not going out with him sooner.

"Where's Cal?" Jana asks.

"He went to the bathroom."

"That was ages ago. I'm ready to go now," Jana says in a whiny voice.

"Hey, I'll go and see if he's still in the bathroom," Brice offers. We both thank him, and he walks towards the bathroom. Moments later, Egon runs over to us.

"Brice needs the two of you right away."

Jana and I exchange wide-eyed looks with one another before running in the direction Brice went, pushing people out of our way. We get to the men's bathroom; the door is being held open by one of the many individuals standing around watching the scene in front of them. My heart drops, and my stomach does a flip when I see Cal lying on the floor. His boyish features are marred with bruises and blood. A few minutes ago, he was lively, and now he's unconscious. What animal did this to him? Only one comes to mind. Kevin.

Brice is kneeling by him with his phone pressed to his ear. He mouths to us that he is on the phone with 9-1-1. Jana and I run over to Cal and Brice motions for us not to touch him. A crowd is starting to form around us in the bathroom.

"Oh, my GOD. Who would do this to him?" Jana cries out.

Brice ends his phone call. "No one was in here when I came in." He looks over to Egon, who is standing nearby. "Bro. Go outside and wait for the ambulance." Egon nods and leaves.

"This is my fault. I insisted we all go out tonight. If I didn't do that, he wouldn't be here," Jana cries into my shoulder.

"It's not your fault. It's the asshole who did this to him," I try to soothe. I hold her for a few moments, rubbing her back.

"Paramedics are here," someone yells.

Egon ushers the paramedics into the bathroom. They check Cal's vitals and ask us a few questions before placing him on the stretcher. Jana rides with Cal in the ambulance, while I ride with Brice and Egon to the hospital. We pace in the waiting room when the cops come to take our statements.

"Did he have any arguments with anyone at the club?" Cop number one asks.

"Yes, he did. With someone from the Cougars," I explain.

Both cops let out a whistle. "What about?"

"Someone bumped into Cal. He stumbled backward and bumped into the guy. The guy got upset and called Cal a lot of derogatory names. Cal apologized, but he wouldn't let it go. The player made some comments referencing Cal being gay."

"Is he?" Cop number two asks.

"What difference does that make?" Jana asks in annoyance.

"Then it becomes a hate crime," Cop number one answers.

"Yes, he is. Cal had a run-in with members of the team a few weeks ago on the field."

"Was that same person he had the argument with part of that altercation as well?"

"Yes," I answer truthfully. Brice places his arm around my waist, pulling me into him. I feel myself relax under his touch.

"What is this player's name?" Cop number two asks.

"Kevin. Kevin Shore," Jana responds.

Brice's hands tighten around my waist. I place my hand on top of his, and he relaxes a bit, kissing the top of my head.

"Whew." He does a low whistle, "Kevin Shore? The defensive tackle?" Cop number two says.

Jana nods her head as a doctor walks through the swinging doors and ambles towards us. "Are you with Calson Deysine?"

"Yes, we are. How is he? Can we see him?" Jana asks.

He looks hesistantly at us, "Are any of you his family?"

We each look at one another and shake our heads.

"Well then I'm sorry, I won't be able to discuss his condition with you."

I open my mouth to protest but Brice holds me in place and speaks.

"We understand, but his family won't be here until tomorrow. We are the closest thing he has to a family. Can you please make an exception?"

The doctor's eyes narrow and then recognition hits him. "Are you Brice Walker? Quarterback for the Cougars?"

Brice nods slowly. "Yes, yes I am."

The doctor moves forward and shakes his hand. "It's a pleasure to meet you." He pats him on the shoulder, "Good game last week. Looks like you got a real shot at the championships."

Brice smiles and nods. "That we do." He gives me a gentle squeeze, "About my friend?"

The doctor looks behind him and then back at Brice. "I shouldn't be doing this but I don't see any harm in letting you know. He has a concussion and two broken ribs. You can see him, but only for a few minutes. He needs to rest."

"Thank you, greatly appreciated." Brice shakes his hand and we all follow the doctor through the swinging doors to where the patients' rooms are located, and head into Cal's room.

Cal looks so small in the hospital bed. One of his eyes is swollen shut, and his face is a patchwork of bruising.

"How are you feeling?" My voice takes on the tone of a person who is in a library, afraid to disturb others, even though Cal is in the room by himself.

"Not too good," Cal responds in a barely audible whisper. His good eye settles on the cops standing at the foot of his bed.

"Are you okay to answer a few questions?" Cop number one asks. Cal nods slowly. "Did you see who did this to you?"

Cal looks at the cops, and then over at Brice. As if he is trying to make a decision of what to say. "No. I didn't get a good look." Jana and I both gasp audibly, not believing what Cal has said.

Both cops look warily at Cal, clearly not believing him either. "Are you sure? We were told that you got into an argument with a Kevin Shore earlier. Was it him?" Cop number two asks.

"No. I said I didn't see the person. Look I'm tired. Can we finish this another time?" Cal says, closing his eye.

Cop number one places his card on the table next to Cal's bed, telling him to call if he remembers anything, and they both leave.

I sigh heavily. "Why did you lie to the cops? I know you saw who did this to you. I see it in your face." I try desperately to reign in my emotions, and look at it from his point of view, but still come back to the fact he should've been honest with the cops. *Why would he lie to cover for Kevin?*

"Leave me alone. I'm exhausted."

I open my mouth to argue, but Jana shakes her head. The room suddenly becomes so silent you can hear the clock on the wall ticking away. Perhaps counting the seconds that his attacker goes free.

"Fine, I'll drop it for now." I spin around and rush towards the door. Jana places a kiss on Cal's forehead and walks out behind me, Brice and Egon close behind. "I don't understand it. Why would he lie?"

"I don't know. Maybe he's scared," Jana cajoles.

"So we just let that animal get away with it?" I rage as Brice pulls me into his chest.

"Listen, do I feel he should have told the cops, yes. But whatever his reasons are, we have to respect it. Give him a few days," Brice says to me as he strokes my hair.

A part of me knows that Brice is right. I need to respect Cal's decision, but it doesn't make it feel right. I exhale, letting out the pent-up tension, but not the hurt and anguish that my friend is laying in a hospital bed.

I lean deeper into Brice's arms and give in to the fact that this feels good. Everything with him feels right. The last of the wall that was standing between him and me comes crashing down around my feet, leaving the two us standing together.

But still, in the back of my mind, I can't help but wonder if it was Kevin Shore who did this to Cal.

Chapter 9

Brice

Cal has been in the hospital for a few days, and still has not told the cops who did this to him. Favor and Jana have been working on getting him to talk to the police, but he refuses, for whatever reason. His parents are now in town, waiting for his release from the hospital, to take him back home to Virginia so he can recuperate there. The cops spoke to Kevin, and of course, he denied having anything to do with what happened to Cal.

Rumors are swirling around in the locker room about Kevin being questioned by the cops. Coach had a team meeting and addressed the issue of some of the team making derogatory remarks about gays. We are scheduled for sensitivity training in two weeks. The coach and school are taking what happened to Cal very seriously as they do their own investigation into the incident.

Egon walks into the gym and watches me finish my reps on free weights. Placing the weights back in its cradle, I grab my towel to wipe the sweat off my forehead.

"Going at it kinda hard, bro." Egon leans on the wall, smirking at me.

"Yeah. Gotta keep pushing myself." I stand and grab my bottled water.

Egon sits on the bench and starts lifting the weights. "Did Cal come out of the hospital yet?"

"No. From what I hear, he should be released soon."

"He still not talking?" he grunts as he pushes a weight above his head.

"Nope. I think Kevin did have something to do with it. Just not sure why Cal won't say something."

"Maybe he's scared? Or maybe he didn't see anything."

I give Egon a look, shaking my head. "Scared, yes. But he saw the person. That I'm willing to bet on."

"Well, one thing is for sure, bro. No one can make him talk unless he's ready." Egon places the weight into its holder before standing and grabbing his towel.

"Yeah. Just wished I understood why he wouldn't want to say something. Why protect the person?"

"Who knows, but he has to have his reasons. Hey, you remember when we were in the seventh grade, and that girl that had the stutter?"

I think back for a moment, and then the image of her face pops into my head. "Oh yeah. Katie...or..." I try to remember her name.

"Kathy. Remember how some of the kids used to pick on her."

"Yeah, I remember. On the school bus. They used to pull her pigtails or something."

"Yeah, and that time when we were in the cafeteria, that same group knocked her food out of her hands and made her pick it up, only to knock it out of her hands again."

I do remember that. Egon and I went over to her when they wouldn't stop harassing her in the lunchroom that day. I nod my head at him.

"Remember when the principal asked her who was doing that to her. She said she didn't know."

"Yeah, I do. She was already being teased about her stutter and didn't want any more attention."

Egon gives me a shrug. "Not to compare the two exactly, but it could be slightly the same thing. I don't know, but people have reasons for doing things." He grabs his gym bag, and we stroll towards the exit.

I wonder if Egon might be on to something after all. Later in the day, after we showered and had lunch, I decide to go over to the hospital to pay Cal a visit. Egon comes along with me. Not so much as to check on Cal, but because he saw a really hot nurse the night we came here before, and he wants to see if she's on duty. *Some things never change.*

I knock on Cal's room door. A woman's voice says to come in. I walk in and introduce myself to his parents. Instantly, his parents sit upright in their seats.

"So, you're a friend of Calson?" his mother asks with a slight southern lilt.

"Yes, ma'am. How're you doing Cal?" I ask, switching my attention.

"Getting better, I guess. I should be released tomorrow, hopefully."

91

"Yes, we're bringing Calson home with us to recuperate," his mother adds, as she pats Cal's shoulder.

Cal's father frowns at me. *What did I do to him?* I turn my attention back to Cal. "Good. Have Favor and Jana come by today?"

"Oh, those two girls are so sweet. They come here faithfully every day, and sit with Cal," his mom chimes in.

"Yes, they came earlier today. I think Favor is supposed to be coming by again later. Jana has cheerleading practice, so she won't be able to."

"I have practice later tonight, also."

"Cheerleading? How exactly do you know my son?" Cal's father stands abruptly, his hands clenched.

"Dad, he's just my friend."

"*I'm speaking to him, not you,*" he growls out.

"Umm, sir, I'm Cal's friend, that's all. I came to check on him."

"Dad, he's the quarterback for the Cougars."

Cal's father looks me up and down, almost questioning his son's words. "It's true, sir. I am. I was the one that found Cal that night also."

"Oh my," his mother cries out.

"Just friends?" his father accuses.

"Yes, sir. Just his friend."

92

His father looks me over again, then back at his son, before he exits the room. Cal's mother gives me a sad smile. "If you'll excuse me, I'll check on him." She leaves the room.

I stare at the door, not believing what I just witnessed. "Sorry about that," Cal says, as he shifts himself on the bed.

"Are they always that intense?"

"Yes." Cal lets out a sigh. "Thanks for coming. I never got a chance to thank you for that night."

I hold up my hands. "Nothing to thank me for. Sorry I didn't get to you quicker, or else I could've caught who did this to you."

He looks away and stares at the wall.

"Do you remember anything yet?" I press him.

"No, nothing." I may not know Cal well, but I can see that he is hiding the truth.

I shake my head. "Cal, I have the feeling that you *do* know who did this. You shouldn't let this person get off without some type of punishment. Listen, your friends are here for you, no matter what. If you want, we can all be with you when you talk to the cops."

Cal shakes his head violently. "*No.* I told you, I don't know who did this. Why can't everyone just leave me alone?"

"Alright. I'm sorry I didn't mean to make you upset. I'll drop it."

He bows his head. "Thanks."

His room door opens, and his mother walks in. "Cal, you really should be getting some rest."

I turn to look at her and nod my head. "Sorry, I didn't mean to stay so long." Turning back to Cal, I continue, "If I don't get a chance to get out to see you before you leave, hope you feel better soon."

Cal smiles and nods his head at me as I leave the room in search of Mr. Loverboy Egon.

Chapter 10

Favor

Cal has been finally released from the hospital, and his parents have taken him home to finish his recuperating process in Virginia. Cal told me that Brice stopped by to see him and my heart was full when I heard. He was excited that Brice took the time out to go to visit him, and insists Brice is a keeper. I cannot deny that my feelings for Brice are growing more and more by the day.

Friday night is here, and I can't figure out what to wear for my date with Brice. I've been staring at my outfit choices, and just can't make up my mind. *I wish Cal was here.* Jana and Regan step into the room.

"What're you doing? Going out tonight?" Jana asks, as she picks up one of my discarded choices.

"Yeah. Dinner and a movie. Can't figure out what to wear," I say as I toss yet another outfit on the bed.

She bounces on her bed. "Who with?"

"Brice," I respond absentmindedly, as I debate my outfits.

"Brice Walker? Oh, my God." She jumps up and down in the middle of the floor while Regan gives me a dirty look.

"I don't see what you see in that loser," Regan snarls.

Did that bitch just call Brice a loser? She better be careful because I am about to throw down in a minute.

"Stop it, Regan. Brice isn't a loser, and you know it. You're just salty because he told you the truth. Everyone knew you weren't dating Egon, but yet you were spreading the rumor around because of one night of sex." I could kiss Jana at that very moment for defending my man. *Wait.* Did I just call Brice my man? Oh God, I need to push these crazy thoughts out of my head.

"How could you be with someone that was mean to one of your closest friends?" Regan complains again.

Is she for real? "Jana? Brice was mean to you?" I ask, as Regan gives me a pissed off look.

"No, not me," Jana plays along.

"Well, then Regan, I don't know what friend you are referring to because my closest friend just said no."

Regan stands up in a huff, opening the door with so much force that it slams into the wall before she slams it shut behind her. *Good riddance.*

"Oh, my God. She's pissed." Jana laughs.

Ehh, fuck her. "Really? I didn't notice. Now help me pick out an outfit."

Jana stands up and rejects all my choices I left on the bed. She reaches into my closet and finds a dress I forgot I had. "Here. That's the outfit." She and Cal know my wardrobe better than I do.

"Shit, you're right. It's perfect." I put on the form-fitting black dress that hugs my curves in all the right places. I top it off with some black heeled boots.

I spin around, and Jana applauds. "Amazing."

"Thanks," I say honestly.

"You know, since we've been rcomies, I have never seen you go out on an actual date before."

I pout as I think about what Jana has said, and realize she's right. I've never dated. My stomach now feels like it is being tied into a knot. "This is just two friends having dinner and a movie, that's all." I throw those words out in hopes of settling my now-bubbling nerves.

Jana rolls her eyes and shakes her head. "Then why the extra effort of getting dressed?"

"No reason. I like to look nice." I bat my eyelashes at her in an exaggerated fashion.

Crossing her arms over her chest, she huffs. "For a dinner and a movie?"

"Yeah. I'm starting a new trend for everyone on campus to follow." I shrug.

"Riigght."

I jump at the sound of a light knock on the door. Placing my hand over my racing heart, I look over at Jana, who is all smiles. Oh God, it's him. I glance in the mirror and see my chest rising and falling rapidly. I inhale deeply, and slowly exhale to calm myself before I hyperventilate and pass out. Fainting on a date isn't exactly a good first impression.

Jana stands behind me and gives me a reassuring squeeze. "You'll be okay. I'm going to answer the door before he leaves." I look up and see her smiling reflection in the mirror, and nod.

She walks over to the door and holds the knob, turning to give me a thumbs up, and opens it. Brice murmurs a hello before walking in. I turn around slowly and set eyes on him wearing a heather-gray sweater and black jeans. He looks so damn delicious, I want to skip dinner and have a bite of him instead. I wonder if that could be an option.

"Wow. You look stunning," he says as his eyes rake over my body, and my sense of propriety slips another notch.

"So do you." I bend my head, trying desperately to hide my blush. "I meant, you look handsome." I look back up to see his brown eyes pulling me in deeper.

"Thanks." His voice a low rumble and my heart is officially silly putty in his hands.

"Umm, shouldn't the two of you get going?"

My breath hitches. I forgot Jana was in the room with us. I grab my clutch from the desk and turn to look at Brice, and instantly I want to jump on him like a pogo stick. I nibble on my bottom lip, debating if I should try.

"Shall we?"

My eyes widen. *Did I accidentally say my thoughts out loud?* But then disappointment hits me when I realize he is talking about leaving to go to dinner. "Umm, yeah." I push my hair behind my ear. "Of course." I turn towards Jana, who is giggling at me. No doubt this will be a topic of conversation later. "Be back in a bit."

"Have fun. And by the way, I won't be back till tomorrow morning, so the room is all yours." She winks at me and I give her the fake angry glare as I walk towards the door, and accidentally bump into Brice.

"Looks like we're always running into each other."

"Sorry," I mutter.

"No worries, I like running into you." His voice is like silk, and now my panties need to come off, along with my clothes.

I look heavenward and pray to God that I can keep a sense of decorum when I'm sitting near him in the car.

Outside, the cool air wars with my internal heat that is burning up for Brice. We stroll down the pathway to his car, side by side. I have to hold myself back from reaching out and taking his hand. Perhaps he's just as nervous as I am and he is waiting for a signal from me. We're at his car before I reach a decision, and he holds the door open for me, helping me inside. With his hands in his pocket, he walks over to the driver side and gets in. The scent of his Acqua di Gio cologne fills the small car, hypnotizing me. I close my eyes and inhale deeply, briefly transporting myself through time. So many futures pass through my brain, futures with him, so vivid and clear that it scares me. I open my eyes with a start, my breath caught in my throat. I turn slowly around to see him staring at me. My cheeks warm and I feel dizzy.

"You okay?"

Not wanting to break the spell, I say, "Mmmhmm."

"I've waited so long for this night with you." He holds his steering wheel and looks ahead for a moment before turning back to look at me with his warm brown eyes. "I guess I just want to say, thank you for giving me a chance."

"Brice, you don't have to-"

"But I do, or at least I want to. I want to show you that I am a good guy, and that I want to be with you. I promise to not rush anything."

I've always felt incomplete, never good enough, not worthy. But somehow his words have molded the different layers of me back together again. If I wasn't already, I feel complete now. If I wasn't good enough before, I know I am now. If I wasn't worthy, I'm worthy now. It's not because of him, but because of his belief in me.

I turn my head towards the window, not wanting him to see the tears of happiness in my eyes. "Thank you for that." I wipe at the corner of my eye. "We really should get going." My voice is raw with emotion.

He clears his throat. "You picked a movie?"

A giggle escapes my lips. "Actually no, I didn't." I was so anxious about tonight, I forgot.

He laughs. "Okay, so dinner and…?" His eyes search my own.

I gulp loudly. "Umm, no clue."

"Okay. We can wing it." He starts the car and pulls off, breaking the spell, but not the hold he has on me.

We arrive at a quaint Italian restaurant. *How did he know I love Italian?*

As if reading my mind, he says, "Jana mentioned Italian is your favorite."

My eyes widen. "She did? When?"

"A few days ago. It is, isn't it?" His brows knit together as he waits for my response.

"No." I close my eyes. "I mean, yes, it is my favorite."

He gives me a satisfied grin. "I knew we were meant for each other. Italian is my favorite too." He hops out of the car and comes around the other side to open my door.

Once we're inside and seated, some patrons come up to him and ask for his autograph, which he signs with a smile and thanks.

"Don't you ever get tired of it?" I ask, as memories of going places with my dad and him being rushed by fans for autographs invade my mind. Somehow, I always got pushed to the sidelines and forgotten.

"Never. I doubt I ever will. Football has always been my dream." A look comes over his face that I've seen dozens of times before, on my father's face, whenever he spoke about the game.

Could there really be room for me in Brice's life? Football...it always comes to football. "Really? Why?" I straighten in my seat. Placing my hands on my lap, I twist the cloth napkin under the table.

He puts his hands on the table top, clasping them together. Looking down, he begins, "Well, I love and have a true respect for the game. That is part of the reason why I model myself after my idol, Kyne Hollister."

My face slackens at the mention of my father's name. Does he know? But how? He looks up briefly, and the frown that was on my face is instantly replaced with a smile. He nods and finishes.

"He's a living legend in the sport. I met him once when he came to Philadelphia. Mom waited with me for hours in that line, just so I could meet him and have my football signed. I still have that ball to this day." For a moment, as he retells his story, he looks to be as youthful as he must've been that day my father gave him his autograph.

It never ceases to amaze me the hearts of the many kids my father has touched. Each one of them has better stories to tell of him than I do. I tug at my clothing. "You grew up in Philly?" Unable to mask the emotions in my voice, my voice is clipped. Brice looks up startled, and I give him a reassuring smile.

"Yeah. Me and Egon. We lived around the corner from each other. I spent more nights than I can count at Egon's house when my mom was pulling a double shift."

My head tilts to the side. "What about your dad?"

He shrugs. "Never met him. It used to bother me, not having a dad when I was growing up. That's when I started to pretend that Kyne Hollister was my dad. It helped to cope with life without one, or better yet, not knowing him."

He is so honest and no regrets. I feel a bit petty about always complaining about life at home. Hell, at least I had both parents around, even though they were just about absent from my life.

"So, what about you?"

Oh great, we've moved on to me. Should I tell him that his childhood idol is my father? If I do, would I stand a chance of keeping him to myself? Or would my dad and football always be between us? "Well, I grew up in a nuclear home. You know, a mom, a dad, and a brother."

"Older brother or younger?"

"Older." The dull ache in my heart that always holds me back from absolute happiness begins to throb heavily. My throat becomes scratchy, so I reach a trembling hand to grab the glass of water.

"Are the two of you close?"

I take a few swallows of the liquid, and it turns my stomach. I place the glass on the table and clear my throat. "Yes, we were. He died three years ago."

"My condolences." His tone is soothing.

"It's okay. Some days are harder than others."

He reaches out his hand to touch mine on the table. A gesture so innocent, yet so intimate, and he says, "If you ever need a shoulder to cry on..."

I give him a weak smile as my vision becomes blurry from the tears that are building up. "Thanks."

The waiter hands us our menus. I gladly accept mine, lifting it in a guise of reading it. I let the tears fall freely, wetting the white table cloth. Each droplet widens the damp spot on the cloth, as well as the hole in my heart. I feel so overwhelmed that I have to fight the urge to run. But where would I run to?

"Favor?"

I can't answer; I'm choking on my emotions.

I hear the scraping of a chair and feel his closeness. His hand gently tugs on the top of the menu. I don't have the strength to hold it any further, and it releases into his hand. He places it down on the table and cups my chin.

I avert my eyes. "Don't. Don't look at me." I can take almost anything else, but his pity...I just can't handle that right now.

"But-"

I stand abruptly. "Please, just give me a minute. I'll be right back." My voice is a throaty whisper. I rush to the bathroom, thankful to have the room to myself. Staring at my reflection in the mirror, my eyes are red and puffy, and my skin is blotchy. The person I'm looking at has become a familiar face in the past three years, and I'm tired of looking at her.

"No more." My voice is weak, but I feel a sense of relief. "No. More." My voice is a little stronger. "NO. MORE." I command myself at will. I won't let the pain of the loss of my brother stop me from happiness. I need to try, I *want* to try, to heal. An invisible needle and thread is mending the hole in my heart, slowly. The last of my tears fall into the sink, and I turn the faucet on to drown them. I place my hands under the stream of water, and my fingertips become numb from the cold. I reach for the knob and turn it off. Lifting my hands to my face, I smear the cold droplets against my skin, closing my eyes and relishing the feel of it.

I take one last look at my old self in the mirror, a self that I won't mourn or miss. I open the bathroom door and step back into the dining area. Brice is facing me, his brows drawn together. I stop in front of him and brush my lips against his.

"I'm fine." He stands and helps me with my seat, his hand brushing ever so lightly on my shoulder, sending a shiver up my spine.

"Are you sure you are okay? I can take you back to your dorm." His voice is hesitant when he asks.

Do I want to go to the dorm? Should I? I stare into Brice's eyes and I know in my heart I'm that I'm not ready for this night to end. "No. I'm where I want to be. It's just hard sometimes, that's all."

He closes his eyes momentarily before opening them. "Okay, I understand. Just know that I'm here whenever you need me."

I reach out and hold his hand, the tiniest of a spark firing up between us. "I know, and thank you."

"Fresh start?"

I nod. "Fresh start."

As if to confirm our deal, the flame from the candle on the table dances, and then settles into stillness.

The mood lightens, and we place our order with the waiter before having some of the most enjoyable conversation I've ever had. The talk flows so easily, it scares me. When there is silence, it is comfortable and not because we ran out of things to talk about. Brice tells me more about his plans of being recruited by the NFL. He says that he gets up early most mornings to get some extra training in. He tells me all about his mom and what it was like growing up in Philly. He promises one day to bring me to the best place to get a Cheesesteak hoagie. We talk about how he and Egon are more like brothers than friends, and how Egon forced him to learn to play bass because he wanted to start a band. Unfortunately, Brice was horrible, and Egon had to drop him from a group that wasn't even created, at fourteen years old. We talk long after we finish dinner and dessert.

I share stories about my family without bringing up football. I'm not ready to talk about that yet. One day, but not today. I just want tonight to be about us and not who my father is.

He pays for dinner, and we walk with dragging footsteps, back to his car.

"Anywhere else?" he asks.

"I don't know. I guess you can take me back to my dorm."

He has a hesitant smile, but he doesn't protest. He starts the car and drives me back to campus.

Brice walks me to my dorm, his hand at the small of my back. When we reach my room, I unlock the door, and a pang of fear hits me that this evening is coming to an end, and I'm not ready to let him go. It's now or never. "Would you like to come in?" I ask the question but plead with my eyes.

He has a dazed look and nods his head. I open the door further and am thankful to see that Jana is out. I flip on the light and flop on my bed, patting the seat next to me. Sitting down, he says, "Your room sure is neater than mine and Egon's."

I laugh at his comment, releasing the tension that I was suddenly feeling. You ever wound up a coil as tight as it could go until the pressure of it builds up? That is how I feel right now. "Thanks for dinner."

"Thanks for coming," he replies, flashing his brown eyes at me. We both turn to face each other, and I feel a pull I can't resist. Before I have a chance to wonder if it feels the same for him, his mouth consumes mine, hungry and fierce.

Why was I fighting this for so long with him? He was right; there is something between us, and there has been for quite some time. Right now, being drawn deeper into his orbit, I feel that all the other times of fighting it was a waste. The time we could have been together, had I not been running scared. He groans into my mouth, and I pull him closer. He rips himself away from our kiss, leaving me wanting and missing him. "If we don't stop now, I don't think I'll be able to later."

"I don't want you to stop," I murmur, dragging him back to my anxious lips.

Pulling away from me briefly, he rubs his hands over his face. "I can't believe I'm about to say this...but I don't want to rush this. I've waited so long for you and I don't want you to think that's what I'm after. I'm willing to wait for as long as needed."

His words carefully sink in, syllable by syllable. I think long and hard about it. Am I rushing things? I know I feel something for him. Ever since that day he defended Cal, I've been in that careful little nook between like and love. It's something, it's more than I ever had with Jameson. I didn't even have a lust for him, yet I gave him the most intimate part of myself. I thought I knew what I wanted, but right now, I'm questioning myself. Perhaps I'm not thinking things through the way I should.

He kisses me on my forehead and rises. "I should go. Thank you for the most incredible evening of my life. I really hope that you give me a chance at a second date." He turns and walks towards the door, and that's when I know.

"Stop." My voice is calm and sure because I know in my heart this is right.

He turns around. "Are you sure?" His eyes searches mine.

Deciding the best way to reassure him is to show him, I stand and slowly lower each strap of my dress. I turn my back to him and playfully tap on the zipper's metal tab with my fingernail. I hear him move across the carpet, and instantly feel his warmth behind me. So close, yet so far. Too far. His fingers fumble with the zipper, and finally, he pulls the metal piece down, releasing me. I take a deep breath at the instant relief of being freed from the burden of the tight dress, and let my inhibitions fall to the floor in a heap, along with my clothes.

I turn to face him, standing in my bra and thong, without an ounce of regret. "I'm sure." I make sure he sees me, all of me, the *real* me. I once read that a person can pick up on the energy you give. I concentrate on this energy, and I will him with every fiber of my being to receive it. As if he reads my mind, he offers me his hand that I take, willingly and without hesitation. This is meant to be, and I can feel it. My heart beats steady in anticipation of him, of us. Because that's exactly what this is; the beginning of us. A word that I used to be so afraid of suddenly becomes a word I can't live without.

Brice is the sun, and I am the moon that orbits around him. That's how great the pull I feel is, as I take a step closer to him. I wonder for a moment if a simple touch by him will burn, forever marking me as his. I want to absorb this moment with him in every way imaginable.

Reaching behind me, he unclasps my bra with one hand, releasing my breasts and I yearn for the warmth of his touch. I look over at the door in a panic that Jana might walk in, but just as quickly, I remember that she said I had the room to myself this evening. Perhaps Jana knew how this evening would end. I know that I wanted this, but did I foresee it? Did he? Oh God, does it matter? I focus on the here and now and forget the rest.

My breath hitches as his hands travel down my back so gently it's like a whisper of a touch. I lean into him, feeling his firm body against my softness. It was like I was molded just for him, and notice how strong his hands are as they settle on my hips and playfully tug at my thong.

I throw my head back in laughter. "You going to play with it or take it off?"

"Hmm. I'm thinking both," he says with a devilish gleam in his eyes. He pushes the lace gently with his thumb, the anticipation building to the point of bursting inside me. I reach down to shove the obstructing material out of the way, but his hands cup my own, preventing my hurried movements. "Oh no, I want to take my time with you."

Did the world just suddenly stop moving, because I feel frozen in time. "Umm, what?" Why am I so breathless?

He leans into me, his warm breath coating my neck as a thin sheen of sweat covers my body. "I said, I want to take my time with you. I've waited a year for you, and I don't want to rush this. I want to make love to your body, your mind, and your soul."

I open my mouth to speak, but no words come out. It's hard to form coherent words when your mind turns to silly putty. Soft tingles run all over my body, and my heart thrums against my chest. This is how it's so supposed to feel. If I never experience this feeling again, I'll be forever grateful to him for this.

His mouth gently touches my already open one, his tongue searching for mine until the two meet. Our tongues dance, almost like a ballet, in complete synchronization. He tastes like cappuccino and tiramisu, triggering my sweet tooth for more. More of him. His arms are firm around my waist, and I'm thankful because my legs are wobbly from his kiss.

He slowly moves my thong past my butt cheeks, and gravity does the rest. His voice is raspy when he says, "Leave the boots on," and I almost come just from those words.

I help him remove his clothes as best I can without losing the contact of his lips on mine. Lifting me up and placing me on my bed, he hovers over me.

"Open your legs for me...wider." His voice is slow, like a lazy day in the summer.

I shift on the bed into a more comfortable position, his smoldering eyes watching - no, worshiping - my every movement. I reach my hands out to touch him because the ache is so deep.

He shakes his head. "Not yet. I want tonight to be about you, and only you."

"What are you going to do?"

"I have a taste for an after-dinner snack," he teases as he lays on his stomach, eye level with my womanhood.

My head feels fuzzy as if I've been drinking, and I begin to quiver. He places a calming hand on my trembling stomach. "What's wrong?"

"I...ugh." How do I explain this? "I've never had someone go down"- I tip my chin - "you know, down there before." My cheeks warm. Why am I so embarrassed?

If he were a rooster, his feathers would be standing on end. "I just got harder. Didn't think that was possible."

"But-"

"No buts. Just lay your pretty head back and enjoy the ride."

He places his hands under my ass cheeks and pulls me closer to him, inhaling my scent. "Mmm, you smell like heaven." Those are the last words I hear because my screams of pleasure drown the rest out.

Hours later, after making love too many times to count, we both lay, panting and sleek with sweat. A delicious odor of sex hangs in the air around us, and it makes me want more. I lightly stroke my fingernails down his back as he licks the side of my neck lazily. "I don't want to ever lose this feeling." It comes out of my mouth before I have a chance to stop it. I bury my face in his shoulder.

Pushing up on his elbows, he looks me in my eyes. "I don't want to, either. I know you felt the connection. Please don't deny it."

How can I deny it anymore? "I felt it. I always felt it."

"The club?"

I nod.

"Then why didn't you admit it?" He smirks at me.

"I couldn't. I was scared." It's the most honest answer I can give.

"And now?" He waits patiently for my reply.

"I'm still scared, but I'm willing to face the possibilities with you," I admit.

He kisses me gingerly, and we make love well into the early morning hours, before I fall asleep in his arms.

****

"Oh, my God." Jana yells when she opens the door in the morning.

I blink back the sleepiness from my eyes, and my heart leaps because I'm still in Brice's arms. He hasn't even stirred from Jana's yell. "Shhh. He's still sleeping," I say, whispering to her, and she gives me a thumbs up.

"I'm not sleeping anymore," he replies in a deep groggy voice, rubbing one of his hands over his face, his other one still wrapped around me. "What time is it?"

"Eight o'clock," Jana says in her usual sing-song voice.

"Shit, baby. We only went to sleep about an hour ago," he complains to me.

"I know." I stretch in his arms, and let out a little yelp from the soreness below. He smiles at me knowingly.

"Sore?" he whispers in my ear. I nod. "Want me to kiss it and make it better?" He nibbles on my earlobe. All thoughts of Jana standing and watching us leave my head. I'm about to tell him 'yes please' when Jana clears her throat.

"I'm standing right here, guys." She snaps her fingers at us.

Brice and I look at each other and laugh. "Jana, can you give Brice and I a minute? He needs to get dressed."

"Sure. I need to take a shower anyway." She grabs her things and leaves us alone in the room.

We begin kissing, and that delicious feeling begins to build up to the point of me wanting more. Soft tingles travel from my toes to my stomach as I try to do a quick mental calculation. Maybe we can squeeze in a quickie. "She's only in the shower. She can come back soon." I halfheartedly try to pull away, but he brings me back into him.

"Girls always take forever in the shower," he murmurs against my lips, in between kisses.

"Well, she won't. She is going to rush it so she can come in here and ask me questions about you." My eyes flutter as he kisses me in the right spot. What was I talking about again?

"How long you need with her?" he asks.

How long will I need with what? Oh, that's right. We were talking about Jana, weren't we? "I don't know. I guess I need to shower also. She'll most likely want to grab breakfast so we can have girl time."

"Alright. I'll give you until noon. Come to my dorm, and we can spend the rest of the day in bed. Egon has band rehearsals today." He kisses me on my jaw, working his way down my neck.

I smile at him. "All day in bed, huh?"

Leaning in, he says, "Yes. Plan on using cushions to sit on tomorrow," and then winks at me.

Mmmm, the thought does things to my lady parts. "Yes, please." We kiss again. "We have to stop for real this time. We're running out of time."

"Okay. Noon. Don't make me come look for you, woman," he jokes as he stands to get dressed.

"Wait," I call out. He stops just as he is about to pull on his boxers. I get on my knees in front of him, taking his length in my mouth till it hits the back of my throat. *Thank goodness for great gag reflexes.* I pull my mouth away slowly until I get to the tip, which I give a swirl with my tongue. I slowly stand up with a smile on my face.

"Tease," he says, pulling me into him, kissing me softly.

Brice is fully dressed, and I'm in my robe already missing his body next to mine. We walk to the door of my room. "Baby. No one else but me. Got it?"

"No one else but you, Brice. I promise. And no one else but me for you."

He kisses me again. "No one else, baby. I promise."

Jana bursts through the door, only minutes after Brice leaves.

"Dish," she squeals.

"About?" I joke.

She throws her towel at me. I think she is getting ready to throw her slipper at me next, when I tell her we can have breakfast and talk, after I take a shower. She smiles and bounces around in happiness. I swear, she is just too damn cute at times.

Chapter 11

Favor

Brice and I have been officially together for two weeks now. Because of his popularity, we haven't made it official on campus yet, outside of Egon and Jana. Girls would purposely throw themselves at him just to start a rumor that they took him away. It is a beautiful cocoon that we're eventually going to have to break.

I'm sitting at one of the campus cafeterias with Jana and Regan eating lunch, and receive a text as I am joking around with the girls.

Brice: Baby, where are you?

Me: West cafeteria, having lunch with Jana and Regan.

Brice: On my way.

Five minutes later, he shows up with Egon. The moment the two of them walk into the cafeteria, all eyes are on them. They make quite a striking appearance together. Brice is tall with an athletic build, and he always looks clean and crisp, as if just coming from church. Egon is slightly shorter, but not by much, and he has the bad boy rocker look, with tats up and down his arms and on his neck. Where one is light and airy, the other is dark and mysterious. Brice takes the seat next to me, and Egon sits next to Jana. Everything is going well with our group lunch up until Jana makes a mistake.

"I swear, you and Brice make the cutest couple," Jana gushes.

Regan drops her fork. "What?"

Jana quickly realizes her mistake and gives me an apologetic look. I give her a shrug. Hey, it was bound to get out someday. I'm surprised we were able to keep it a secret this long.

"Thanks, Jana. My girl and I think we look cute also," Brice jokes as he steals a French fry from my plate. His action reminds me of something my brother would do.

"When did this happen?" Regan asks, as she looks from me to Brice and then back to me again.

"Oh, I guess about two weeks ago. Isn't that right, babe?" I ask Brice, and he nods his head as he chews another French fry he has stolen from me.

"Oh. Guess that was to be expected," Regan says, folding her arms over her chest.

"What do you mean?" Jana asks.

"You know, the two most popular kids in school are bound to date one another, but I doubt it'll last. You have a reputation around campus as a player, Brice," Regan says, as she looks at him through narrowed eyes.

I open my mouth to lay into her, but Brice, who was holding my hand under the table, gives me a gentle squeeze. "Careful Regan, your claws are showing."

"Fuck you, Brice," she snaps angrily.

Brice returns a wave to someone who passes by before he responds. "No, as I recall you offered before, and I turned it down."

She gets red in the face, as Jana and I give each other a passing glance. Egon laughs, taking a bite of his pizza.

"You're going to let him talk to me like that?" Regan turns to Egon.

"Yep." He swallows. "Regan, you're so caught up in trying to be a version of Favor, it's sad. Everyone in school knows it. You're just the only one who hasn't bought a clue yet." He reaches into his pocket and flips a quarter to her. "There you go. Now you can go and buy one." We all erupt in laughter at her.

"I slept with you because I felt sorry for you," Regan stammers, fighting back the tears.

"I slept with you because I was too lazy to find something better," he responds back.

Regan's mouth drops open.

"And also, if I were you, I would stop repeating that I slept with you. I have a reputation to keep up. I may have to announce what a lousy lay you were," Egon says, in between bites.

"And *loud*. Don't forget *loud*. Lousy and loud is so much worse," Brice chimes in for the final kill shot.

Regan storms off, leaving her tray of food on the table. "Babe, that was brutal," I tell Brice, not feeling sorry for her in the least.

"Bitch deserved it," he replies with no remorse.

"I never really noticed that she's really just that mean," Jana muses.

"Aren't you a cute little pixie," Egon says, looking at Jana.

"Uh, pixie?" Jana asks.

"Yeah, pixie. You're a cute little pixie." He leans in closer.

Jana blushes. "I gotta go, guys." She stands and takes hers and Regan's trays to empty.

"Wow, the two of you sure know how to clear the table," I say.

"Who us?" they ask in unison, as they give each other a fist bump.

"Babe, I gotta get to class." Brice squeezes my hand under the table and stands to leave. Egon remains seated, still working on yet another slice. "Later, man," he says to Egon as he walks away. But at that moment, I feel the need to cut the crap and make this shit official in front of God and campus. Let's give the rumor mill something to talk about, damn it.

"Brice," I yell out, and all eyes turn to me as I stand from the table. I sprint to him, still standing in the middle of the cafeteria, and jump into his arms. We give the crowd a kiss to remember as he swings me around. Everyone is cheering us on. "Guess I just outed us," I say, smiling into his lips.

"Damn baby, you can out us anytime like that again." He gives my butt cheeks a squeeze.

"I have an idea. Let's skip classes and go to bed."

He gives me a look, letting me know he's considering it. "God, woman, you're going to be the death of me."

"Go to class. When you're done with practice tonight, come to my dorm."

He kisses me again. "I will. And baby, get ready to be fucked, and well." He kisses me one last time before he turns to leave.

Spinning on my heels to walk back to my seat, I bump right into Jameson.

"So it's official? The two of you?"

"Yes, not that it is any of your business."

"You know your parents want you with me." His eyes turn to narrow slits.

"Since when do I listen to what they say?" I try to walk around him, but he steps in front of me.

"Yo, Favor. All good?" Egon calls out as all eyes are on Jameson and me.

I look at Jameson. "Yeah, Egon it's all good. My buddy Jameson here was just wishing Brice and me all the best wishes for our future together." I smile at Jameson and walk past him, as hushed whispers flow by me.

Chapter 12

Brice

Practice is brutal. Coach has us training harder than usual today. We have a chance at the Championships, and he wants to make sure we are ready for whatever comes at us. I push myself hard on the field, harder than the rest of my teammates. Jameson tries to match me with everything that I do, but I always outdo him. I'm just a better player than he is. Where I feel one with the football, Jameson always manages to look like he's still trying to remember a play in his head. He may have the family background for football, but this stadium is my house.

I take a quick water break and look up in the stands to see Favor watching me. I think to myself how feasible would it be to grab her, fuck her in the locker room, and get back out on the field before Coach realizes I'm gone. One of my teammates comes over.

"Hey, man. I've never seen Favor step foot in the stadium until you two started dating."

What? Is he checking for my girl? "You've been looking for her up there in the bleachers or something?" I ask, ready to tackle him to the ground if he gives me an answer I don't like.

"Naw, man. It's just that she has been notorious for avoiding the stadium and football games. She also used to stand firm by her decision that she doesn't date football players."

That is true, now that I think back. I never did ask her why that was. I'll have to remember to ask her one of these days. "Yeah. But hey, I'm not just your ordinary football player," I say as I flex my muscles.

The cheerleaders out practicing start catcalling. I yell out to them, "Sorry ladies, I'm already taken."

Some of them act like they are crushed, and others still taunt with whistles. "Hearts all over the campus are breaking," my teammate says to me.

I place my hand on his shoulder. "Only one heart around here I care about, and she is sitting in the bleachers. Wearing my jacket, waiting for me to warm her bed tonight."

"Man, you are one lucky son of a bitch. You know how many guys tried to..."

"Don't say it, bro. Just to put it out there for you and the world to know, I'm a very jealous man. So don't go putting thoughts in my head. When I hear it, I might take it for truth and start pounding some heads together."

He backs away with his hands in the air. "No worries, bro." He jogs back over to the rest of the team, and I stand staring at Favor as she waves to me. I want to run over to her and kiss her right now, but I have the feeling our break is up, and Coach will be calling us back. As if on cue with my thoughts, Coach yells for us to huddle. I give Favor a wave and jog over to my team.

We practice a few more plays and scrimmages. By time Coach calls it a day, we are all dragging tail. I walk over to the bleachers where Favor is sitting with Jana. She steps down onto the field, and I pick her up with one hand and kiss her. "God baby, I missed your mouth."

"Is that all you missed?" *Is she for real?* I feel my dick twitch.

"As a matter of fact, it isn't. I missed being inside you also."

She licks her lips at my words. God, I love this chick and those lips, and so many other parts of her body. "Hmm, me too. My place or yours tonight?"

"Yours. Egon is bringing home a girl." As if that's unusual. Egon brings someone over most nights.

"We should think about getting an apartment for next school year." She mentions it so quietly I almost miss what she says.

"Really, baby?"

Looking me in my eyes, she continues. "Yes. That is, if you want." For a moment, she seems unsure of her words.

"I want. I really want. Tired of having to either climb out of your bed because Jana comes back or you having to climb out of mine. We need our own place."

"Are we talking about this?"

"Looks like it, baby. We can start looking during Spring break. I'll be done with football by then, except for a few practices here and there. But other than that, I'm all yours."

She squeals with excitement, and kisses me. "I can't believe this."

"So how did you like me at practice?" I joke with her. She hates football, but I fish for a compliment anyway.

"Oh, you looked exquisite. But next time, when you are getting ready to snap, you might want to pull back a little further with that throw. It'll give you the power that you need."

Huh? My eyes bug out of my head. "Listen to my baby, talking football to me." Did I just hear her correctly?

She blushes and leans her head down. "Oh well, I picked up the lingo here and there."

"Baby, you not only picked up the lingo, but you had the logic down. And you are right about the snap. I was dead tired towards the end, so I was holding back, not giving the full power I could've." Sexy, beautiful, *and* can talk football? Would people stare if I got on my hands and knees and kissed her feet?

"I knew it." She giggles with delight. I grab her around her waist to pull her into me so I can sneak a quick nibble on her ear. Perhaps I can get her to giggle for me again.

"Hey, Brice. I've got some plays that I want to go over with you tomorrow," Coach interrupts as he walks closer to us.

"Oh hey, Coach. This is my girl, Favor Fontaine. Favor, this is Coach Vega."

"Hi Favor. I never met you before, but I knew your old man, and I coached your brother."

What? I turn to look at her, and she looks away. "Yeah well, Favor was giving me some football tips." I try to cover my shock.

125

"Well, she would know, what with her father being Kyne Hollister, and all. How is Kyne?"

The floor feels as if it has reached up and swallowed me. Did he just say Favor's - *my* Favor - father is Kyne Hollister? The childhood idol she has heard me go on and on about countless times? If her father is Kyne Hollister, then that makes her brother...*fuck me*.

I stare at her in disbelief as she tries to avoid my gaze when she responds to the coach. "He's fine, thanks."

"Good. Good. Your parents will be here in a few weeks for the dedication ceremony. Will you be sitting with them on stage?"

"Umm, I haven't thought about it yet, but most likely." At this point, I can barely hear their conversation because my heart is pounding so loudly in my ears.

"You should. Trevor would've wanted it. He was a good kid. Football lost its brightest talent." Coach pats me on the shoulder. "But we still have some exceptional talent out there. Okay son, I'll leave you and your girl to it. Stop by to see me a little earlier tomorrow so we can go over the plays before practice. Alright?"

My mouth forms a tight thin line, and the muscles on the side of my lips twitch anxiously. Too numb to do anything else, I just nod, and Coach walks away. Turning a deliberate gaze towards Favor, those beautiful, soulful eyes that I've gotten lost in so many times refuse to look in my direction. I will her to look at me, even if this is the last time. My prayers are answered, and she faces me, though hesitantly. Little by little, her trembling hand reaches out to me, and I want to lean in to feel her soft hand one more time. I want that touch to explain everything away and make the last five minutes disappear. I want so much from one simple touch...a touch I back away from.

My heart bears the burden of the weight of the revelation and crushes, leaving me broken. She gasps audibly at my slight, and I feel awakened from what seems like a dream. Why wouldn't she tell me about this?

I open my mouth but find I have no air in my lungs to speak. I gulp in mouthfuls of air and try again. "All this time, you heard me talking about him. All this time, and you, not once, said a damn thing that he was your father." I try to steady my voice, but I'm failing miserably.

Her eyes are red rimmed, and her bottom lip quivers. "I-I can explain."

I bend over as a feeling of being kicked in the gut comes over me. She takes a step towards me, but I hold my hand up, stopping her. I breathe in deeply. Was I not good enough? Maybe she's just playing house with me? Fear of losing her, coupled with the pain of her not telling me such an important detail of her life, grips me. Gradually, I stand up. "Explain? We were talking about moving in together a few minutes ago. Shouldn't you have explained *before* this conversation?"

"I'm sorry. I was planning on telling you soon." Her words are rushed and her tone desperate. I fight the impulse to reach out for her, soothe her and make it all go away. I'd rather die than to have her hurt, but...what about me?

"Soon? Soon would've been the days and nights you were in my arms. The times I broke my soul open for you because I was so desperate to earn your love." I throw my head back in a bitter laugh. "I felt that I" - I stab my index finger into my chest, deliberately wanting to hurt myself; anything to make the pain of this go away - "wasn't good enough for you." I point at her, but I lack the energy to hold it there, and it falls back to my side. "Let's face it, the only reason you were going to tell me soon was because the dedication ceremony is coming up. You probably would've broken up with me or something because you'd probably be too embarrassed to introduce me to your parents." My anger and fear take hold when I say those words and I see her visibly flinch at them. How can everything that seemed so perfect minutes ago, now seem to be going to hell?

"*No.* Brice, I was afraid." Tears fall down her face as she speaks again.

"Afraid of what? I told you everything about my family. And you, what? Lied?"

"No, I didn't. Every story I told you about growing up was the truth."

"Isn't that the age-old question? If you purposefully omit information, is it a lie? Hmm, let me think on that." I turn and walk away, needing to put some distance between us. Not wanting to say words I'll ultimately regret.

Soft footsteps fall in line behind me, but I stop, keeping my back to her. If I look into her eyes, I won't have the strength to leave. "I need time, Favor. Just give me some time to think." Saying those words to her cuts me deep, but I don't stop.

The walk to the locker rooms felt like an eternity as I drag my leaden legs towards one future and away from one with her. The pull to turn around and run back to her is so great that, in a fit of rage, I knock over a basket that holds the practice balls. The contents bounce on the ground and spread across the locker room in different directions, a perfect reflection of my state of mind. I begin pacing in circles when I hear the last voice I needed to hear.

"Lovers' quarrel?" Jameson jeers in front of me.

My body tenses at his words. "Now's not the time, Jameson."

"What? Did I touch on a sensitive subject?" he sneers.

I can feel my veins twitching in my temples, and I grind my teeth while simultaneously fighting the urge to ram my fist down his throat.

"I wonder what it could be that the two love birds fought about. Was it the fact that her parents would never accept you? A. No. One."

And just like that, the thread is snapped, and I lose it. A loud guttural roar escapes my mouth as I rush and tackle him to the ground. We both land in an *oomph*. His face goes from stunned to pissed by the sudden attack. He tries to fight me off, but I'm quicker and faster. I throw my fists in coordinated jabs into his ribs and face. Five of our teammates strain to pull me off of him but because I'm used to dragging two-hundred-pound men across a field, it does little to slow me down.

Jameson stumbles a few times before finally being able to stand on his own. He rubs at his jaw, where a red mark appears. "Looks like I touched a sensitive subject. You know she was always meant to be with me, deep down. Even her mother and father know she and I belong together."

His words resonate with me. Is that why she didn't tell me sooner? Anger takes hold of me again, as his overuse of words and her lack of them, go through my head. I try to get at him again, but our teammates hold me back. "*Fuck you, motherfucker*. You stay away from her, you hear me?" I'm positive I sound like a madman. All I need is to start foaming at the mouth for people to have a reason to cart me away.

"Did she send you packing because mommy and daddy will be here for the dedication ceremony? You know who will be up there on that stage with her? Me. Not you, asshole. *Me*."

Again, his words hit their mark like a sucker punch. All this time, I've been passing Jameson off as a sore loser and not paying attention to his words. Was he speaking words of truth? Wisdom? This pain in my heart makes me want to smash something, and his head is looking like the first stop on the crazy train. *That's it*. I break through and rush towards him. One of my teammates tries to block me, but I fake a left and go around him. I tackle Jameson back to the ground and begin to pound my fists into various parts of his body, until I'm pulled off again. I fight to get back to him again, snarling as I try.

"*Enough.*" Coach yells out.

Coach's words fall on my deaf ears. I push and shove, frantic to get my hands on Jameson, as teammates try once again to hold me back. Coach steps in front of me.

"I said, *enough*. You want him? You gotta go through me. And that means you're throwing your career away, because you'll be off my team." Coach squares his shoulders and waits for me to either make a career-ending decision or take the life preserver he is offering me.

As if doused by cold water, my anger begins to cool slightly. I shrug off my teammates who were holding me back. The room is silent, and all eyes are on me as I grab my bag from my locker and leave. I get in my car and drive to my dorm. Unlocking the door, I slam it behind me, startling Egon and the girl he is with.

"*Out*," I say to the girl. She looks at me, half-naked, and then to Egon.

"You better go. I'll catch up with you later. Gotta talk to my boy."

The girl mumbles some curses as she gets dressed and leaves.

"What happened?" Egon asks as he reaches for his t-shirt.

"Her father is Kyne fucking Hollister."

His eyes narrow as he crosses his arms over his chest. "Bro, what? Whose father is Kyne Hollister?"

"Favor. Favor's father is Kyne Hollister," I say through gritted teeth. I feel my veins pumping in my neck.

His arms drop beside him as his eyes widen. "*The* Kyne Hollister? Your idol?"

131

"The one and only. She never, not once, told me the truth, as many times as I spoke about him and what he meant to me as a kid."

"Bro. She must've had a reason." *Whose side is he on here?*

"What?"

"Did you ask her?"

I look down at my feet, and he has his answer.

"Dude, you blew your gasket and didn't even give her a chance to explain?" This is the part where I hate having a friend that knows me so well.

"I found out through Coach. How were you expecting me to react? One moment, she and I are talking about moving in together this summer, and next thing I know, she isn't who I thought she was."

"You didn't find out she is an alien from outer space, Brice. Calm the fuck down, and then go talk to her. And you guys are moving in together? What a way for you to break that one to me, asshole."

I stare at my best friend in disbelief. How the hell did he just flip this on me? He did the old Jedi mind trick or something because somehow, I feel like I owe him an apology also. I think about this for another moment before I burst out laughing. *"Dammit.* I fucked up." Regret takes over. Shit, am I still on the team? I hit the top of my head. Fuck, fuck, fuck, *fuckety, fuck.*

"What else did you do?" He shakes his head at me, as if I'm a five-year-old who made a boo-boo.

"I beat Jameson up in the locker room." I don't regret that. Fucker had it coming.

"Dude. Are you going to get kicked off the team?" His brows furrow with concern.

"I don't know. I stormed out of the locker room and came here," I say, throwing my hands up in the air.

"Bro, you gotta go back and set this shit right with the coach. And *then,* go see your girl."

"That's if she still wants me after the way I acted."

"Flowers."

"What?"

"Flowers and candy and shit like that. Chicks love that stuff. And me? Just buy me a six-pack and all is forgiven." This asshole here stays with a girl long enough to flush the condom when he is through, and he's giving me relationship advice? And I'm about to listen to him. Is the world coming to an end?

"All is forgiven?"

"Yeah, you kicked out a hot piece of ass I was going to bang tonight. And you told me, in the worse possible way, that our bromance is coming to an end by moving in with your girl." He clutches his hand to his chest.

I pick up the pillow from my bed and throw it at him. "Fuck you, man." I look at the door and turn to leave.

"Yo, Brice." I turn around. "Umm, you might want to shower first. You're a little ripe."

Fuck me. I forgot I didn't shower at the locker room. "Yo, good looking out, dude." We give each other a high five, and I head to the shower.

After I shower and change, I drive over to the stadium. *Time to pay the piper*, I think to myself, as I knock on the coach's door and wait for a response. He calls for me to enter.

"Hey, Coach. Do you have a minute?"

Removing his glasses, he sits back in his chair. "Well, I see that you calmed down some. Sit down."

I take a seat and prepare myself for a piece of humble pie. "Coach, I want to apologize for my behavior today. I was out of line."

"That you were, son. I've never seen you out of control like that. What happened? You seemed happy when you were outside with your girlfriend."

"Well Coach, I was caught off guard with the information about who Favor's father is. She never shared that with me, and the dedication ceremony is coming up in a few weeks..." My voice begins to trail off.

"Damn. I was the one who broke it to you?"

"Yes, sir. And it didn't help that Jameson saw that I was upset, and knew all the right buttons to push." I try to play the sympathy card.

"Shit. I understand. And Jameson can be an asshole most of the time. But you still owe an apology to him, and your teammates. And you owe me some extra pushups tomorrow." So much for the sympathy card.

Fuck, he couldn't just accept the apology and move on? "Yes sir, of course. I'll apologize to Jameson and my teammates tomorrow on the field."

He stands and offers me his hand to shake. I rise and take it, before leaving to make the drive over to Favor's dorm. Climbing her dorms steps two at a time, I say a silent prayer that she won't slam the door in my face. I knock and wait.

Jana opens the door instantly, blocking my view inside, and doesn't step aside to let me in.

"Is Favor inside?"

"No, she isn't. She went for a walk around campus." Jana's normal chipper disposition is gone and replaced with annoyance...directed at me.

"Where does she normally walk to?"

She shrugs her shoulders. "I'm not sure." She knows, she just isn't telling me. My heart pounds in my chest.

Fuck. I pull out my cell phone as I run down the stairs and call Favor's phone, but it goes straight to voicemail. *Double fuck.* I leave a message and head to the parking lot. I look around for her car and can't spot it. That means she must've driven somewhere. But where? I'm at a loss, so I make a decision to camp out in front of her building. She has to return sometime. Four hours later, I'm still sitting in my car, waiting for her, when she finally pulls into the parking lot. She walks towards her dorm, and I sprint over to her.

"Favor," I yell out.

She stops and looks at me. My heart drops to the pit of my stomach. She has been crying, and I'm the asshole who made her cry. "Baby." I run over to her and pick her up in my arms, kissing her sweet lips. "I'm sorry for losing my temper and not giving you a chance to explain."

"I'm sorry too. You were right. I should've told you a long time ago."

Cupping her face in my hands, I ask, "Why didn't you?"

"It's a long story."

"Well, I got time, baby. Let's get a hotel room, and we can talk in private." I kiss her forehead.

"Yeah, that would be a good idea." I take her hand and walk her towards my car. Screw grabbing a change of clothes.

We drive to the hotel and the first thing I do is undress her, and make love to her. I was so desperate to feel that connection with her again before our talk. Favor is laying across my chest, when she begins her story of what it is like growing up as the daughter of Kyne Hollister, who she calls Joe Football. She also tells me both of her parents want her to be with Jameson, but she has never liked him. She called him a total tool. Her words, not mine, but I don't disagree.

I told her about my fight with the tool, and she laughed once I told her I got off with an apology that I have to make tomorrow. She said if Jameson does anything stupid, she'll call his father on him, and we both laugh at that.

"So, let's address the other elephant in the room. Do your parents know about me?"

She stills in my arms. "I haven't mentioned it yet. But I will. I'll call them tomorrow."

"What about the dedication ceremony? Will Jameson be sitting with you?"

"He'll be sitting with my parents, yes."

"With you on stage as well. Giving everyone the impression the two of you are together." Perhaps I'm shallow at this point, but I don't give a damn.

"But we aren't, you know that."

"Baby, *I* know that, but the entire campus will think otherwise. I'm going to look like a fool." This will also give Jameson something to hang over my head.

"I'll figure something out. Don't worry, okay?" She leans in for another kiss.

"Damn girl, I'm feeling like I'm whipped."

"Whipped? Why?"

"You just shut up my bitching with a kiss." And I wouldn't have it any other way.

We both laugh. This dedication ceremony will be interesting.

Chapter 13
Favor

It is the day before the dedication ceremony. Brice is at my dorm as we wait for my parents to arrive. I told my parents all about him, and while they were not very receptive to the idea of him, I held my ground. I have the feeling the next few days will be interesting. Meanwhile, the rumor mill at school is abuzz. Everyone, and I mean everyone, now knows my father is Kyne Hollister. It's not like they weren't going to figure it out after tomorrow anyway.

Me and Brice's relationship is tighter than ever after our first argument with each other. I made a promise to him that I'll never keep a secret from him again. We are still making plans about moving in together. Between my allowance and the leftover money he gets from his scholarship, we should be able to afford a decent place not far from campus. I haven't mentioned our plans to my parents yet. One step at a time.

"Oh, my God, Favor. I think your parents just pulled up," Jana squeals as she looks out the window.

Brice and I break away from our kiss so we can look out the window. Yep, that's Mom and Dad a.k.a. Mr. & Mrs. Joe Football.

Brice kisses my temple and murmurs, "Ready, babe?"

I gather my strength from being in his arms and nod my head. I give myself a quick onceover in the mirror, making sure my appearance will pass the test of my mother's disapproving eyes. We link our fingers together and head downstairs into the lion's den.

Outside, we meet my parents. "Hi, Mom and Dad," I say, giving each of them a peck on the cheek. My parents and I are good at putting up false pretenses for the sake of the public.

"You put on some weight?" My mother places her hands on my shoulders and turns me around, appraising me, like she was shopping for a dress. Geez, she couldn't wait five minutes.

I look down at myself. "No, I doubt it. I exercise every day."

"Hmm, I don't know. I think you have. You need to cut back on those carbs, Sugar." She pinches my chin, as if I was a five-year-old asking for a lollipop.

"Yeah. Sure." I roll my eyes so slowly that, for a moment, I thought they would get stuck mid-roll. I squeeze Brice's arm. "I would like you to meet my boyfriend, Brice Walker. He's the quarterback for…"

"Where's Jameson?" My dad interrupts.

My lips tighten together, and I count to ten before responding. "I don't know, I didn't invite him today. I thought it would be a great time for you to get to know my boyfriend…"

"Oh, there he is." My father interrupts again and walks towards Jameson, who is walking down the pathway. They give each other a hug and walk over to my mother. Jameson gives her a huge hug, and my mother gushes.

I stand, watching the scene before me unfold. Brice's arms tighten around my waist. He is pissed; I can feel the anger vibrating off his touch. I watch my parents as they have a conversation with Jameson, and completely forget that Brice and I are standing here.

"You weren't kidding me," Brice murmurs.

"Nope. If anything, I might've tried to sugarcoat it," I whisper back my reply, as I continue to stare.

"Oh Favor, honey, you didn't tell us that Jameson bulked up some," my mother says as she squeezes his biceps. I choke back a gag.

"Mom, Dad, are you fucking kidding me? I'm trying to introduce you to my boyfriend, and you are being blatantly rude by ignoring him. You can't be bothered enough to say hello?"

"Language, dear, language. You know I raised you to be a lady," my mother admonishes me.

Is she for real? I look up at Brice, and he just shrugs his shoulders. I don't think he can believe what he sees either.

"Favor. It has been explained to you time and time again. You will date someone at your level," my father says through gritted teeth.

"What does that mean, Dad? You didn't come from money. Neither did mom. Brice has an incredible future ahead of him. He is a good man, and I love him." *Shit, did I just say the "L" word out loud?* Hell, I haven't even admitted this to Brice yet.

"He is a scholarship student. Who are his people?" my dad asks.

"Un-fucking-believable. You were a scholarship student also, Dad. Who were your people? Let's not put on airs."

"Favor, language. People are going to think wolves raised you." My mother once again tries to correct my foul language.

Okay, am I the only one who feels like they got transported in time? Are they the *Stepford* family of football? God, I wish my brother was here. He would've made a joke about it, and welcomed Brice into the family with open arms.

"Let's go to lunch." My dad looks over at Jameson.

"No problem, sir. I had a feeling you would be hungry by now. I took the liberty of making reservations for the four of us," Jameson says to my father.

"Five."

"What is that, dear?" my mother asks.

"Jameson said the four of us. There are five of us, unless Jameson plans on sitting lunch out?"

"Favor, I think we should stick to family only," my father says.

"Oh okay. So then, it will be the three of us instead, because Jameson is no family of mine." I fold my arms over my chest. This is an obvious stalemate, and I wait for my father's next move.

"The two of you grew up together. We are close friends with his family," my father tries to argue.

"Never mind, Dad. Why don't you, Mom, and Jameson go to lunch. I'll catch up with you tomorrow after the ceremony."

"What? What is this, you say?" my mother asks.

"I'll catch you after the ceremony tomorrow. Then the four of us can have dinner before you leave."

"But you are sitting with us onstage, dear. So, that's not after the ceremony. Actually, I want you to meet me at our hotel room in the morning. I bought some outfits for you to choose from for tomorrow," my mother says, as she reaches into her purse for a handkerchief.

"If Jameson is on the stage, I'm sitting in the audience."

"Now, Favor. This is not the time to discuss these things. Don't be ridiculous. You will take your place on the stage with us," my father roars.

"You choose. Jameson or me." I dig my feet deeper on this, not willing to budge. I feel my blood pumping through my veins, as my father and I standoff against each other.

My father glares at me and then looks at Jameson. "Fine. Sorry, Jameson. It seems my daughter is more spoiled than I remember."

"That is fine, sir. She'll grow out of it one of these days," Jameson replies as he glares at me as well.

I look around and realize that our group has grown quite the audience. People are snickering and taking photos. My mother did raise me to be polite, so I smile and wave at the people. Brice tugs on my arm. "What the hell are you doing?"

"Being polite and minding my good southern manners, dear sir," I say in a very fake, drawled out accent.

Brice spins me around and slaps me with such a powerful kiss I feel my knees buckle. "There. Now we gave everyone something to talk about."

My father looks as if he is about to have a coronary from our very public display of affection. My mother signals to me that my lipstick is smudged. People gradually come up to my father and ask him for his autograph, as Brice and I stand off to the side and watch.

"Wow. And to think I thought of him as my idol all those years," he says, still in shock.

"Not anymore?"

Looking at me directly in the eyes, he shakes his head. "Not anymore."

We begin to kiss again, and he lifts me up to get better access to my lips. I hear a loud gasp from my mother, and I pull away from Brice, assuming her gasp was meant for us. Brice puts me down, and I turn to look. Wayne is walking towards my parents. He looks horrible, like a man who is the walking, breathing dead.

"What are you doing here?" my father demands.

"Mr. and Mrs. Hollister, I just want to say..."

"There is nothing you can say that we care to listen to. You *killed* our only son. It's because of you that we have to do a dedication ceremony instead of cheering him on in a stadium," my father roars at him.

Jameson moves forward and pushes Wayne away. Wayne stumbles, but does not fall. I watch him as the crowd laughs at him. He walks slowly away, an utterly broken man. *Oh, my God.* How did I not see this before? We never allowed him to move forward. Me, my mother, and my father; we never gave him permission to move forward and live. He may have been driving the vehicle that killed my brother, but we are the ones that are killing *him*. I make up my mind in this moment that I will try to move on and forgive him. This anger we are harboring is doing no one any good, and it is tarnishing my brother's name in the end. My brother was always a forgiving person. I am positive he'd be ashamed of us right now.

My mother begins to cry, and my father holds her, rocking her in his arms, as Jameson stands next to them as their acting guard dog. I look at Brice. "I'm so embarrassed of my family right now."

Kissing my forehead, no words need to be spoken between us, to understand the weight of that statement.

Chapter 14

Brice

I can honestly say I'm not a fan of Favor's parents, and they will not be sending me any well wishes either. When she told me about them a few weeks ago in the hotel room, I thought she was exaggerating. Boy, was I wrong. Hell, they are worse than what she said, if that's at all possible. Kyne Hollister is a douche of the class-A variety, right up there with Jameson. Who the hell names their kid Jameson anyway?

After yesterday's fiasco, Favor was extremely worked up about her parents' behavior towards me. I'm a big boy, so I just shrugged it off. But I didn't want her to feel bad about it, so I took her out to dinner, and then made love to her until the early morning hours. When she left my bed just after dawn, it instantly felt cold and empty. I miss her touch, her scent. I just miss her.

"What time do you have to be at the dedication ceremony with the team?" Egon asks from his side of the room.

"Coach wants all of the players to show up at one."

"Good. It gives us time to grab something to eat."

The glaring red light on my digital clock flashes eleven o'clock. "Let me take a quick shower." I stand up and stretch my sore muscles, courtesy of yesterday's practice.

"Dude, you bulking up?"

"Coach has us training hard. We have a shot at the Championships. The away game in the next couple of weeks will seal the deal for us."

"Sweet. NFL, here you come."

"I hope so. If I can keep the momentum going, yeah, I don't see why not." I shake my head in disbelief. I've worked hard all these years for this moment, and this moment alone. Finally, it's about to become a reality, and I can't believe how lucky I am. I have a beautiful girlfriend and a sensational career in my future.

"It would've been helpful if your girl's dad would give you a good word."

"True, but hey, I made it this far based on my hard work and skill, so I expect it to carry me the rest of the way. Besides, I wouldn't want Favor to ever think that I used her or her family's connections to get in."

"You really like this girl."

"No bro, I love this girl."

Egon's eyes bug right out of his head. I don't think either one of us ever thought we would see the day when we would utter those words. "You love her?"

"Yeah. And she loves me."

"Damn. She is good for you. I like her. And your kids will be so gosh darn pwetty." He crosses his arms in front of him, batting his eyes, hamming it up.

"Fuck you, bro. Let me hit the showers. Be out in a few."

****

When we left our dorm, we were hit with the hushed whispers about what went down in front of Favor's dorm yesterday, so we opt to go to a greasy spoon restaurant off campus to eat. Grabbing the first seats we set our eyes on, the waitress comes over and pours us some coffee.

"Y'all from the campus, right?" the waitress asks in her southern lilt.

"Yes, ma'am." Egon puts on the charm. She smiles and her cheeks turn a bright pink before she turns to me.

"You're that quarterback for the Cougars?"

Guess it's my time for the charm. "Yes, ma'am."

She clutches her notepad to her chest and smiles from ear to ear. "My son is a huge fan. He goes to all your games. Says he wants to be like you when he grows up." Her voice turns high-pitched, and for a moment, I wonder if she is a fan of mine as well.

"Thank you, ma'am. Perhaps, one day, I can meet your son, and sign his football for him," I say honestly. Hell, I used to be just like her son when I was a kid. Looks like it's my turn to pay it forward.

Her eyes turn star struck. "You'd do that?" she whispers, as if I told her a dirty joke.

"Absolutely."

"That is just so sweet. He'd love that."

"It would be my pleasure."

"I'm going to call my husband now and see if he can bring him over with his football. Thank you so much. And the food is on the house for you and your friend here."

"Why thank you, ma'am, from both of us," Egon chimes.

We give her our order, and she rushes off to the back; I guess to make her phone call.

"I love hanging out with you," Egon says while taking a slurp of his coffee.

"Why, because of the free food?" I smirk.

"Yep, why else?" He smiles, giving me a toothy grin.

We always tease each other like this. The shoe is usually on the other foot when we go to clubs where he's played before. "Going home for Winter break?"

"I might have a meeting with a record company around that time. So, I don't know. I'm still up in the air."

"Damn, bro. That is incredible. Congrats."

He holds up his hands. "Well it's just a meeting, but we're keeping our fingers crossed."

"You worked hard for this. They'll make you an offer, I know it."

"Who would've thought, all those years ago in Philly, when you and I were playing out in the streets and talking about our dreams, that all this shit would happen?" We had a lot of odds going against us, especially growing up in the rough side of Philly. Instead of making drug deals, Egon and I dreamed of a future without orange jumpsuits. Most of our old crew is either locked up, dead, or still on the same street corner, talking about missed opportunities.

I sit back and reflect. "Yeah, you're right. But I think it was something in me that kept pushing for it, and I just knew." It was evident to me the day we found out our friend in the seventh grade was killed by a stray bullet from a drug buy that went wrong.

"Yeah, same here. We've been best friends since we were seven years old."

"Yep." Neither one of us talk about it, but we both know that was a day that changed us.

"Man, at the risk of sounding like a chick...our lives are going in different directions pretty soon..."

I cut him off. "Don't even think that shit. We're more than best friends, we're family. We'll find a way to keep the bromance alive." I had to throw in a joke. This mushy shit is too much.

"Well, I heard long distance relationships are hard." He mock cries.

"As long as you don't cheat on me."

"Cheating on Favor already?" Regan interrupts, standing over our table.

This chick is like an insect, always popping up when you got company. "What do you want, Regan?" I groan out.

"Where's Favor? Two of you broke up?"

149

Is it just me or is this chick delusional?

"None of your business where my girlfriend is."

"You know, Regan, you're making me regret fucking you more and more," Egon responds.

"Just thought you'd be with her, getting ready for the dedication ceremony."

"I'm sitting with the team. I think that is a given." I straighten in my seat.

"Are you two going to ask me to sit down?"

You see, I was right. *Delusional.* "Fuck no. I don't want to give people the impression that we're slumming it."

Her eyes grow hard toward me. "I don't know what Favor sees in you. You're so rude."

"What she sees in me is a man that loves her. End of story."

"Puhleeze Brice, I think it's that other L word, and its not love."

I open my mouth to spit out some harsh knowledge for her, but our waitress suddenly appears.

"Let me grab you a chair, honey." She turns to a table and takes a chair from it, placing it at our table so Regan can sit. "What will you have, sweetheart? Are you one of these boys' girl? You're pretty enough to be."

Regan sits, and a huge smile appears on her face. "Oh, why thank you. I'll have a western omelet please, with turkey bacon."

The waitress walks away to put in Regan's order.

"What the fuck?" Egon complains.

"What? She was so sweet, who am I to correct her?"

Fuck me. Thank goodness no one from school is around to see her sitting with us. It wouldn't look good.

We finish our breakfast, and the waitress's son comes over with his dad. I sign the football for him, and promise to get him box seats for my next home game. Me, Egon, and Regan step outside into the cool afternoon air. Egon and I begin walking towards the car, and Regan is walking behind us.

"What are you doing?" Egon asks.

"Coming with the two of you," she responds.

"What?" My eyes narrow, wishing my death glare would make her disappear. "How did you get here?"

"My ride left me. I saw the two of you through the diner's windows, and came in."

Fuck. I give Egon a look, and he shrugs his shoulders at me. Good looking out, bro. "Well, call your friend, and have them come back to get you," I say.

"Come on. You would leave me out here in the street to wait for a ride?"

"Yeah, that is pretty much what I'm thinking." Am I a dick for saying yes? Probably, but I don't care.

"I'm going to be late for the dedication if you do that to me," she pouts.

Fuck. I better get into heaven for this good deed. "Fine. I'll give you a ride, but just don't talk. I like to pretend that you don't exist."

She rolls her eyes at me at first, but then it seems something catches her attention. She takes a step forward but trips, right into my arms. I hold her up until she gets her footing. She smiles and places her hands on my biceps.

"Brice?" I hear Favor's voice.

I turn around to see Favor, and her mother and father, dressed for the dedication ceremony. This does not look good. Fuck, can my day get any worse?

I remove Regan's hands from me and walk over to Favor and her family.

"Good afternoon, Mr. & Mrs. Hollister." I nod to her parents and look at my confused girlfriend. I step closer to Favor and give her a kiss on the cheek, whispering that I'll explain everything later. She searches my eyes and nods.

"Shouldn't you be on campus for the dedication?" Mr. Hollister's voice has a tone of irritation and boredom.

"Yes sir, I'm on my way back now. Egon and I came out for breakfast."

"And what about your girlfriend?" Mrs. Hollister asks, looking at Regan, who is smiling and waving behind me.

My actual girlfriends face turns crimson. "Favor is my girlfriend, as you know, ma'am. Regan is-"

"Regan is with me. Hi, I'm Egon. I'm Brice's best friend." Egon holds his hand out for Mr. Hollister to shake and he kisses Mrs. Hollister's hand. Forever the Romeo, he is.

"Oh, she didn't look like she was with you the way she held on to Brice," Mrs. Hollister adds, looking from Regan to myself.

"Mom, Dad. We should get going. We have to meet with the dean before the ceremony," Favor interrupts, giving me another look.

"Yes, you're right. The car is just up the street," Mr. Hollister replies.

"You're riding in your parents' car?" I ask.

"Yes. I can pick my car up later."

Time to look like I'm a good boyfriend by pulling out the charm. "I'll take your car back to campus. I'll park it in your usual spot."

She smiles at me and hands me her keys. Stepping closer to me, she places a loving kiss on my lips. *Score.* "Thank you. I'm parked across the street."

Favor and her parents walk down the block to her father's car. When they are out of earshot, I look to Regan. "What the fuck kind of stunt was that?"

She smiles and shrugs at me. "What? I tripped?"

She is lucky that she isn't a guy, or I would lay her out. "The fuck you did. That was on purpose. Did you plan this whole thing?"

"How would I know when Favor and her family would come out of the hotel?" Her eyes widen, as if that would help proclaim her innocence more.

She might have a point, but I don't trust it. It's too much of a coincidence. "Well, guess what? Your little stunt just cost you a ride back to campus. Hope your cell phone is working, so you can make that phone call."

"But..."

"No buts. Egon, here are my car keys, and don't let this fucking bitch in my car. I'm going to take Favor's car back to campus. Can you just follow behind me, so I can have a ride to the dedication? I can't be late."

Egon takes the keys from me. "Sure, no problem." We both walk away, leaving a stunned Regan behind.

I arrive at the dedication ceremony on time, and take my place with my team in the front row with the cheerleaders and faculty. Various people give speeches about Trevor Hollister, Favor's brother. Kyne Hollister gives an emotional speech towards the end of the dedication. You can see the genuine pain in his eyes. I don't believe a parent ever recovers from the death of a child. That is a pain that you will always carry with you, and it is evident in both of Favor's parents. In spite of how everything went between us yesterday, I wouldn't wish that on them, or anyone.

When I found out who Favor's family was a few weeks ago, I asked her if she would be giving a speech at the ceremony, and she told me that it would be too hard for her, so she wouldn't. That's why my jaw dropped open when her father finished his speech, and she stood and walked to the podium. Her mother and father both look shocked, and Favor has a haunted look on her face. Was she staring at something? I turn around in the direction she's staring. Wayne Anderson. He stands in the back, close enough to hear but far enough not to be noticed. He looks disheveled, as if he hasn't slept.

"Hi, I'm Favor Hollister," she begins, using her family surname. "Many of you may know me as Favor Fontaine." She takes a deep breath before proceeding. "Trevor Hollister was my older brother."

She pauses momentarily. I will her to look at me, so I can give her the strength to carry on. She does, and a silent message passes between us. We're so in tune with each other, words are no longer needed. I wordlessly tell her she has the strength to do this, that I'm here if she needs me, and that I love her. With a slight nod, she proceeds. "I listened to the many speeches that were given today in honor of him, and I couldn't be prouder of how loved he was by all." She turns her head and nods behind her at the people who gave speeches, smiling gently.

"He had a caring and giving personality, one that generated warmth, and people just naturally gravitated to him." She looks in the direction Wayne is standing.

"But one thing that I did not hear about my brother today, that I would like to point out, has to do with forgiveness.

Trevor had the wonderful ability to forgive." Her hands tremble at the sides of the podium.

"When we were kids, my brother had a toy that he loved. One afternoon, when he was out with friends, I snuck into his room to play with it, and I accidentally broke it. I cried and cried when my brother came home, and I tried to apologize. He was upset at first, but he ultimately forgave me. He told me he could always get another one, and that it wasn't worth my tears." She chokes up at the memory and breathes through her grief.

"Trevor was taken from our lives too soon, and it has left a hole in our hearts. But I believe my brother is staring down, begging us to forgive, and make peace with his death. If we can each find it within ourselves to forgive, it will give us all the ability to move forward."

She straightens to her full height and, with determination in her voice, she says, "I'm doing that today, right now. I forgive Wayne Anderson for that night. He was my brother's best friend, and I remember many summers he would spend at our house. Wayne was a good person then, and I believe him to be so now. My brother would want this, I'm sure. Let's stop holding back our own personal growth as individuals, and learn the art of forgiveness. Thank you."

She pauses, gripping the podium as if she's too weak to make it on her own back to her seat. Her mother and father sit, dumbfounded at her speech, unmoving. I see Favor look so frail at that very moment, and I'm on the move before I know it. I climb the stage steps and walk over to her, still gripping the podium. Standing behind her, I place my hands over hers. She tenses at first, but slowly releases the podium. Leaning into my chest, she is trembling. I lift her into my arms and carry her off the stage. A thunderous applause rips through the audience as I hold the woman I love in my arms, and carry her into the building behind us. I sit her down on a bench and kneel in front of her. Looking at her haunted eyes, I grab her and lay her head on my shoulders.

We sit there for long moments as she cries into my shoulder, releasing all her pain. My heart is breaking for her, and I want to make it better, but I don't know how. At that very moment, I know she is my everything. She is my heart, and my soul. Nothing is worth having without her.

"I love you," I say into her ear as she sobs on my shoulder.

Lifting her head, she looks at me. She wipes the tears away from her eyes. "I love you too." She smiles gently at me, and I feel as if I just melted into a puddle, and was reborn.

"Your speech was amazing."

"I wasn't supposed to give one." She sniffs. "But when I saw Wayne yesterday, I promised myself I would let it all go and forgive him. But it was seeing him at the dedication ceremony that convinced me I had to say it in public."

A wide smile spreads across my face. "You're an incredible woman, do you know that?"

"Well, I'm sure I'm not looking very incredible." She smiles.

"You're right, you're not looking very incredible at all. You look stunning." I kiss her gently.

"Well I don't feel very stunning, but I'll take your word for it." Her eyebrows furrow with worry.

"My parents are going to be pissed by my speech, but I don't care. It needed to be said."

"Well, I'm standing behind you, no matter what."

She kisses me. "I'm lucky to have you. You helped me to face my demons in ways that you don't even know."

"I will always be there for you," I promise her.

"What was that about, Favor?" Jameson asks, as he walks towards us.

"This is not the right time, Jameson." I stand and block Favor from his view.

"The fuck it isn't. Her parents are beside themselves at her little speech."

"Too bad. It needed to be said. She's right."

"Favor. You need to speak to your parents."

"Tell them I'll see them at dinner tonight. I need to be alone with Brice." She stands and holds my hand.

He stares at us in disgust. "Fine. I'll go tell your poor mother, who is sobbing right now, that you don't have time to see her because you are too busy getting ready to have sex with your boyfriend."

I punch him in the face for his remarks. I'm sensing a pattern with me and Jameson. He speaks, I see red. I hit him, and he usually ends up on the ground, as he is now. "Get out of my sight, Jameson. *I mean it.*"

Jameson stands and adjusts his suit jacket, walking away. I wait until he is gone and I turn back to Favor. "Do you want to go and check on your mother?"

She shakes her head. "My father will just rip into me, and I don't have the strength. Let's just go back to your dorm."

I kiss her forehead. "Okay, baby. Let's go."

Alone, back at my dorm, I just hold her because I'm a kickass boyfriend, and it isn't always about the sex.

"What time is dinner tonight with your parents?"

"Eight. We can meet them at the restaurant."

"Do you need to go back to your dorm to change?"

"No, I think I can just wear this," she says, linking her fingers with mine.

"Okay. So, on a scale of one to ten, how bad is dinner going to be tonight?" I already have a feeling, but I want to hear her say it.

"Hmm, ten being the worst? I would say it'll be at least a hundred."

Dayum. "Shit, do I need to bring a crucifix and holy water or something?" I semi-joke with her, but try to figure out the closest church, just in case.

"You might, just in case my dad's head begins to spin around, and he spits out pea soup." Looks like my girl and I are both on the same page.

"Yeah, this is going be great for the digestion system."

"You know what works wonders for the nervous system?"

"What?"

"This."

She sits up on the bed and slowly takes off her dress. Remember when I said earlier that it isn't just about the sex? Yeah well, scratch that. It's all about leading up to this moment, and making love to the woman who completes me.

My eyes follow her every movement as she unbuttons my pants and pulls them off, along with my boxers. My body stills when she unbuttons my dress shirt, seductively kissing my chest for every button that she undoes.

Straddling me, she continues to trail her lips across my body, and I feel her moisture on my shaft. And then I wonder how she would feel going bareback, though we've never approached that conversation before. Reaching over to the drawer next to my bed, she grabs a condom. Rolling it over my more than hungry cock, she positions herself over me, and I hold her waist as she begins to lower herself on to me inch by delicious inch. When she is fully seated, I give her a minute to adjust.

The sunlight shining through my window hits the top of her head, and for a moment, she looks like an angel sent here for me. I wonder where she hides her wings?

I close my eyes momentarily because the sensations of her touch have me wanting to explode prematurely. "Babe, you feel so fucking good."

She throws her head back. "Oh, my God, Brice, so do you." Her voice is breathless, and it turns me on even more.

Lifting herself slowly and lowering back down, I buck my hips with a little bit of a swivel to give her the deeper penetration that I know she likes. *Who knows how to satisfy his woman?*

Her nipples are hard and begging me to have a taste. I place my hand at the small of her back, so she doesn't fall, because the need to have her breasts in my mouth is overwhelming. I sit up, deepening our connection, and she gasps.

"Brice." Her voice is like a whisper.

I take one perfect nipple into my mouth, and I suck while playfully pinching her other nipple. She wiggles and squeals her delight, and I realize that I'm content with just making her happy. Holding her tight against me, I push inside her with short quick thrusts.

She places her hands on my shoulders and gives a gentle push. I lay on my back, never losing our connection. With the grace of a dancer, she places her hands on either side of her on the bed and builds up momentum, to a tune that she has created. Arching her back, her breasts the size of large grapefruits push out, and the sun's beams shine on them like a spotlight.

Her pace picks up as I feel her walls contracting around me, and I feel the pressure building in my balls.

Taking complete control, I roll us over without breaking connection, and place her on her back. Lifting one of her legs in my hand while placing kisses on the side of her calf, I place it on my shoulder and then repeat with the other. I thrust the tip of my penis in and out a few times before deepening from tip to scrotum. Releasing one of her legs back onto the bed, I hold her other leg with my arm as I begin deep thrusts into her that earn me screams of pleasure. Letting go of her other leg, I brace on to the headboard and give her everything I have. She screams out her orgasm, which is music to my ears. I lean over to kiss her and, with a few more thrusts, I shoot over the edge.

I lift her up so she can lay on my chest, both of us panting as I stroke her hair. We stay like this until our breaths finally even out. "Baby, how would you feel about going bareback?"

She sluggishly lifts her head. "I've never done that before."

"Neither have I, but I would like to with you."

She smiles at me. "Me too. I'm on the pill, so no worries on that end."

"Good. I'll get tested. Once I get my results, we should be good to go."

"I'll do the same. We can go to the clinic together."

I kiss her again. Thoughts of dragging her to the clinic right now goes through my head. But no, I won't spoil the moment. I'll drag her tomorrow instead.

"We need to get ready for dinner. And now, it seems I'll need a shower after all. I smell of sex."

"Correction. You smell of good sex."

"No, you are wrong. I smell of mind-blowing sex."

"Damn. That just might have earned you a quickie before dinner."

"I sure hope so." She smiles, and guess what, it does.

Chapter 15
Favor

Walking hand and hand with Brice towards the restaurant to meet my parents, my heart is so full of love for this man who has become my rock. He knew exactly what I needed today after the speech I gave. And I am not talking about the sex, but just holding me, letting me cry and talk through my pain. We stop in front of the restaurant's door, knowing that once we walk through, all hell will break loose at the table. I take a deep breath and look at him. "You ready?" *I hope one of us is.*

"I guess I'm as ready as I'll ever be. It's not me I'm worried about, you know. It's you. I never want to see you hurt. I want to shield you from everything. Having to sit across the table from your parents while they tear you apart is hard. But I'll give your parents the respect, and not say anything."

I stand on my tiptoes and kiss his lips gently. "I love you for that." He lifts my hand to his lips and kisses my fingers lightly. Opening the door for me, I step into what I know is going to be the depths of hell. The maitre d' shows us to the table where my parents, and of course, Jameson, are already seated.

"Nice of you to show up," my dad says in a brisk tone.

Wow. I didn't even get a chance to order before the jabs start. "Nice to see you too, Dad. You know Brice already," I say as Brice holds my chair out for me.

"Good evening, Mr. and Mrs. Hollister," Brice replies, with not a hint of anger. "Hello, Jameson." Wow, he was even nice to Jameson. Jameson, on the other hand, just scowls at him.

The waiter hands us our menus.

"So, you caused quite the scene there with your speech earlier," my father scolds.

"Favor? Whatever possessed you?" my mother asks, as Jameson tries to stifle a laugh behind a napkin.

"Well Mom, I thought it was time. Wayne used to be Trevor's best friend. Hasn't he suffered enough? He'll always go through life knowing that he was the one who was driving that night. Why add to his pain? I think Trevor would have been proud of me." My words come out of my mouth, as a sense of calm goes through me. In my heart, I know this was the right thing to do.

Slamming his hands down on the table, as patrons seated near us jump, my father argues, "You had no right. You should have discussed this with us before."

"The decision was spur of the moment. I had no idea I was going to do it." My voice shakes slightly, but I am able to steady it in the end.

My father looks at me as if aliens just deposited me from their spacecraft right in front of him. He closes his eyes, exhaling loudly, before looking across the table. "So, Jameson, your team is almost to the Championships." My father deliberately says this, knowing full well that the Cougars making it this far is riding on Brice's shoulders. His tactic is to try to hurt Brice, knowing it will destroy me. I bristle at his comments.

"Dad, as you know, Brice is the starting quarterback that brought the Cougars out of their slump," I point out, as Brice smiles lightly at me. "Jameson doesn't get the playing time he used to anymore." I add that in there for my own amusement.

"Favor, that was rude. How could you say such a thing?" my mother asks in a shocked tone.

"Was that rude? Oh, I'm sorry, Jameson. I thought I was just stating the obvious." I lift my glass of water to hide the blatant smile on my face.

Jameson's entire demeanor goes rigid. "Yes, it is true I do not get the playing time that I used to, but I'm training harder than ever to regain my spot."

Brice, to my astonishment, did not even give him a response in return. I'm proud of him for that. I mean, what for? We all know it is just a pipe dream for Jameson. The crowd loves Brice. The team loves him, the coach respects him, and he has the skills and the talent. Jameson never had any of those qualities because he relied too heavily on his family's name, rather than putting in the time and effort that was needed to earn that type of respect.

"I can give you some pointers, if you like," my father says.

"That would be greatly appreciated, sir," Jameson says as he stares directly at Brice.

Brice just rolls his eyes and twists his water glass around on the table.

"So, Brice, where are you from?" my mother asks.

He jerks his head up at the sudden question directed at him. "I'm from Philadelphia."

"Oh. Philadelphia is a beautiful city. Your parents are still there?" she asks.

"My mom is," Brice hedges.

"Oh? Is your dad no longer with us?" my mother asks, with a slight look of concern.

Brice looks at me. I just nod my head. "Well, Mrs. Hollister, I never met my father. When my mother found out she was pregnant with me, my father walked away."

The table is silent for a long moment. "I'm so sorry. Have you ever tried to look him up?" my mother pries.

"No. I never felt the need to. My mother became both a mother *and* a father for me. I can't say that I truly missed him because I never knew him."

"I understand," she says, sympathy in her eyes.

"Favor, when should we expect you for Winter break?" My dad switches the subject.

"Umm, I don't know. I haven't figured out when I'm heading out. I'll make a decision after the away game." I want to speak to Brice about his plans for Winter break before I make any concrete decisions.

"Jameson, if your parents aren't back by the time Winter break comes, you are welcome to spend it with us," my father says.

"I'll let you know. Thanks for the offer."

The rest of dinner consists of semi-polite conversation, with my father mostly ignoring Brice and directing his conversation to Jameson. And of course, dinner would not be complete, unless my mother corrected me constantly on my table manners. Thankfully after dinner, Brice suggests we go to a party that the football team and cheerleaders are throwing by the lake. We head straight to the party instead of changing because, let's face it, if we went back the dorm, we would have ended up in bed. And I don't mean to sleep.

Parking near some of the other cars at the party, we walk hand in hand.

"You know, this will be our first party together since we have been a couple," I tell him.

Grabbing me by the waist, he kisses me. "Let's just have fun and leave the drama from today behind us."

"Well, that I can handle. Let's go." We stroll right into the thick of the party crowd. Of course, people are chanting our names when we enter.

"I thought you would never show up." Jana rushes over to me.

"Sorry, got caught up at dinner with the parents."

"Oh, that's why you're dressed like that?" She takes a step back, appraising my outfit.

"Yeah. We came right over instead of changing."

"Babe, I am going to get a beer. Want anything?" Brice asks.

"No, I'm fine. Go hang out with the boys."

"You're the best." Kissing me, he runs off.

"Just us girls?" Jana claps.

"Just us." I smile at her.

I look around at the utter chaos of the party, with some girls walking around half-naked. I just got here, and I am already ready to leave.

"Come on, let's get closer to where the band is playing, so we can dance." Jana grabs my arm and drags me in the direction of where Egon and State of Mind are playing.

"I didn't know they were playing at this party," I say as I listen to the music playing.

"Well, Egon was already at the party and said we needed some good music, so he called up his band, and they set up," Jana explains as she starts moving her body to the beat.

I begin to dance with her, like girls dance together, fooling around and looking sexy while doing it. People are starting to crowd around us and some of the cheerleaders that Jana cheer with are dancing with us. I'm getting lost in my head

169

as I dance to the music with my eyes closed. Jana tugs on my arm. "Come on, let's go up on stage with the band and dance."

I shrug my shoulders and follow her. We climb onto the makeshift stage and begin dancing around while Egon belts out another song. The band and the crowd are eating it up as Jana and I twirl around and dance. The more the crowd cheers, the more Jana and I put on a show with our moves. I feel hands snake around my waist from behind. The crowd erupts. But the hands around my waist don't feel like Brice's hands. Brice's hands are longer and leaner. I stop dancing and turn around to see who is holding me.

Jameson. He gives a drunken smirk. I try to pull away from him, but he holds on to me, lifting me up as I try to slap his face. He places a kiss on my lips, and I struggle to push him away with my hands. Suddenly the singing has stopped. Again, I feel hands on me, and this time, I'm being dragged away from Jameson. When I'm placed on my feet, I see it is Egon who has pulled me away. "You okay?" His voice is full of concern, I nod my head. "Good." Then he steps around me and punches Jameson. Jameson stumbles backward, but recovers quickly, and they start trading blows.

Jameson's team mates and Egon's band join into the chaos. I jump into the thick of the fight. Hell, I grew up in a football family, so it's not like I haven't been tackled by my very own brother before.

I find Egon, who is still throwing jabs at Jameson. I stand in between them to hold them each away from each other. Egon lifts me up to place me behind him, and I see that Jameson is about to sucker punch him. I quickly go around Egon to try to get him out of the way, but I end up right in front of an oncoming blow. Jameson's fist lands directly on my face, and I fall backward and off the stage. The fighting stops as someone screams that I'm dead. Egon jumps down to where I lay sprawled on the floor.

"*Fuck. Favor.* Are you okay?" Egon rubs his hand over his face.

I try to sit up while holding my hand to my eye. Someone is going to have a black eye in the morning. "Yeah, I think."

"Favor." I hear Brice yell, followed by his running footsteps.

"She's over here." Egon stands and calls out.

Brice runs over and kneels by me. "Baby. What the fuck happened?"

"Jameson is what happened. She was dancing, and Jameson grabbed her. I pulled her away from him."

I see Brice's expression grow cold. He's trying hard not to lose it in front of me. Trying to diffuse this situation before it gets worse, I explain as quickly as I can get the words out. "I'm fine. I'll just have a black eye in the morning. I've had worse." And I have.

His nostrils flare. "He grabbed you? But why would you have a black eye?" Brice's voice is tight, as his muscles and veins strain against his skin.

"He umm..." Hell, I don't even know how to explain this one.

"Favor, I'm so sorry," Jameson says from the side, looking down on me.

"You grabbed her? How did she get the black eye? How did she end up sprawled out on the ground?" Brice is asking the rapidfire questions through gritted teeth.

Egon looks at me with sympathy in his eyes because he knows what is about to come next. "Egon and Jameson began fighting," I answer him.

"And?" he prods. I look heavenwards. He couldn't let it go at that.

"I didn't know what to do."

"And?" His patience seems to be hanging by a slender thread.

"I got in the middle of them, hoping to stop the fight."

"And?" His teeth are bared now.

"Egon placed me behind him, so I wouldn't get hurt." Why do I feel as if time has suddenly frozen?

"*And?*" He's cracking his knuckles as I say a silent prayer in my head.

Nowhere else to go with this but to tell him the rest, so I try my best to explain. "Jameson was going to punch Egon. I was trying to help Egon because he wouldn't have been at that disadvantage if it wasn't for him moving me behind him. So, I moved around him, quickly thinking...oh hell, I don't know what I was thinking. Jameson's fist connected with my face, and I

172

went flying off the stage and onto the ground." I rush out the last part in hopes his mind won't catch up with his ears.

"What?" Brice stands and rushes towards Jameson, but Egon blocks him.

"Take care of your girl. Let it go," Egon rationalizes.

"I told you before, you stay the fuck away from her." Brice screams out over Egon's shoulder as he tries to push Egon out of his way.

Jameson stands his ground and says, "She was mine before *you*."

"She was never yours, and you know it. You're fucking pathetic. She never wanted you."

Jameson throws back his head and begins laughing. Oh, my God. I know exactly what is coming and I don't know how to stop this trainwreck. I brace myself.

"Who do you think was her first? *Me*. Who do you think was keeping her pussy moist before you. *Me*."

Brice flinches and looks at me on the ground. I never told him about my on and off sexual history with Jameson. It never seemed like a thing to talk about...until now. Now I realize the error in my thinking. He turns back to Jameson and rushes him, landing a punch to his stomach. Jameson bends over, but Egon drags Brice back. Brice is fighting to get back to Jameson, who stands back up to his full height.

"Guess she never told you, but like I said, she belonged to me first." He spits blood out of his mouth onto the ground.

Hushed whispers are all around us, and I stand with the help of Jana. She gives me a sympathetic look; my second one of the evening. I walk over to Brice. "Brice, let's go," I whisper to him. He doesn't respond, as he is still in a stare down with Jameson, so I tug on his shirt. Looking down at me, he looks at me as if he has never seen me before. "Brice, let's go," I say again, louder this time. He eventually nods, and we walk away from the crowd.

Brice walks ahead of me but in the opposite direction of the cars. He walks towards the lake, and I try to keep up with his long strides. We reach the lake, and he stands at the edge, looking at the water, not saying a word. I open my mouth to speak but close it instantly.

"You know, our freshman year was the first time I saw you, here at the lake." He points to a spot near some trees. "Over there. You were sitting with a group of girls by a fire and laughing. I thought you were the most beautiful thing I ever saw." He laughs. "But I was also a cocky freshman. I was the backup quarterback at the time, but I knew I had the skills to change that eventually. I remember, I came over to you and your friends with Egon. I tried to talk to you, but as soon as you heard I was on the football team, you stood up and walked away." He rubs his hands over his face and I watch his back muscles flex underneath his shirt. "I had always watched you from afar. I ended up calling you my Golden Unicorn."

"Golden Unicorn?" I ask, remembering Egon's words at the pizza spot months ago.

"Yeah. You were mythical to me. Something I wanted, but I could never have."

"Oh," I hang my head.

"When I saw you that night at the bonfire, months ago, I thought, 'Wow, I finally have my chance with her.'" He turns and looks at me, his eyes red.

"I've committed every first with you to memory." He points to his head and then his heart.

I remain silent as I take in everything he is sharing with me.

"I think I must have loved you all along, but I just didn't know it." He looks away, and my heart is breaking.

"I figured, when I finally got a chance with you, the best way to keep you was to show you the real me. Not the bullshit persona I put on for everyone else. Because I knew, in order to keep a woman like you, I could never bullshit you ever, or I'd run the risk of losing you."

I bend my head and feel my cheeks burn. I never afforded him the same respect.

"When you didn't tell me about your parents, I was upset at the way I found out. But once you explained, I understood it."

A tear falls down my cheek. Because he did understand, and we were able to work through it and come out stronger for it.

"I guess that's the reason why I'm having a hard time wrapping my head around this right now. You've had plenty of opportunities to tell me that you and Jameson were bed partners at one time. But you never told me. It's like the two of you were in on a secret that I was never privy to. But now I see things differently. I get it. He, in his own way, was telling me. Every single time he would say you were his before you were mine."

His words pierce my heart. "I'm sorry, Brice. I'm so sorry. I should've told you."

"That's all?"

"No, that's not all." My voice cracks as I speak. "At first, I didn't say anything because we were so brand new. But as time went on, I was embarrassed by it. I never even liked Jameson. He was just..." My words drift as I search my brain for how to explain it.

"When did the two of you stop having sex?"

"The end of freshman year. I explained to him after freshman year that I didn't want to have sex with him anymore. We were never exclusive. He wanted to be, but we weren't. The first time we had sex was a few weeks after my brother's funeral. I was hurt and lost without my brother. He was there, and we ended up having sex. We didn't again until freshman year. It was random hook-ups, nothing regular."

"You must've known this was going to come out eventually." He remains still, his voice devoid of any emotion.

"I guess I did. But I hoped it wouldn't. I have always regretted having sex with him. But I regret not telling you more. I was wrong. I should've told you."

"Favor, I love you. I am *in love* with you. But I just don't know how to handle this right now."

I walk over to him and place my hands around him. Standing on my toes, I kiss him. He grabs me and kisses me back. We begin tearing at each other's clothes to get them off, not caring that there is a party a few hundred yards away from us. I lay on the ground, and he hovers over me. I reach for his neck to pull him closer for a kiss, but he suddenly pulls away.

"I can't." It's all he says as he kneels beside me.

"But..."

"I can't. I need to get my head straight." He stands and gets dressed. When he is finished, I'm still sitting on the ground. "I'm going back to campus. Coming?"

I swallow deeply. "So we can talk some more?" My knees feel weak as I wait for his reply.

"No." His tone is clipped. He looks in my direction, but not at me. "I'll drop you off at your dorm."

My head reels back as if I've been slapped. "B-but..." I try to focus on getting my words out. "Why does this feel like we are breaking up?"

He looks away. "Favor."

"Are you breaking up with me?" My voice cracks, as does my heart.

"I don't know." His shoulders slump and his voice is somber.

It feels like an artificial hand is squeezing my heart. Oh God, this hurts…it hurts so bad. "I promise you, there aren't any more secrets. That was everything." I start to move towards him, but stop myself, not willing to suffer another rejection. He can't leave me. He is all I have.

He spins around, nostrils flaring. "Isn't that what you said the last time? No more secrets?" He runs his hand over his face. "But it seems that you still had important ones that you didn't share with me. And once again, I find out, not from your lips, but from someone else's. I don't know what I have to do to gain your trust." He turns his back to me, hands on his hips and staring at the ground.

"I trust you. I love you."

"You can't possibly trust me. You never trusted me with the truth." He turns his back on me, rubbing the back of his head.

"Okay, the truth. I've always been the second-class citizen in my own family. I have always lived in my brother's shadow, both in life *and* in death. I gave my virginity to a family friend who was there for me when I needed a shoulder to cry on. Had my brother never died, I probably would've never slept with Jameson. But I was at the lowest point in my life. When I came here during my freshman year, I was still reeling from my brother's death from the year before that. Jameson, again, was there because he was the only one who knew Trevor was my brother. I had built a cocoon around myself here, and Jameson was my only sense of reality. We hooked up a few random times, but I shut it down after freshman year because I knew it wasn't healthy for either one of us. He wanted more, and I didn't want to depend on him." I pause. "But then you came

178

into my life. You changed everything for me. I felt more like who I am with you; who I am supposed to be. I felt alive, and I felt loved for once in my life, other than my brother. If I lose you, Brice, I'm losing myself. That is the truth."

He stands, staring at me. I begin to get dressed. When I am finished, I walk towards the party. "Where are you going?"

"Something I should have done long ago," I call back, as I set off to find Jameson.

I find him talking with some friends. Bruising around his face is becoming more prominent. I am about to add to that bruising. I walk over to him. The group quiets as they see me approaching with Brice behind me. I walk over to Jameson, and slap his face. He gets mad, but then I knee him in the balls. Jameson bends over in pain.

"You son of a *bitch*." A crowd begins to draw around us.

"You left out some details in the pathetic excuse of a sexual relationship we had."

Jameson, who is still clutching the family jewels on the ground, stares at me with a pained expression.

"Each time we had sex, I was grieving for my brother."

People snicker off to the side.

"You, a family friend who was supposed to be offering me support during that time, was just interested in getting in my pants. You know it, and I know it."

The snickers grow louder.

"You ride on your daddy's coattails. You think you are something on campus, but you are just the joke of it. You lost the top spot on the team yourself, so stop blaming Brice. He put in the work and the time to hone in on his skill."

Taunts towards Jameson come out of the crowd.

"You are a sad individual who hangs on to my family in hopes of, what? Getting me? You will never have me. I belong to Brice and only him. I know you were hoping your little outburst would turn him against me, but guess what? It has turned most girls against you. What girl is going to want to spread her legs for a man who will put her sexual business out there for a crowd to hear? What girl will spread her legs to someone who would take advantage of her? Grow up and get a life. Never speak to me again. Oh, and by the way, I *will* be telling my father about this."

I push through the crowd as everyone laughs at him. I walk past Brice, not sure where I'm going at this point, but I need to get away from here.

"Favor." Brice yells. "Favor, wait up."

I stop and wait for him. He jogs over to me. "You belong to me and only me?" he asks with a smirk.

The anger I felt towards Jameson leaves me instantly when I set eyes on Brice. "Out of everything I said to him, that's all you got out of it?" I smirk back, folding my arms over my chest.

"Was there anything else more important?" He pulls me into his hard chest.

"No, I guess not," I say, as my heart skips a beat.

"Say it again." He leans in close to kiss me.

"I belong to you and only you."

"That's the way I like it." And he kisses me. With that kiss, I knew our relationship had just passed yet another hurdle.

Chapter 16
Favor

Today is the day the Cougars leave for their away game in North Carolina. This is a very important game on the road to the Championships. No classes today so students can have the opportunity to support the team. Brice says he isn't worried about the game, but I know it must sit in the back of his head as they get closer and closer to the Championships. This game will have scouts sitting in the bleachers. Brice will be riding with the team, and I'll be driving with Jana, following behind the team bus. Walking hand and hand, we are headed to the meeting place in the stadium parking lot.

"Okay, baby. Drive carefully, and I will see you in North Carolina." Brice tips my head for a kiss.

"Get some rest on the bus. I know I kept you up last night," I tease and clench my legs together as I remember our activities of the night before.

"You can keep me up like that anytime." He smiles and places another tender kiss on my lips. "You should let Jana drive though, because you didn't get much sleep either."

"Jana is probably hungover. I'll be okay."

"Walker, any day now." Coach Vega yells.

"On my way, Coach," Brice calls out. "I love you, be safe. Text me when you check into your hotel."

"I will. I love you too." I kiss him again, and watch him turn to board the bus with his team.

God, I miss him already, as he gives me a final wave goodbye. Turning around to walk over to my car, I see Jana stumbling towards me with a group of her fellow cheerleaders. Most of the cheerleaders will be riding the bus with the team, but Jana opted to make the drive with me since Cal isn't back from Virginia.

"Oh, my God, I'm so hungover," Jana complains as she walks towards me, with her Gatorade dangling in her hand. Her normally perky disposition is gone and replaced with pain and nausea. *Knew it.*

"Why am I not surprised?" I say to her, my eyes focused on Regan standing next to her.

"Can Regan catch a ride with us?" Jana begs, giving me a bashful look.

"Why do you need a ride, Regan? What happened to your car?"

"I have transmission problems."

"Is that so? You're telling me you don't have anyone else to go with?"

"I told you she wouldn't," Regan speaks to Jana.

"Sorry, Favor. It's my fault. I told her I would ask you, when she said she had no way to get to the game. I would've taken her myself in my car, but I already said I would drive with you."

"Regan, you insult my boyfriend and me at every turn. A few weeks ago, you tried to leave me with the impression that

183

you were with him by pretending to trip and fall into his arms. You can see why I'm a little wary of a four-hour trip with you." I cross my arms over my chest.

"Okay, I get it. You're right. I apologize. But I really would like to go to the game to support our team. Can I please catch a ride with you?"

I look at her and then at Jana. "Your idea, huh?"

"Yes. I should've called you last night to ask. But I didn't want to disturb you because you were with Brice," Jana says, giving me an impish grin. I could never say no to Jana. She has done me countless favors without so much as a cross word.

"Fine, but this is definitely against my better judgment. You do anything to piss me off or insult me, you're out, and I don't care if we are in the middle of nowhere. Got me?" I narrow my eyes at Regan.

She smiles. "Got you. Your car, your rules."

"Alright then, let's go. The team's bus is going to be pulling out soon, and I want to be directly behind it." Spinning on my heel, I walk towards my car. As I open the door, I see Wayne staring at me from a distance, his car door already open for him to get in. He smiles slightly and gives me a wave. I haven't seen him since the dedication ceremony. This is the first time I feel my heart is truly healing, as I lift my hand and give him a wave in return.

Jana stares at me before entering the car. "Are you okay?"

"Yeah, I am." I smile at her.

Four and a half hours later, we arrive, and I drop Jana off at her hotel first, where she's staying with her fellow cheerleaders. Regan and I check into our individual rooms at another hotel. A party atmosphere is evident in the hotel as students check in for the big game tomorrow evening. I still can't believe that I am going to a football game that isn't for my dad or my brother. Brice would've understood if I didn't come, but I wanted to be here for him to offer my support.

Inside my room, I flop down on my bed and shoot off a quick text to Brice, letting him know that I've checked in. As I am about to close my eyes for a nap, my phone beeps.

Brice: God I miss you, baby. Think you can come over for a few hours? Got practice in another hour or so but you can stop by afterward.

Me: Miss you too. I'll stop by later. But I won't stay that long. You have to keep your head on the game and not me.

Brice: It's always about you baby and don't you ever forget that.

I smile at his words, pressing my phone to my chest. Oh, this man of mine.

Me: It's always about us. See you in a few hours. ☺

While I wait, I've taken full advantage of the time. I slept and ate some lunch. Looking at the clock, I realize that Brice should be back in his room from practice, so I decide to drive over to his hotel. Walking through the lobby of the hotel where the team is staying, I see Wayne talking to some of his former teammates. Since my speech at the dedication ceremony, he is no longer as ostracized as before. It is good to

185

see him smiling and looking better. Some cheerleaders are hanging around him and the players. I walk over to them because Jana is part of the group.

"How did practice go?" I ask Jana, who is looking much better than she did a few hours ago.

Shrugging her shoulders, she says, "It went well, I guess. One of the girls did puke on the field, though." She scrunches up her nose at the memory.

"Eww. Disgusting." We both laugh.

"Here to see Brice?" Jana gives me a knowing look.

"Yes. I should be heading up now, actually." I wave bye to everyone and walk over to the elevators. As I am waiting, I look over to see Jana leaning in closer to Wayne. An outsider looking in would say those two look quite intimate. The chime of the elevator interrupts me from my thoughts, and I step in.

Getting off on the team's floor, I see Jameson talking with Kevin Shore in the hallway. Glaring at both of them, I walk past without a word. Jameson, of course, glares back at me and Kevin laughs out loud. I know we don't have proof, but I feel it in my gut that Kevin is the reason Cal ended up in the hospital. Standing in front of Brice's door, I knock and wait for him to answer. The door opens, and I can't believe what I see before me.

Regan answers the door. A *naked* Regan answers the door and gives me a look.

"What are you doing here?" she asks me.

Is this bitch for real? Did she really just ask me what am I doing in my boyfriend's room? "Shouldn't I be the one asking *you*?"

She looks me up and down, as if sizing me up for competition. "I didn't know Brice was into threesomes, but hey, I'm down if you are. Besides, I thought I wore him out already. Guess that stud has more energy than I anticipated."

What the fuck? As I step forward to slap her, I see Brice walking out of the bathroom with a towel hanging low on his hips, drying his face with another towel. He comes to a sudden stop and looks up, taking in the scene unfolding before him.

"Regan? What the fuck are you doing in my room?" he snaps angrily.

This bitch doesn't flinch or bat an eyelash. I survey the room from the position where I'm standing. I take in the rumpled bedsheets, the empty condom wrappers around the floor, and a used condom discarded on a nightstand. My heart breaks in two. Backing my way to the door, I open it and run down the hallway to the elevators. I hear Brice yelling after me, screaming for me to wait. *Damn elevator is going to take too long.* Spotting the staircase, I make a run for it, passing Jameson and Kevin on the way.

Once in the hotel lobby, I don't bother to break stride as I head towards the exit, my vision blurred from the tears. Jana calls out to me, but I don't stop.

"Favor, *wait*." Brice yells after me.

I turn and glare at him. He is still wearing nothing but a towel. His muscles bulge as he lifts his arms, almost like he is approaching a wild animal. Perhaps he is. I'm feeling quite wild at this moment. Wild with anger.

"Favor, I don't know how she got in my room. You have to believe me," he says, as he walks over to me slowly.

A crowd begins to form around the two of us. Jana is now standing at my side, along with Wayne. Jana instantly places herself in front of me. "She doesn't want to talk to you. Give her a moment," Jana says to him.

Brice looks crushed. "Favor, please baby, you have to believe me."

I shake my head as fury builds inside of me. "I can't do this." I turn and walk outside. Brice doesn't come after me, but Jana and Wayne follow behind. When I get to my car, I fumble with my key and feel Wayne's hand touch mine, removing the keys from my fingers.

"I'll drive you back to your hotel," he says to me. Unable to speak, I just nod and get into the backseat with Jana. Instantly, I lay my head on her shoulders and cry.

You ever had that friend that knows when to talk and when not to? Jana is that friend right now. She doesn't bother asking me questions I'm too emotionally spent to answer. She only saw her friend who was in need, and she was there. No questions or answers are needed. I'll always be thankful to her for that moment.

Chapter 17

Favor

Bang, bang, bang. "Favor, I know you're in there. It's Egon. Open up."

I shake my head at Jana and Wayne, and bury my head in my pillow. The two of them stayed up with me last night as I cried and explained what I saw. Jana, ever the cheerleader, said I should talk to Brice. She doesn't believe he slept with Regan. Wayne said he doesn't know Brice, but he will follow my lead on how to handle this. Brice has called several times throughout the night all the way into this morning. *Looks like I'm not the only one who lost sleep over this.* Of course, I refused to answer any of his calls or text messages.

"He isn't going to stop knocking. I'll answer it, okay?" Wayne says as he stands, walking towards the door.

"I don't want to talk to him," I cry into my pillow.

"No worries. If you don't want to talk to him, you don't have to. Wayne will do the talking," Jana responds.

Wayne opens the door, and Egon tries to push past him. Wayne holds his hand to Egon's chest. "Listen, it's been a rough night for her. She doesn't want to talk. If you need to say something, just say it to me, and I'll give her the message."

I hear Egon exhale deeply. "Favor, he didn't do anything. You have to believe him. He hates Regan, and always has. As his best friend, I know him, and he would never do this to you."

I don't respond; I just cry harder into my pillow as Jana strokes my head.

"I think you should leave now," Wayne warns.

"Today is a very important game for his career. His head is not in the right place. They need to sort this out before the game." Egon stresses his last words.

"I understand. But she isn't ready to talk to him," Wayne says.

"Favor. I've come to think of you as my friend. As your friend, I'm asking you to please believe me when I say Brice would not do this to you. I've never seen him so hung up on a girl before in all the years I've known him. Don't throw it all away. Give him a chance to explain." Egon makes a last-ditch effort.

I sit up on my bed, and turn to face Egon standing in the doorway. "How did she get in his room without him knowing?" I ask.

Egon closes his eyes and shakes his head. "We don't know."

"Just leave, Egon. Please. Just leave." I turn back around and throw myself onto my pillow again.

Egon lets out a breath. "Okay, I'll leave. But promise me you'll talk to him."

I don't say a word, and I hear the door close.

"I think you should talk to Brice," Jana confides, stroking the back of my head.

"I can't. It hurts too much."

Jana sighs. "Listen, I have to get to the stadium and change clothes. Are you going to the game, at least?"

"No."

"Not for him, but for me. Please go to the game and support me, at least. I'll be cheering, and it would mean a lot to me. Besides, it will cheer you up."

I turn and look at her. "For you, I will." Jana smiles and gives me a hug.

"I'll drive you to the stadium, and come back to pick up Favor later," Wayne offers.

Jana beams at him. She gives me another quick hug, and they both leave. Sitting up on my bed, I see my reflection in the mirror. Oh my goodness, I look like hell. I shower and change clothes, finishing just as Wayne arrives. In his car, we drive towards the stadium.

"Listen, I don't know Brice. But from what I hear, he is a really good guy. Do you believe he would do that to you?" Wayne asks me.

"I don't know what to believe anymore. It's hard not to believe it, with all of the evidence in the room, staring me in my face."

"Listen, some buddies of mine on the team are stressed about this also. This game is riding on Brice's shoulders. They all said his head isn't in the right frame of mind. As a former player, trust me, I know what that is like. He could make a mistake on the field that could not only cost the team the game, but he could get injured."

"I know. You know I, of all people, would know that." I'm slightly stunned I'm sitting in Wayne's car having this conversation at all.

"Like I said, I'll back your play, no matter what. But to tell you the truth, I'm starting to believe he got set up."

"Set up? By who?"

"Jameson, perhaps. He has it out for Brice. He knows how important this game is, with all of the scouts watching. If he could get Brice to the point where he doesn't perform well, it could damage his career."

"Jameson is a lot of things, but he wouldn't sink that low." Would he? As soon as the words leave my mouth, I begin to question them.

"Wouldn't he? Brice took his spot on the team. How does that look regarding his career? Besides, trust me, there is a lot more to Jameson than you are fully aware of."

Sitting back in my seat, I close my eyes to contemplate what Wayne has just shared with me. Would Jameson sink so low? He has always been arrogant, obnoxious at times, and self-absorbed. But would he do something like this?

Arriving at the stadium, Wayne helps me find my seat.

"Do you miss it? Football. Do you miss it?" I ask him, genuinely interested.

"I do. There isn't a day that doesn't go by that I don't think about all that I have lost. But I'm making the best of it. Thanks to you," he says and offers me a warm smile.

"Thanks to me?"

"Yes. When you rejected me initially, I spun out of control. But once you were able to accept my apology, it was as if a weight was lifted. I felt that I was able to begin to live again. It still hurts and bothers me what I've done, but each day, I'm trying to do the right thing and prove that I'm worthy of your forgiveness. I hope to be a better man for it." Tears are in his eyes as he says those words, and I hug him.

"Wayne, I can already tell you are a better man. You didn't have to sit with Jana and me last night. The way I treated you before, you had every right not to want to get wrapped up in my drama. But you placed yourself at the heart of it, and I thank you for that. Trevor would be so proud of you."

"He would be proud of both of us. I miss him. He is the only best friend I've ever had."

We both stare at each other, caught in our memories of my brother. I settle in my seat and Wayne leaves to find his own. We both make plans to meet in front of the ticket office after the game, so he can give me a ride back to my hotel.

****

It's almost halftime, and the team is struggling. Brice's throws are off, and he is not connecting with his receiver. From the times I've seen Brice at practice compared to now, I know his game is not what it usually is. Brice has always thrown with a confidence that he doesn't seem to have at this moment. The halftime bell rings and the teams head to their locker rooms. Egon's band begins their setup to play.

"Favor. Come with me." Wayne motions to me.

I turn to see him standing on the steps of my row. I stand and walk over to him. "What's going on?"

"I found someone who can help." He grabs my hand, and we walk past the concession stands and take the stairs down, walking towards the teams' locker rooms. "What is going on?" I ask, partly because I'm confused but mostly because I am stalling, not wanting to run into Brice. That is a meeting I'm not ready to have.

"Trust me, okay?" He looks at me and gives me a reassuring smile.

We stand in front of the locker room as he pulls out his cell. Moments later, a Cougars player walks out of the locker room.

"Favor, this is my friend Joel. He has something he has to tell you." Wayne steps back as Joel looks me over quickly.

"Listen, I wouldn't be doing this if it wasn't for the fact that the game might be riding on it," Joel a tall, somewhat handsome man, says. "Jameson and Kevin put Regan up to setting up Brice. Jameson has been gunning for Brice ever since he took his spot on the team. Things escalated when you started dating him." He looks down at his feet as he tells the story.

I gasp. "Jameson and Kevin? But how did they get Regan inside of his room?"

"They were able to swipe the extra keycard from the coach. Coach has the second key card for all our rooms. We get mandatory checks now and then. Drugs and shit, you know?"

My head feels as if it is spinning. He didn't cheat after all. I was such a fool to fall for the trick.

"Yo. Is that all? Can you two, like, kiss and makeup or something? We're getting our asses handed to us out there."

"What? Oh yes. Can you please send Brice out?"

Joel and Wayne bump fists as he turns and heads into the locker room.

"How were you able to do that?" I question.

"I asked a few of my buddies on the team. They weren't willing to talk at first. But I think the game helped change their minds. You know how football players are. They're like a wolf pack. They might fight each other, but will protect one another from outsiders. Since I'm an outsider now, they weren't willing to tell me at first." He pushes his hands into his front pockets and looks at the floor.

"Favor?" I hear Brice's voice, and I look away from Wayne and over to him. I mouth my thanks to Wayne, and walk over to Brice. He takes me into his arms and kisses my forehead. "Baby, I would never do anything like that to you. Please believe me."

"I do. I'm sorry for not giving you the chance to explain. I was just so hurt by everything that I saw." Tears fall down my cheeks, and he wipes them away. "I, unfortunately, must ask

195

you once again to forgive me. Looks like I'm starting a trend." I try to smile.

"None needed, baby. I love you. Let's promise to find out all the facts before jumping to conclusions for now on." He holds my face in his hands.

"I promise. Now I need you to do something for me."

"What's that?"

I hear Egon's band playing in the background. He is playing the song Brice and I danced to that night in the club when we watched his band play. "For God's sake, man, I need you to win this game. Please don't tell me that I wasted a trip, for the team to lose," I joke around, pushing him lightly.

He smiles at me and picks me up in his arms, kissing me. His kiss leaves me dizzy and wanting more. "I have to go back. Looks like I have a game to win." He winks at me and jogs into the locker room.

Relief washes over me as I stare at his retreating figure. Wayne walks over to me. "Listen, we should be getting back to our seats. I had to call in some favors to even get us back here."

Nodding my head, I follow Wayne back towards the seating areas. He walks me to my seat, and I turn and give him a hug. "Thank you so much."

"No problem, little sis." He smiles and turns to leave. *Little sis?* I guess he is like an older brother. We were close at one time. He could never take the place of Trevor, but it is good to know that I can count on him.

I take my seat just in time for the second half to begin. Brice leads his team out onto the field, an air of confidence to him I didn't see during the first half. In Joe Namath fashion, he points his pointer finger in the air, declaring he is going to win this game. The stadium erupts in applause and cheers. I stare at the jumbotron as he and his teammate's huddle.

"Oh, my God, he is so cute," a very drunk girl slurs in front of me.

I sit back and listen to the smashed girls talk about Brice. My Brice. At first, I bristle at their words as they describe in detail what they would like to do with him. But I remember, the things they would like to do with him, he will be doing with me later tonight. A smile of satisfaction spreads across my face.

The team wins the game, crushing their opponents in an 8-point lead. I stand and cheer the team as they shake hands with the opposing team. Brice did a great job on the field and rallied his team down to the last minute. He showed true leadership skills on the field. I'm almost positive his play in the second half of the game has more than fixed the play from the first half in the eyes of the scouts.

Chapter 18
Brice

Coach gave Jameson and Kevin each a two-game suspension. Regan, on the other hand, received an academic probation. The team, for the most part, backed me because, no matter how Jameson feels about me, he affected the game. I had to convince Favor not to hit Regan. It seems the lady in my life has a temper. Favor walking out on me that day almost broke me. Never have I felt so lost in my life. I owe Wayne a huge favor for having both of our backs and bringing us together again.

Leaving Favor's dorm, I walk towards my car. "Brice, do you have a minute?"

I look up and see Wayne jogging over to me. "Yeah sure, bro. What's up?"

"I know this is a huge thing to ask. But, I miss the game. Was thinking about giving it another try."

"Have you been practicing?"

"No. Was hoping you could practice with me a few days a week. If I can get myself back up to par, I'll then speak to the coach. I know all the spots are taken, but maybe I can get a temporary spot."

I look at him for a moment, and remember hearing about him and Favor's brother playing. They were called the dream team at that time. Wayne has a reputation for being a really good receiver. "Yeah sure, bro. I can help you. For me, it's just more practices. I'm always down for that. But yeah, you're going to have an upward battle to get on the team. We are mid-season. If you want, I can speak to the coach with you."

"You would?"

"Yeah, of course. I still owe you for uncovering the truth, so hell yeah, I got you, bro."

"Thanks, man. Truly appreciated." We shake hands.

"I thought you were heading to your dorm?" Favor says, as she walks over to the two of us talking. Even though I just left her moments ago, I'm excited to see her. She comes over to me, giving me a kiss.

"Hey, baby. Yeah, Wayne just needed a favor from me." I tilt my head in Wayne's direction.

"What kind of favor?" she asks.

"Brice is going to help me train to get back on the team."

A look of surprise forms on her face. "Wow. So, you're going to go for it?"

"Yeah." He looks down, rubbing the back of his neck. On some level, I understand why this would be hard to talk to her about.

She places her hand on his shoulders, giving him reassurance. "It's okay. It was both of your dreams. No reason why you can't pursue it. I'm happy for you." She smiles and gives him a quick peck on the cheek.

"Thanks. It means a lot that I have your blessing," he admits.

"Is this a private party or can anyone join?" Jana calls out as she walks towards us.

"Anyone can join," I respond, squeezing Favor to my side, and she giggles.

"What's everyone up to?" Jana asks.

"Wayne and I are going to toss the old pigskin around. You ladies care to watch and drool over the magnificentness of the two of us?" I say, as Favor slaps my chest lightly.

"Yeah sure. Count me in," Jana chimes.

Favor shrugs her shoulders. "Sure, why not."

"Alright, kids. I'll drive us to the stadium. It should be free right now," I reply, as I turn to open my car door, and everyone piles in.

Wayne and I don't bother with changing clothes, since we are just tossing the ball around a little. We can work on some other stuff later, and I'll see if I can get some of my teammates to help with training him. Favor and Jana sit on the astro turf but, in true Jana fashion, it's no time before she is jumping up and down, rooting for us.

Wayne falls right back into the groove of the game. It's like he is a natural at receiving. I sure could have used him a few weeks ago. Taking a quick water break as we stand with Favor and Jana, I hear a voice that I have learned to hate.

"What are you doing here, Wayne?" Jameson accuses.

Wayne turns around to look at Jameson. I place a hand on Wayne's arm and walk forward. "What's it to you?" I ask.

"He is a disgrace to this sport. What is he doing on the Cougars' field?" Jameson spits out.

"No, you're the disgrace to this sport. Don't think that I forgot your little antics from a few weeks ago," I respond in anger.

"Favor, you, of all people, should be ashamed of yourself." Jameson directs his attention to my girl.

"Don't you talk to her. You lost that privilege, you son of a bitch." I roar, about to lunge for him.

Wayne holds my shoulder. "He isn't worth the suspension, man. Let it go. He is just sounding off."

"Jameson, go away. This is none of your business." Favor walks over and stands next to me.

"The hell it isn't. All of those nights you cried in my arms after what he did."

"Oh, stop it, Jameson. Not like you didn't enjoy taking advantage of the situation," Favor responds.

Jameson flinches at her words. "It wasn't like that," he says slowly.

"It wasn't? From my point of view, it was." she throws back at him.

"Fine. Let's see how your parents like the fact that you're hanging with the enemy." He turns to walk off the field.

At that very moment, I feel as if a Pandora's box of sorts has just been opened. Favor places her hand on my chest. "Are you okay?" she asks with a look of concern.

"Yeah. I just had a feeling that someone just walked over my grave," I say, shaking the reverie out of my head.

"Let's call it a day with practice. My treat for pizza, if there are any takers," Wayne interrupts.

"I'm down." Jana bounces up and down.

Favor and I both nod and we head out of the stadium.

****

A few days later, the four of us, plus Egon this time, head to Favor's dorm to drop her and Jana off, after dinner and a movie. Walking towards the girl's dorm, we see a tall male figure pacing in front of the dorm building. Favor looks at me because we both know exactly who it is. Kyne Hollister.

"Dad?"

"Where have you been? I've been waiting out here for nearly two hours," Kyne snaps at his daughter.

"Why didn't you just call my cell? I wasn't expecting you," she retorts in a snarky tone.

She wasn't expecting him but somehow, I knew he would come. I knew it the day Jameson spotted me practicing with Wayne.

Kyne's eyes move over to where Wayne stands with Jana next to him. "So, it's *true*. Jameson wasn't mistaken. You

202

are hanging out with the trash." His tone is thick, and his arms hang to the side.

"Dad, he is…" Her voice sounds like a little girl's.

"*Enough.* You have a choice." He points a finger in Wayne's direction. "You stop hanging out with this piece of shit that killed my son, or I cut you off. You'll be no daughter of mine."

Her eyes widen, and her mouth is agape. "Dad? We need to forgive and move on."

"To hell, we will. He killed my son. My only son. You expect me to forgive that? And you stand here," - he points his finger in my direction now - "and let *him* influence you into accepting him?" He points a shaky finger back to Wayne.

"No one influenced me. I made that decision on my own."

"You would date a man that has no regard to your brother's memory?"

"Mr. Hollister. Please don't blame Favor or Brice. If you want to blame someone, then let it fall at my feet, and mine alone," Wayne pleads.

"I blame all three of you. Your mother is beside herself. I need an answer now, Favor. These two, or your family?"

Without any hesitation, Favor responds. "Then I choose them, Dad. They've been more of a family to me than you or mom."

Spittle builds up on the corners of his mouth. "Then you are no daughter of mine. Starting now, all of your accounts will be closed. You will have to figure out your way to pay for all of this," he says, as he stretches his arms out. Giving us all a final look, he walks away.

"Oh, my God, Favor. How are you going to pay for school?" Jana cries.

"Babe, we will figure this out," I say, holding her to me.

"It's...it's okay. It has been a long time coming. Looks like I just expedited it, that's all." She gives a slight laugh. Looking at all of our concerned faces, she continues, "Listen guys, it will be okay. I'll see if I can get financial aid, or student loans. I can also get a job."

Today, I learned my girl was Superwoman. Here she is, her world crumbling around her, and she is reassuring us that things would be okay.

"I can get a job also, to help," I tell her.

She shakes her head. "I want to do this on my own. Don't worry about me. I would've had to learn to do things by myself eventually."

"Favor, I'm so sorry. If I thought, for a moment, this would've happened, I would've stayed out of your life," Wayne sympathizes.

"Wayne, I stand by my decision. I don't feel that I have done anything wrong. It's fine."

I hold her to me and kiss the top of her head. At this moment, I know things will be okay because I won't allow for anything else.

Chapter 19
Favor

The days following my father disowning me have been a whirlwind. Lucky for me, I am fully paid up for the school year. I will have to receive financial aid and student loans for next year, though. Next on my list of things to do is to find a job, since I still need money for day-to-day living expenses. Unfortunately, I do not have many skills since I have never had a job before. Lucky for me, Egon's band needs someone to handle their expenses. It doesn't pay much, but at least it gives me some spending money for gas and things.

Brice and Wayne have repeatedly apologized to me. Thing is, I feel that by my father forcing my hand, I have a huge weight lifted off my shoulders. Finally, I feel free and more like the real me. Or should I say, I've rediscovered myself?

Brice stayed true to his word and went with Wayne to visit the coach. Coach Vega was surprised by this request, but said Wayne would have to go through tryouts, just like everyone else. If he gets in, then he will be playing next year, for his senior year. He most likely will not be offered a spot in the pros, but at least it's something for him to strive for.

Jana has been very mum on the question of her and Wayne. Brice and I both have our suspicions about the two of them being a couple. If they are, then I am happy for them. Wayne has changed so much from that person he used to be when my brother was alive. He used to believe he sat on top of the world. Now he is humbled by it all, and you can see his personal journey. It feels great to be able to let go of all the animosity I held towards him at one time. I never knew how tiring holding on to anger could be.

Winter break is coming up, and I'm not sure what I'll be doing. For obvious reasons, I will not be going to my parents' house. Brice offered for me to come home with him to Philadelphia, and Jana asked if I would like to join her and her parents in Georgia. I haven't made up my mind yet. I have been in touch with Cal, and I was thinking about spending Winter break with him and his family. He should be back to school after the break. Cal still refused to say who beat him up that night and I have stopped pressing him for the information.

Walking hand in hand with Brice on campus, we are enjoying the unusually warm weather we are having. Our relationship has survived so much turmoil in such a short period of time. We are just enjoying each other and being together as we take a walk. Goofing off, he chases me around the campus quad. Of course, since most of what he does in football is run, he catches me with ease, throwing me over his shoulder as I screech with surprise. I love days like today with him. Young and without a care in the world. It feels great.

"So, lunch?" Brice asks, as he steals a chip from my bag.

"Sure. Town or campus?" I nuzzle into his shoulder.

"How about town. Tired of campus food."

"How about that Italian restaurant?"

"Okay, now you're talking." He pulls my hand as we walk in the direction of his car. My cell phone rings, and I see it is my mother. I have to take the call, and Brice steps away to give me some privacy.

207

I hesitate before answering. "Hey, Mom."

"Oh great, you picked up. I thought I'd be leaving a message."

"I was cut out of the family, not the other way around." My fingers begin to cramp from the death grip I have on the phone.

She's silent for a moment before she speaks. "About that. I'm in town. I'd like to talk to you."

I look over at Brice, standing a few feet away from me. Some people are gathering around him, chatting, and I don't know how he stands it. He never gets a break from people wanting to talk to him. "Umm well, I'm on my way to have lunch with Brice. We're going to that Italian restaurant in town. I guess you can meet us there."

Again, she is silent for a moment. I begin to think I lost our connection and I look at my phone to check for a signal. Nope, full signal. "Mom?"

"Oh, yes. Well, I was hoping to talk with you alone."

"Look, Mom, I'm with Brice, whether you agree with it or not. Whatever you have to say can be said in front of him because he's a major part of my life. But I'm really hungry, and I'd really like to see you." I say with all honesty. Brice smiles and gives me a wave. I blow a quick kiss to him. God, he holds my heart in his hand.

"Alright. Fine. I will meet you there in, let's say twenty minutes."

"Okay. See you in twenty." I hang up and stare at my phone. Brice walks over to me.

"Everything okay?"

"Mom. She's in town. Guess who's coming to lunch?" I try to make a joke out of it.

Perking up one eyebrow at me, he says, "Your mom is joining us for lunch? Shouldn't the two of you talk without me around?"

"No. I need you for moral support, if anything else."

He bends to kiss me. "Your wish is my command."

Walking into the restaurant, I spot my mother already seated. She looks impeccable as always, in her Ralph Lauren dress and perfectly manicured nails, not a hair out of place. We walk over and I kiss her on her cheek, as Brice says hello to her. I'm surprised she acknowledges him and says she's glad that he could join us. Menus are handed over, and we begin deciding on something to eat, trying to pretend that we are not studying each other.

"So, what brings you to town, Mom?" I ask, taking a sip of my water.

"Can't a mother want to visit her child?" She snaps her purse closed and hangs it on the back of her chair.

"Yes. But this is out of the ordinary for us." I smile coyly at her.

Ignoring my comments, she proceeds, "I wanted to discuss Winter break. What are your plans?"

I shrug my shoulders and slouch in my seat. Before she has a chance to correct my posture, I reposition myself in my seat. "I haven't made a decision. I might spend it in Philadelphia with Brice and his mom, or maybe with Cal and his family in Virginia."

"I see." She raises her hand that showcases some of my father's expensive gifts to her and signals for the waiter. "I was hoping you would spend it with your father and I. Christmas won't be the same without you."

Since when? When Trevor was alive, my father would do "manly" things with him, like play football or talk about football or something revolving around that damn sport. My mother was usually busy entertaining guests and correcting me. After Trevor died, I spent most of the time in my room, only coming down to eat and disappearing immediately afterward. So basically, if ignoring me throughout the holiday is not going to be the same, then I'm more than happy to not participate.

"Do I still have a father? I recall being disowned."

My mother has always been one to keep up appearances, smiling and waving in the public eye. Beatrice "Birdie" Hollister has always been considered the perfect southern lady because of her poise and manners. Rarely does anyone get to see the real Birdie, the one who made an appearance just now. Gone is her smile, now replaced by a frown, tears forming in the corners of her eyes.

For the first time, I notice lines of age around my mother's eyes and mouth. She clears her throat. "I've lost one child. I'm not willing to lose another." She picks up her napkin and dabs at her eyes. "I know your father and I haven't been the best parents to you. Your dad, because you were not a son, and myself..." Her words linger before she inhales deeply to finish her sentence. "And myself, because you've always been so independent. From the moment you could walk, you haven't needed a soul."

A lump forms in my throat and drops to the pit of my stomach like a rock. *You will not cry, Favor, you will hold yourself together.* "That's just it, Mom. I *have* needed you. Both of you. All those years growing up, I felt invisible to the two of you. Trevor always had your full attention."

She looks at her lap. "Trevor and your father bonded over football. Your brother was a natural quarterback, but he hated the game."

My gaze shoots over to her to see if this is true. It is. He did? That's news to me. "He never told me."

"I know. He would cry to me very often, about how your father would push him to be better than himself. You see, when your father retired, he lost his identity. Being part of a team was the only thing he knew. He didn't know how to be a husband or a father. So, his way of connecting was through the game." She lifts her glass of wine and takes a sip. "Your brother was one of those people who needed the support and love from his family and friends. He hated playing, but it made your father happy, and that was the only way to get your father to be interested in him. So, he would play and talk to me about his true feelings."

How did I not realize this before? Was I really that caught up in my own feelings that I missed what was going on with my brother? I thought he enjoyed those moments with Dad. "Why didn't he talk to me?" Was I not as close with him as

I thought? Did I imagine it all? A stab of pain goes through my heart, opening up another wound.

"Because, Favor. He was your older brother. He wanted to shield you always. He was such a kind and giving soul." She chokes on her last words.

I reach my hand across the table, and she takes it. I squeeze her hand gently.

"Trevor was slightly jealous of you. He knew that out of the two, you were the strongest. You always went to your own beat. In some ways, I'm envious as well. I've never had the courage myself to go against the norm. So, in my own way, I shut you out. I don't believe it was done intentionally. It was a gradual buildup until, I guess, I'd destroyed whatever chance at a mother-daughter relationship I could have had with you. For that, I am sorry." Tears fall down her face. I stand up and hug her. This ordinarily would have caused a rebuff from my mother, but today, with her walls falling down, she accepts my hug. Her arms are warm and inviting, and I wonder if I could have had this all along.

"Mom, please don't cry," I choke out.

"It's okay. It took your father's temper tantrum to snap some sense into my head. Favor..." She places her hands on my cheeks. "You are my beautiful baby girl. I am so sorry for all those years of being absent from your life. But this stops today. I want to be a part of your life and get to know you. I know I can't make up for all of those lost years, but I would like to wipe the slate clean, and have a new start. Let's call it the path to forgiveness."

Looking into my mother's eyes, I see myself. She has offered me an olive branch; the one thing that I have always wanted. "But what about Dad?"

"He will come around eventually. But for now, you and I will have our start." She reaches into her pocketbook as I take my seat again. She pulls out a checkbook and card, and hands them to me. "I've opened up an account for you. I will be paying your monthly expenses and don't worry about school. I will be paying your tuition going forward."

I hold the checkbook in my trembling hands. I look at Brice, who has sat silent this entire time. My silent but strong wall that I have come to lean on. Turning back to look at my mother, I say, "But, Mom, it's okay. I've figured out a way to support myself."

"I had no doubt you would. But I will still be doing this for you anyway."

"What about Dad? Won't he be upset if he finds out?"

"You leave your father to me." She gives me a wink. "Now, back to Winter break."

I look over at Brice, who shrugs his shoulders, leaving the decision up to me. "Can I think about it?"

"How about this." She looks at Brice. "You and your mother are both invited to spend Christmas with us. It will be my treat, of course. Besides, from the look of the two of you, I would imagine you will become part of the family in a few years." She winks at him, and he smiles.

"What do you think?" I ask Brice.

"I think mom would be thrilled, Mrs. Hollister. I'll call and ask her. Thank you for the invitation."

"Please allow me to call your mother to extend the invitation myself. It would make me happy to do so."

"Of course, Mrs. Hollister."

"Birdie. All of my friends call me Birdie." She gives him a genuine smile. And the Birdie of public appearances is back, albeit a warmer version of herself.

Chapter 20
Brice

My mother was thrilled to be invited to the Hollister house for the holidays. Not just because Kyne Hollister is my childhood idol, but because she wants to meet Favor. She knows how much Favor means to me. Believe it or not, Birdie and my mother hit it off during their initial phone conversation and over the weeks that followed, they have spoken a few times. Favor is in just as much shock as I am. Kyne decided to invite Jameson over for the holidays, and this action doesn't go unrecognized by me, Favor, or her mother. He wants to make me feel as uncomfortable as possible, but what he doesn't realize is, as long as I have Favor by my side, I feel I can conquer the world.

Birdie extended an invitation to Egon as well. She said that there is strength in numbers. Behind that quaint, southern charm is a cunning woman. Though Birdie said at lunch that she felt that Favor was the stronger one, I feel that Favor perhaps gets her strength as a result of her mother. Egon, whose meeting with the record company was pushed back, accepted the invite, mostly just to piss Jameson off. I can be a force to be reckoned with, but with my brother, Egon, with me, I am virtually unstoppable.

We pile into Favor's car for the trip to her parents' house. It is just a two-hour trip, but from the way we packed snacks, you would think it was a fourteen-hour trip instead. The three of us are looking forward to this road trip together. The only thing that would make it truly complete is to have Jana, Cal, and Wayne with us. My mother's flight should be arriving later today, and Egon and I will meet her at the airport.

Favor has been going on and on about how this will be the first holiday that she is looking forward to. I'm looking forward to spending our first of many holidays together. We arrive at Favor's parent's house in pretty good time, with a jovial holiday spirit. Who knew things would go downhill from there.

Receiving the nickel tour of the house, it is interesting to see where Favor grew up. Kyne is not home, and isn't expected until later in the evening. This gives us a few hours of peace, or so we think. Wishful thinking, I guess.

"This is my dad's man cave, of sorts," Favor says, as we walk into a massive room with every sports memorabilia that you could think of.

"Wow your dad is really into all sports, isn't he?" Egon asks, looking at a basketball jersey signed by Michael Jordan.

"Yes, I guess you can say that," Favor says absentmindedly.

"Does he keep his Super Bowl rings in here?" Egon asks.

"Yes, over there, in the glass case in the corner." She points to a corner to our right.

Egon and I both walk over to the case and stare at the enclosed rings.

"It's like the holy grail," I joke. Favor walks over to join us.

"Yes, I guess. He only wears them on very special occasions."

"He has so many of them. How does he pick and choose?" I laugh.

"Beats me," she smiles, flipping her hair over her shoulder.

"Have you ever touched them or tried them on?" Egon asks.

She touches her throat. "Oh no. That privilege was never bestowed upon me. My brother, on the other hand, has tried them on. Matter of fact, we have pictures on the wall from when my brother was young, trying on the rings."

We look at the pictures that she's referring to. They hang above the glass case. Pictures of what appears to be a very young Trevor at different gatherings, held in the arms of his father, trying on the rings. You can see the love and devotion on Kyne Hollister's face for his son. At that moment, I feel instantly sorry for Favor. That love and devotion has never been given to her. I look over and see her staring at the images with a haunted expression. Grabbing her by the waist, I pull her into me and kiss the top of her head. She relaxes at my touch and lets out a breath.

"If it is too hard to walk down memory lane, we don't have to, babe," I whisper in her ear.

She looks up at me and smiles gently. "It hurts, but I think I need to stop being afraid of the past. It's okay, really." Taking me by the hand, she leads Egon and me out of the sports room and back upstairs to the main floor of the enormous house. Reaching the foot of the steps, we hear talking coming from the kitchen area. The three of us walk into the kitchen to see Jameson has arrived and is talking to Birdie.

"Oh, you guys finished the tour of the house?" Birdie smiles at the three of us as we enter the kitchen. She is standing by the kitchen island, sipping a cup of coffee. In that instant, Birdie looks young and carefree. She is standing barefoot with perfectly manicured toenails, wearing an ivory-colored sweater, and long trousers. Her hair is up in a ponytail.

"Yes, ma'am. Your house is incredible. Thank you once again for inviting us," I say to her.

A warm smile spreads across her lips. "No ma'am here. Remember, please call me Birdie. It is my pleasure to have you here."

Favor, Egon, and I take various places around the kitchen island. No one has said anything to Jameson as he scowls at Egon and me. Egon gives Jameson a wink, which further annoys him.

"Are you kids hungry? I can whip up something quick, or we can order," Birdie offers.

"No thanks. I'm still stuffed from all the junk food we ate on the road trip down here," I reply, patting my stomach.

"Eating junk food while in training?" Jameson quizzes.

I pointedly ignore his remarks and smile at Birdie.

"Yeah, none for me either, Mom. I'm still stuffed as well."

"Me three," adds Egon, as he stretches.

Birdie looks at Jameson. "I guess I can eat a little something, but please don't go through too much trouble on my behalf."

"Oh, no trouble at all. Why don't you kids go and watch a movie? What time do you have to leave to pick up your mother?"

"We should probably leave in another hour or so, just in case there is traffic," I respond.

"Good. I can't wait to meet her. She seems like such a lovely woman over the phone."

"Thanks, m...I mean, Birdie. Mom is looking forward to meeting you too."

The four of us head into the media room. After a huge debate on what to watch, mostly because Jameson wanted to be difficult, we finally settled on something. Egon and I watch part of the movie before we leave to go pick Mom up from the airport. When we arrive back at the house, Kyne Hollister is back. I introduce Mom to Favor and her family. Favor instantly gives my mother a hug and a kiss on the cheek. She's the first girl that I have introduced to my mother, which is a major step for me. A coming of age, of sorts. Birdie welcomes mom with open arms. Kyne, on the other hand, says a very brisk hello and heads into his office, with Jameson following behind. Thankfully, my mother doesn't take offense at all because she was warned beforehand.

Lying down in the guest room, I toss and turn because I have gotten so used to sleeping with Favor by my side. Or even better, making love to her and then falling asleep with her.

Either way, I am having trouble sleeping. Finally getting tired of counting sheep, I decide to go downstairs and watch a movie in the media room. When I reach the foot of the landing, I hear a voice call out from the kitchen.

"Having trouble sleeping also?" Birdie asks as I walk into the kitchen.

"Yes. I thought I could watch a movie to pass the time." She points to a seat across from her, and I sit.

"Would you like anything to eat or drink?" She is ever the proper lady, no matter what time of the night. I shake my head. "I am glad that you came downstairs. I wanted to have some time with you, to talk."

My stomach tightens as I get ready for whatever she has to say. I try to keep my face neutral.

"Don't worry, it's nothing bad. I know my husband and I were pretty hard on you when we initially met you. I can see now how wrong we were for not giving you a chance. It warms my heart to see how happy Favor looks when she is with you."

"Thank you. I appreciate that. She makes me happy as well. Mrs. Hollister, I just want you to know that I love your daughter very much."

She smiles at me. "A blind person could see how much the two of you are in love. Which brings me to the second reason for this conversation. My husband is not happy about your relationship with my daughter. He sees her with Jameson, as you already know. Coupled with you training Wayne, it is not exactly helping."

I instantly feel bad sitting in front of her, knowing how much pain Wayne has caused her. "I am sorry if I have caused any discomfort to you and your husband by training Wayne."

"Thank you for saying that. But, in all honesty, it is not necessary. When Favor forgave Wayne during the dedication ceremony, it was a tough pill for me to swallow. But listening to her words about forgiveness, and this being what Trevor would have done, helped me to understand better. I just wasn't willing to accept that at that time. Trevor is gone, and he is never going to come back. I am proud to have been his mother, and to have had the privilege to see him become a young man coming into his own. There isn't a day that goes by that I don't think about him. But I also know that I would dishonor his memory by not forgiving Wayne. So, I have made my peace with it all. One of these days, I will have the courage to say it to him myself." Tears fall down her face as she talks.

"I am sorry I did not get a chance to meet him. He sounds like he was an incredible person."

"He was," she replies, and looks away momentarily before focusing her eyes on me again. "Now my dear boy, I need to know if you are going to fight for her."

"Fight?" I give her a quizzical look.

"Yes, fight. You will have to fight for her. She is a strong woman, stronger than I, in so many ways. But she has been fighting a battle alone for so many years. I have just joined the fight, and I need to know you will too. She is going to need both of us."

Fight for Favor? Of course I would. "I will always fight for her."

"Good. Because she will need you in her corner."

****

It's Christmas Eve, and the house is feeling anything but festive. The battle lines have been drawn...Kyne and Jameson in one corner, and the rest of us in the other. At every twist and turn, Kyne or Jameson make comments to try to throw Egon or me off our game. We both smile and laugh at them, taking it in stride, as last night's conversation with Birdie echoes in my head.

Walking past Favor's room, I see her standing by her window, staring. I knock on her door startling her, and she smiles at me, waving for me to join her. Standing behind her, her head resting on my chest, we both look out the window, watching the lightning and listening to the thunder.

"Looks like we are going to have a wet Christmas instead of a white one," I murmur into her hair.

"I used to be afraid of the rain when I was a kid."

"The thunder and lightning would scare you?"

She nods her head. "Yeah. Trevor would let me crawl into the bed with him, and he would talk to me, or read me a story, to get my mind off of it."

"Want to crawl into bed now? I don't know any fairytale stories, but I do know of other ways to distract you."

Turning around, she pushes at my chest. "I'm no longer afraid of thunderstorms, thank you very much." She smiles at me.

Taking a step closer, I pull her into me. "You sure? I was hoping to distract you for a bit."

"You're incorrigible," she says and places a quick kiss to my lips. "Listen, we should go down for dinner. Dad is very punctual." Grabbing my hand, we walk out of her room and head down the stairs to the dining room.

Everyone is seated, as Favor and I take our seats. Kyne says grace over the table and our meal begins.

Everything starts out pretty normal, with light conversation around the table. Kyne and Jameson are keeping most of their discussions confined to each other. That is, until they hear the conversation between my mother and Birdie.

"I wouldn't be surprised if I hear wedding bells soon for these two." Birdie points to Favor and I.

Instantly, Favor hangs her head down, her hair covering her face like a veil, no doubt hiding some very red cheeks. For me, it starts the wheels turning in my head.

My mother's eyes dance with excitement. If Favor and I got married, I would be the first in her family to do so. "You know, she's the first girl that Brice has ever spoken to me about. And when Egon grabbed the phone from him to chime in, I knew then and there she would be the one. Now that I've met her, I second that." My mother gabs on as if the subjects of her conversation were not sitting just mere inches away from her.

Favor slides down in her chair further, while I sit up straighter. Instead of feeling trapped, it feels right, this conversation with our two mothers. I look over at Egon, who isn't paying any bit of attention as he scoops a second helping of stuffing on his plate. He burps loudly then mutters his pardon, reaching for a hot buttered biscuit.

"I can't wait to start dress shopping," Birdie announces, clapping her hands together.

"Mom. You're going to scare Brice off," Favor says in a flustered voice. I honestly think she would have banged her head on the table if it wasn't for her plate being in the way.

"It takes a lot more than that to scare me off, baby," I cajole.

"Wedding? What is this I hear about a wedding?" Kyne, who for the better part of the day has done everything in his power to make myself, Egon, and my mother feel as uncomfortable and as unwelcomed as possible, finally speaks.

The table instantly quiets, with the exception of Egon, who is still chewing, loudly and apparently oblivious to what is about to go down.

Birdie looks across the table at her husband and, without missing a beat, plasters a smile on her face. Not the same one that she had for my mother; no, that one was genuine. The smile she gives her husband is strained, her tone no longer holding the warmth it had a moment ago. "I was talking about the possible wedding between Brice and Favor." She dabs her napkin on both sides of her mouth and carefully folds it, placing it on the table. Anyone looking in would probably think this would be a gesture of giving up. After my talk with Birdie last night, I know this is a declaration of war.

Slamming his hands on the table, the crystal glasses shake, their sound reverberating through the air like the tensions coming from all of us. "I do not approve. No daughter of mine will..."

"I thought I was no longer your daughter. Didn't you make that declaration weeks ago?" Favor's head still hangs low, and her voice sounds dead. Not defeated, but not full of life either.

Kyne glares at Favor, but she doesn't lift her head. I reach under the table and grab her hand to let her know that I'm here with her, no matter what. I wait for her to return the squeeze, but she doesn't. And, in this moment, I'm scared.

He throws his napkin on his plate and rises from his seat. "You do everything in your power to embarrass this family and me. *Everything*. If your brother were alive, he would know how to handle you to make you behave yourself like a member of this family."

I think back to the conversation we had with Birdie on her surprise visit to the campus a few weeks ago. She spoke about how Trevor hated football, but played it to get his father's love. I wonder how would Trevor react to this. Would he protect his sister, or sit silent and say nothing, the way it seems this entire family behaves.

Favor looks up, and I expect to see tears in her eyes, but there aren't any. "Don't you dare throw that in my face. You've done everything you possibly could to make me feel like I wasn't worthy enough to be in your presence." Her voice is tinged with something, but I can't put my finger on it. It isn't hate but something much deeper.

Birdie stands and has her hands out in a peace offering. "Now Kyne, please. Let's just all calm down."

I guess, because he's done tearing his daughter down, he decides to turn on Birdie instead, pointing at her. "This is your fault. You forced this...this...down my throat. I didn't want her here, *or* for her to be in my sight." He now points in Favor's direction, never breaking eye contact with Birdie. "She chose who she wants to be with. Her brother's murderer. You, of all people, should have backed me up."

"I was not going to lose another *child*." Birdie's voice cracks as she screams the words out. My mother jumps out of her seat, accidentally knocking her wine glass over. The crystal stem breaks and the red wine spills across the white table cloth. I stare at the red stain as it gets bigger and bigger; such a small glass and yet a large stain comes from it. She stands behind Birdie, placing a hand on her shoulder.

"Another child? Since when did she ever act like a child of ours? Trevor knew how to behave himself, at least."

"You never wanted me, did you? Because I wasn't him." Favor's voice is soft.

Kyne looks at her. Actually, he looks through her, never saying a word. What feels like minutes or hours, in actuality was just seconds before we hear him say, "No, I never wanted you." The silence around the table is deafening. Favor, receiving the answer to her question, stands to leave the table, but I hold her in place. I stand up instead.

"Mr. Hollister, you should be ashamed of yourself. You still have a wonderful daughter who wants, no, *needs* your love, and you are too selfish to give it to her. I never had the luxury of growing up with a father. When I was a kid, you used to be my idol, and I would pretend you were my father. It helped me in so many ways when I was growing up." I hear my mother let out a sob. I turn to her and say, "It's okay, Mom. You know why? Because even though I didn't have a father, you more than made up for it in so many other ways." My mother nods as she wipes tears away from her eyes. I focus back on Kyne. "I am embarrassed that you were ever my idol, or any other kid's idol. *You* are the one who is an embarrassment to this family, and to Trevor's name."

"How dare you." Kyne begins to walk towards me, but Egon stands and blocks his path. "How *dare* you. You don't speak my son's name, ever. You're not deserving of it."

"You don't ever call yourself Favor's father. Ever. You're not deserving of it."

He pauses a moment before saying, "Well, that is one thing she will never worry about me calling myself to her again."

"Kyne, no. Don't say that. Please take that back. She's our daughter. Our only child." Birdie runs over to her husband and pounds her fists into his chest. He holds her hands in place as she sobs deeply, before releasing her hands and walking away. Birdie collapses to the ground, trying to stand but no longer able to.

We all sit in silence as his words still linger in the room like a black cloud.

Birdie, whose back is to the table, kneels on the ground, her body shaking. "He didn't mean that. He's just hurting, that's all." But from the sound of her voice, I can tell she doesn't believe that lie herself.

Favor stands and runs out of the dining room. I look to my mother, and she shakes her head. "Give her a moment."

"What kind of son of a bitch would say something like that to his daughter?" Egon asks as he stands next to me.

I'm about to answer, but Jameson responds before I get a chance. "She brought this on herself. She sided with Wayne. What do you expect?"

I begin to walk towards Jameson, but Egon beats me to it, punching Jameson in the face. "Don't you say a word about her. She's family, and we protect our own."

Jameson lies on the ground, rubbing his jaw. I swear, why does he keep opening his mouth because that is where he ultimately ends up; the floor. Some people just never seem to learn.

Dinner is obviously over, so we all help to clear the table. An hour passes, but Favor still hasn't returned. I stand by the window in the kitchen, looking out for her.

"Thank you for protecting her," Birdie says from behind me, startling me from my thoughts.

"Nothing to thank me for. I would've done that, regardless." I shrug my shoulders and take a seat at the table.

"She needed the support. I had a feeling it was going to come down to this. I just didn't realize it would've gotten this bad." She hangs her head slightly.

"Do you know where she would have gone?"

"There is a place down the back pathway that leads towards the lake house. She and Trevor would go there when she and her father would argue. I would imagine she's there."

I stand up immediately. "I'm going to go there then."

"Wait." Birdie steps out of the room, and comes back moments later with a duffle bag, handing it to me. "Here is a blanket. She must have gotten soaked in the rain. This will keep her warm. There is a fireplace in the lake house, but she never did figure out how to light the darn thing, so I put some matches in the bag as well." She smiles at me warmly. I take the bag and kiss her cheek, and go off in search of my girl.

The lake house is pretty easy to find. I open the door and see Favor sitting on the floor, shivering. Opening up the duffle bag, I pull out the blanket and wrap it around her shoulders. Looking at the fireplace, I debate lighting it.

"Don't bother. Just sit next to me," she says softly.

Doing as she's asked, I sit next to her, silent.

"Thank you for standing up for me," she finally says, as she takes my hand in hers.

"I am just sorry that it came to that."

"It's okay. I was hurt...still am, but...I realized that it's okay. I have you, and I now have my mother. Oh, and I have Egon." She smiles.

"We all have your back."

"I know, and I felt it. So, thank you, Brice Walker, for being my rock." She kisses my lips gently.

"My pleasure. Should we head back to the house?"

"No. Just you and I. No one else." Placing her hands on my face, she pulls me to her and kisses me again. "You know, a great way to generate body heat is skin to skin."

Smiling against her lips, I say. "Is that so?"

"Yep, I learned it in school. Never thought about it too much until now." She murmurs against my lips as she undoes the buttons on my shirt.

Something tells me I'm going to enjoy this lesson on body heat.

Chapter 21

Favor

A few weeks have passed since the Winter break fiasco at my house. I was hurt by my father's words and his actions, but I have Brice, my friends, and even my mom to lean on. After all this time, I no longer feel I am fighting an uphill battle by myself. I still can't believe how Brice stood up for me at Christmas dinner. I never felt as loved as I did that day.

The Championship game is coming up, and the feeling on campus is electric. The Cougars have been training extremely hard for this game. Many nights, Brice has come back from practice too exhausted to do anything but sleep. I've gotta say, I can't wait for this to be over because my libido is in overdrive.

Tonight, we are going to a frat party they are throwing for the Cougars. One of the perks of being on the team is everyone wants to throw them a party. Personally, I think they just want an excuse to party, that's all. Brice and I haven't been to one since the bonfire incident. I really need this night to be drama-free.

Me and Jana have just finished getting dressed. Because Brice loves to see his name on me, I decided to wear his team jersey, with a pair of black leggings and boots to finish the look. After debating for several minutes if I should pull my hair up into a messy ponytail, I decide to let my hair fall in soft waves around my shoulders. Jana helps me with my smoky eyeshadow look because, trust me, if it was left to me, I would have come out looking like a raccoon instead of a sex kitten. Jana and I pose in front of the mirror, giving ourselves a final approval, and I turn around to see how Brice's name and number look on my back. It looks hot, just the way I thought it would. Secretly, I've been toying with the idea of getting his number tattooed on me as a surprise for him. Jana is wearing an ultra mini skirt, paired with tights and a form-fitting sweater. Her hair is pulled up in a messy bun. When she went searching in her closet for a look, she said her options were "slutty" or "sluttier." The fact that her skirt is a good six inches above her knee, I'm going with "sluttier." But it's a cute look that only Jana could pull off.

My cell beeps, and I grab it from my bed. I see Brice's car downstairs and instantly know who the text is from.

"The boys are here." I grab my coat and wristlet from the chair.

Jana, who was practicing her pout in front of the mirror, turns around and smiles. Yes, she practices that otherwise annoying facial expression that somehow looks good on her. She uses it to get guys to buy her drinks. I've even seen her use it to make sure a bouncer doesn't look too closely at our I.D. cards.

I toss Jana her jacket, and we walk downstairs arm and arm. Wayne is already at the party, and Jana and I hop in the car for the quick drive to Alpha Sig house. Upon arriving, we can tell the party is in full swing. As we climb the stairs, we hear someone puking on the front lawn. *Eww, gross.* Walking through the doors of Alpha Sig, Brice is instantly swarmed by people. I give him a quick kiss and leave him to his adoring fans. There is no way in hell I am going to stand and watch girls eye fuck him, and try to touch him. He tries his best to maneuver around the skanks, but it is just too much sometimes. Jana and I move through the partygoers in search of Wayne. Finally spotting him in a corner, talking to some of his former teammates, his eyes light up as soon as he spots Jana. She, of course, bounces right over to him.

"Hey, Favor. How's it going?" Wayne asks, drinking a can of soda.

"Good. Some party, huh?" I look around at the throngs of people dancing and talking.

"If I remember correctly, you never really liked parties too much." He laughs.

"Still don't. But I have to because the other half goes to them on occasion." Truthfully, Brice has never forced the issue about going to parties. I just don't want him to miss out simply because I don't like to go. So, I try to compromise.

"Where is the man of the hour?" he asks, leaning against the wall.

"Oh, he is engaging in meaningless conversations with the ho bags." *Wow, did that just come out of my mouth?* I guess the green-eyed monster just made an appearance.

Wayne throws his head back in a hearty laugh, and I have to join in because, quite frankly, I did sound extremely jealous. Not that I don't trust Brice because I do wholeheartedly. It's the ho bag brigade I don't trust.

After a few hours of mingling, I let out an unexpected yawn, and I know it's time to leave. I begin to search for Brice to see if he is ready, and Jana and Wayne join me in my search

233

efforts. We search the entire first and second floors but cannot locate him.

Walking towards the basement staircase, we hear chanting going on. *"Go. Go. Go."*

I look at Wayne and Jana, and they both shrug their shoulders, not sure what is going on. The fully-furnished basement looks like a type of rec room for the fraternity brothers. It reeks of pot and booze down here, mostly because of the poor ventilation, and I start coughing.

A group of guys is in a circle still chanting. *"Go. Go. Go."*

My curiosity gets the best of me as I push through the crowd. My mouth drops open as I see Regan on her knees in the middle of the crowd, giving a blowjob to Kevin Shore. I turn to look at Jana and Wayne, who have turned away, unable to watch this scene unfold. Kevin ejaculates in her mouth, and she licks it up like ice cream. She stands up on wobbly legs as everyone cheers her on.

"Who's next, boys?" she slurs, and several hands go up.

No fucking way. This has got to stop. She has to be drunk out of her mind to be doing this. I push past the guys and make it to the middle of the circle. One of the guys shouts out, "Sweet, some girl on girl action." I turn around to see if I can figure out who said it. Focusing my concentration back on Regan, I reach for her arm, but she backs away from me.

"Regan, I think you should come with me. You're drunk and trust me, you are going to regret this in the morning," I plead with her.

She stares at me, unable to focus. Kevin walks over to her and pulls her into him. "Yo, leave her alone. She's just having some fun."

"She is drunk, you *asshole*. She needs to come with me." While Regan is not one of my favorite people, especially after her antics with Brice, she is clearly very intoxicated. As much as I don't like her, I don't want any harm to come to her.

"Fuck you, *bitch*. Just because you're Brice's girl, you think you're in charge? You don't run shit around here," Kevin shouts out, holding his beer up in the air. He receives some cheers but, for the most part, the guys keep quiet.

"So, you like picking on women? Let's see how you do with a man." Wayne steps forward and places me behind him.

"Oh, so her brother's killer has something to say?" Kevin spits out.

Wayne punches Kevin so quickly I don't see it coming. Kevin is sprawled out on the floor, knocked out cold. Wayne takes a look around the room and asks, "Any other takers?" He opens his arms, slowly turning around in a circle, beckoning for anyone who wants to step forward. Of course, no one else does. Jana and I stand on either side of Regan and begin to push through the crowd, with Wayne bringing up the rear. When we reach the main floor, I see Brice and Egon standing together, talking. He looks up and sees me, and then Regan. His expression is a *what the fuck* look.

Releasing the hold I have on Regan's arm, I walk over to him. "She was downstairs giving blowjobs for the crowd."

He raises an eyebrow and releases a low whistle. "Are you kidding me?"

I shake my head. He turns and looks at Egon, who bursts out laughing. "We should take her back to her dorm. I'm afraid to leave her here alone with the wolves," I say.

Brice looks down and pulls me into his chest, placing a quick kiss to my lips. "You know, that is why I love you so much. After all that shit she put us through, you are still looking out for her."

I quickly shrug my shoulders. "I may not like her, but I don't want her to get hurt, either."

"Eg, I'm going to split. You staying?"

"Nah. This party is starting to get dull. I'm outta here, bro."

Brice looks over to Wayne, who is now in charge of holding Regan up. "Need some help?"

"I got her. No worries." He bends and lifts Regan into his arms while Jana stares in slight annoyance.

Outside, he places Regan in the backseat of Brice's car, and Wayne and Jana head to Egon's car. Brice drives us towards Regan's dorm. Parking the car, he tries to help her out of the car.

"I can do it myself," she snaps angrily at him. Brice stares at her and then looks over to me.

"Are you okay to walk?" I ask her.

"You always have to put your two cents into *everything*. I wasn't that drunk that I had to leave." She slurs her words. Right, clearly, she was sober.

"Regan, you were giving blowjobs to guys while a crowd cheered you on. I prefer to think that you were too drunk to know better," I argue.

"For once in my life, I was the center of attention. Everything comes so easily for you. You didn't want Brice, but you got him. You don't want to be popular, but you are. You never need anyone, but yet everyone wants to protect you. I'm tired of being last or never thought of." She gets out of the car and stumbles, falling to the ground. Brice bends to pick her up, but she slaps his hands out of the way.

"Regan, just let him help you."

"I. Am. *Fine*." She makes a few attempts before successfully standing. Dusting herself off, she walks towards her dorm without looking back.

Brice and I stare at her retreating silhouette. "Damn, babe. She's jealous of you."

"Seems so, but I don't know why. In the beginning, I tried to be her friend, but she has repeatedly done things that made me not want to be. And that stunt she pulled with you was the final straw for me."

"Yeah. I almost lost you that day."

"Never." I wrap my arms around him. My cell phone beeps. I pull out my cell to see who sent me a text.

Egon: Someone from the party just sent these to me.

There they were. Pictures of Regan. Pictures of her doing the same thing I caught her doing with Kevin. *Damn, looks like I didn't get there in time.* There's also picture of her doing an Eiffel tower with two guys. I am almost positive, by tomorrow morning, this will be circulated all throughout the school. Her life on campus is about to become hell.

Brice looks at me with a questioning look. I show him my phone, and he lets out a whistle. "Oh boy. Believe it or not, I feel bad for her and what is about to happen."

"Me too. I thought I broke it up in time."

"It's not your fault, babe. She should be happy that you stepped in at all."

"Somehow, I have the feeling that is going to be the opposite of how she will feel."

"Come on, let's get out of here." He opens the car door for me to get in, and we drive off, leaving Regan's troubles behind us.

Chapter 22

Favor

The following day, as expected, the pictures had circulated to the mass majority of students and as if things couldn't get any worse, the Dean of Students got wind of the situation. All campus parties have been placed on hold, and we now have a curfew, due to an investigation from the dean. Everyone on campus is now in a sullen mood, and everyone blames Regan.

Brice and I walk into the cafeteria together with Wayne, Jana, and Egon. We see Regan sitting in a corner by herself, completely ostracized.

"I feel bad for her," Jana says.

"Ehh, I don't," Egon replies. We all look at him. "Hey, listen, she has always been a wannabe. She is constantly sleeping around to move up the social ladder. Hell, she even offered a threesome with Brice and me one time." He notices our expressions, particularly my pissed off one. "Well, of course, that was before the two of you were dating." We still stare. He clears his throat. "Umm, we didn't do it." Realizing, he isn't making it better, "Okay, I'm going to shut up now."

"Smart, bro. Real smart," Brice says, and we all erupt in laughter.

"Come on, let's grab a table," I say, pulling Brice with me.

We all sit down with our trays of food. Someone on the football team walks over to where Regan is seated and drops his pants, mooning her. Everyone in the cafeteria laughs, as Regan breaks down and cries. I look at Jana, and we both stand and go over to her. A hushed silence settles over the room as we make our way to her table.

"Hey. Why don't you come and sit with us?" Jana pleads.

Regan looks at us with her red-rimmed eyes. "You guys don't want me. And I'm not a charity case."

"Regan, can you please, just once, stop with the chip on your shoulder. We are trying to be nice to you," I say, annoyed.

Brice and Wayne come over to the table as well. "Listen, just come and sit with us. Strength in numbers. I have been in the position that you are, where everyone hates you. I know what it feels like. If I had the support that they are offering you now, it would have made life easier."

She shakes her head at us. Egon comes over and kneels beside her, placing his hand on her cheek. "Listen, beautiful. Just come with us. If someone tries to fuck with you, we will get you."

"But you never liked me. You said so yourself." She sniffles as she talks.

"Ehh, don't listen to me. I'm an asshole, remember. But right now, I'm trying not to be. So please, come with us."

Regan looks up and at each of our faces. "What about what I did to you and Brice, Favor?"

"Well, you're still not my favorite person for that, but Brice and I are good. Actually, we are stronger as a result," I say.

Inwardly, however I think, *If you try that shit again, I will beat your ass, bitch.*

"Okay," she says and places her hand in Egon's outstretched one. We all walk to the table, and you could have heard a pin drop in the cafeteria at that moment.

We eat our lunch and as usual, our group jokes and teases each other. Regan remains silent for the most part, just watching the way we interact with one another. When we are finished, we all walk outside together.

"Aww shit, this can't be good," Egon says, and we all look in the direction he is.

The Dean of Students is headed towards us with a very serious expression on his face.

"Regan Mathews?" Dean Smith asks.

"Yes, that's me."

"Please come with me, young lady. We need to discuss the events of last night."

Regan has a deer caught in the headlights look. "Umm, Dean, is it alright if I come with her?" I ask. I can't believe the words came out of my mouth.

"Favor? This is a friend of yours?"

I look at Regan and then back at the dean. "Yes. She is nervous, and I would like to go with her."

"I hear you are the one who put a stop to what she was doing, is that correct?"

I look at Brice for moral support. He gives me a look that says *you should have kept your big fat trap shut.* "Yes, Dean Smith."

Dean Smith looks at the rest of our group. "The rest of you were witnesses?"

"Wayne, Jana, and Favor, during the fact. Myself and Egon, after the fact," Brice interjects.

"Alright then. I guess you should all come with me." Dean Smith begins to walk, and we follow behind.

Dean Smith interviews each of us individually. Coach Vega is also called in since some of his players were involved. When Coach Vega steps out of the dean's office, his look would send the devil running scared.

"Right before the Championships?" he says to Brice. "You're lucky, son, that you weren't involved in this. The players that were, are on academic suspension, and being kicked off the team. "

Brice looks as if a ton of bricks just hit him. "*Shit.*"

"Exactly. I'm calling an emergency team meeting in one hour. Anyone who is not in my office by that time will be released from the team instantly." Coach Vega starts to leave but turns back around. "Wayne. You better join us in the meeting. Looks like today has just become your lucky day. Don't fuck it up."

Brice and Wayne pound it out. "Damn man, glad to have you on board. Just sorry that it's under these circumstances."

"Yeah man." Wayne shakes his head in disbelief.

"But what is going to happen to Regan?" Jana asks.

"Well, she is still inside with the Dean," I say, looking at the closed office door.

We all look at the door as if it could speak. A few minutes later, Regan steps out of the office in tears, and I walk over to her.

"What happened?"

"Since I was already on Academic Probation from my stunt with you and Brice a while ago, I'm officially dismissed from this school."

"Oh, my God." Jana cries out and hugs Regan.

"My parents are going to be pissed. I was the first to go to college. My dad remortgaged the house to send me here," Regan cries into her hands.

"Listen, babe. You can apply to another college," Egon states.

"That will never happen. My parents won't pay for it. I'm screwed."

"Financial aid? Student loans?" I ask.

"Oh please. My grades were horrible. I was barely making it."

"That's because you were too busy trying to be the life of the party. Apply to community and get your grades back up," Brice says.

"Thanks, guys. Listen, I gotta go and make a phone call to my parents. Thanks for everything."

"Wait, I'll come with you," Egon calls out, and follows her out of the door.

"Shit bro, we better head over to Coach's office before my ass gets the boot also," Brice says. Kissing me gently on my lips, he asks, "Are you okay?"

"Yeah. Just in shock about the whole turn of events."

"Shit is crazy. I love you. I'll see you later." He kisses me again.

"Love you too, babe." He releases me and heads out of the door with Wayne.

"We should go to her dorm room," Jana says.

"Egon is with her. I think she needs her space. Let's give her a few hours before we check on her."

Jana nods her head and links her arm with mine, and we walk out of the office together.

Chapter 23

Favor

The past two weeks have been a whirlwind of activity around campus. Regan, along with three of Brice's teammates, have been dismissed from the school following the events from the fraternity party. Wayne is officially back on the Cougars team, as a result. Some of the team members who knew my brother are not happy to have him back, while others who heard about his skills on the field, are ecstatic. I hardly see Brice these days because of his training schedule in preparation for the Championship game, and I'm looking forward to having him to myself again after tomorrow. Since all campus parties have been suspended, the atmosphere is a little down. Some students are opting to party off campus, but most do not want to risk a chance of getting caught and placed on academic suspension.

I'm at the stadium, waiting for Brice to finish practice. Coach Vega called quits on practice two hours ago, but Brice and Wayne opted to stay longer and practice harder. They both know how much they have riding on this game tomorrow. If they are able to usher the team into a victory, then NFL deals could be on the table, even for Wayne. This is everything Brice has worked so hard for all his life. He is taking everything in stride and not showing an ounce of worry. But I know him. Deep down, he knows how much is riding on this and that is the reason why he is pushing himself so hard. In some ways, Brice reminds me of my brother and father. When he is out on the field, he gives all of himself, which garners the respect of his teammates and opposing teams.

My father will be coming to watch the game tomorrow; though I doubt I will be seeing him. It hurts in some ways, but I am thankful to have the full support of my mother behind me. He is supposed to make a speech tomorrow and present some awards to the players. It should be very interesting on stage if Brice wins one of the awards. I cringe at that thought alone.

"Sorry to keep you out so long, babe," Brice says as he wipes a towel over his face.

I walk over to him and wrap my arms around him, giving him a quick kiss. "No worries. I like watching you practice." Even though I hate the sport, I do love watching him play. There's something about the way his body moves on the field that gets me horny every single time. Also, the fact that he can still run the ball with a two-hundred-pound man trying to stop him, and later that evening, make love to me in the gentlest of ways, makes me hot.

He gives me a megawatt smile. "Damn babe, you know how to turn me on."

I quirk one eyebrow at him. "Really? That's all I have to say to turn you on?"

Lifting me up in his arms, he replies, "Nah, babe. You just have to look at me, and I'm turned on."

My heart officially just melted, and I now need to change panties. "That comment just got you lucky tonight."

He throws his head back in laughter. "Oh, so there was a chance I wasn't getting lucky?"

"Maybe. You *have* been neglecting me these past few weeks." I playfully bat my eyelashes at him.

"Neglecting?" He nibbles on my ear, before placing a soft kiss to my neck. "How so?"

Wait, what? What were we talking about? My mind drifts as I get tingly sensations from his kisses, my body instantly reacting to his touch. "Looks like you will have to make it up to me."

"Oh, baby, I plan to do that, and then some." He kisses me with searing passion and reckless abandon.

I start to wonder how rough the ground would be if he laid me down and had sex with me right here, right now, when Wayne interrupts me from my thoughts. "Get a room." he says, laughing at us.

Brice turns his head to look at Wayne and then turns back to me still in his arms. He places one last kiss to my lips before setting my feet back on the ground. "You're jealous."

Wayne laughs again and gives me a quick hug. "How is my little sis doing today?"

"Doing good. Will be better once the Championships are over, though." I smile bashfully.

"I bet." He nudges me and gives me a wink. "Not enough alone time with your man?" he teases

"I could never get enough alone time with him," I tease right back.

"Babe. I gotta shower. You okay till I get back in about fifteen minutes?"

"Yeah sure. You two get showered; I'll just hang out here."

Brice gives me another kiss and releases me. He and Wayne head towards the locker rooms, and I take a seat again so I can wait for them.

"That should've been us, you know." I hear Jameson's voice from behind me.

Startled, I jump up to see where his voice is coming from. Jameson walks over to me. I hadn't seen him since Winter break a few weeks ago. "That could have never been us."

Pain flashes over his face. "Am I that horrible? You never even gave me a chance."

Oh boy. Does he want to hash this out? "Jameson. I'm sorry if I hurt you in any way, but you and I were never meant to be."

"I loved you. Still love you. I would have done anything for you." His eyes are pleading with me.

"I'm sorry, but I have only ever looked at you as a friend. It has never been more than that for me."

"Then why...why would you give yourself to me? You gave me your virginity, and I've cherished that. I thought, because of that, it meant that you and I had a chance."

"I was in pain from my brother's death. I wasn't receiving the love that I needed at home, and sometimes...sometimes..." I don't know how to say it. Sometimes you just need something as simple as a touch to help you feel grounded and connected to the world.

He ponders my words, and I see the moment the realization hits. "You know, when you first started dating Brice, I thought that it was a phase you were going through. I thought you would eventually come back to me. But looking at the two of you at that Christmas dinner at your parents' house, and just a few minutes ago on the field, I think I am finally getting it. You two have a connection that you and I never had. At least, I felt the connection, but you didn't." He looks out at the field and shakes his head. "As much as it hurts to see you with someone else, I think I finally understand it."

My eyes widen, and I stare at him for a moment. Standing up, I give him a hug and a kiss on the cheek. Perhaps we can learn to be friends again; if we ever were, that is. Jameson suddenly releases me from the hug. I look at him, and he tips his chin in the direction of the field. Turning to look at what he is motioning towards, I see Brice and Wayne standing there, watching us. I give him one more quick peck on the cheek before I climb down to the field. Walking over to Brice, his eyes are questioning.

"Ready to go?" I ask.

"Umm yeah. But what was that all about?" He pulls me to his side.

"I think it is a beginning of friendship." That is the short and sweet of it.

"Okay. I can accept that." He kisses the top of my head, his eyes never losing sight of where Jameson sits. "I'm starved. Let's get something to eat."

"Pizza?" I ask.

"Sure, babe. Anything you want." He looks at Wayne. "Coming with?"

"Nah, three's a crowd. Besides, I have to meet someone shortly." Wayne and Brice pound it out, and Wayne leaves the field.

"Looks like it's just us." He smiles at me.

"Always." I kiss him quickly, and we walk towards the parking lot.

****

Later, back at Brice's dorm, I lay in his arms on his bed. I love these moments with him. It feels like the rest of the world has faded away and it's just the two of us. Egon is with his band, practicing for tomorrow's show at the game.

"Nervous about tomorrow?"

He inhales deeply before answering. "To tell you the truth, no. I've trained as hard as I could. I'm ready for this, and so is the team." He squeezes me tighter. "Also, I have the added benefit of you in my arms."

"I'm your lucky charm?" I smile at him as my toes curl.

"You're more than just my lucky charm. You are everything to me."

My heart bursts with joy at his words. How did I get so lucky to find a man like him? I hope to always have this feeling. "You're everything to me also. I love you, Brice Walker, with all of my heart."

"I love you too, Miss Hollister." He kisses me gently, but as I wrap my arms around his neck, trying to bring him in for a deeper kiss, he pulls away. "I was thinking about something."

I pout, not a Jana pout, but a 'horny girlfriend gets rejected' pout. "Hmm? What?"

"I don't think I like your name."

I lift to look at him, trying to hold back a smile. "And what's wrong with my name?"

"I think Favor Walker sounds more the way I like it."

"Favor Wal-" Hold up. Wait a minute. Rewind. "Did you just propose to me?" My eyes narrow at him as I try to wrap my head around what he just said.

"I don't know. It depends on what your answer would be." He searches my eyes for the answer.

Without a moment's hesitation, I answer him. "Yes, my answer is yes." I play with my future name in my head. *Favor Walker.* If I was alone, I would practice writing it on a piece of paper. I debate if he would laugh at me if I do it now.

He kisses me again as relief washes over him. "Good. Starting next week, we shop for a ring. I've saved up enough to place a rock on that dainty finger of yours." He lifts my left hand to his lips and kisses my ring finger.

I'll always belong to him, and he'll always belong to me. I already know the date I want our wedding to be. The day we met by the pond on the night of the bonfire. Though technically it would be the second time we met, it's when I knew I had an attraction to him. And then reality hits me; we're still in school. "Let's wait to get married until after we graduate."

"Absolutely. I just want my ring on your finger to show the world that you belong to someone."

"Do you think it's too soon?"

He cups my face in the palm of his hands, and I see myself, or at least my future self, in the pupils of his eyes. "No. I knew you were the one from the moment I set eyes on you. Being with you these past few months has only confirmed what I already knew. You and I were always meant to be."

And he's right, we were always meant to be. I, in my own way, knew it all along. Somehow, I know Trevor would approve of this as well, and that somehow makes it easier to make the decision.

Sitting up on his bed, I straddle him as I take off my pajama tank top. Passion fills his eyes as he sits up, and sucks on my breast before moving to the other one. With my arms wrapped around his neck, I throw my head back and let the sensations carry me away. If my body were an instrument, he would be a world-class musician. My screams from the orgasms he gives would be the music, and together, we make this undeniable harmony; a symphony of sorts.

He sucks on my pebbled nipples until I feel it in the core of my stomach, and even further down. "This belongs to me and only me." He says the words as an affirmation.

He flips me gently on my back and removes my pajama bottoms and panties, letting the rumpled clothing fall to the floor in a heap. Bending his head to my lady parts, he licks as if I were chocolate ice cream, his favorite flavor. "This belongs to me also," he murmurs.

I clutch a handful of the bedsheets and moan loudly, my eyes rolling to the back of my head. He removes his pajama bottoms, freeing himself. His shaft is long and hard, veins pulsating. I lick my lips at the sight of him. He is quite the sight to behold. Body sculpted like a Greek god and the face of one too. And more importantly, he belongs to me. All of him.

"Liking what you see?" he teases me with a wicked grin. He knows I do. I often salivate when I look at him, and tonight is no different.

"And if I don't?" I tease him with my words. He quirks an eyebrow at me.

"If you don't, then we will have to do something to change your mind about that." He bends his head and kisses my belly button. Oh God, that is my spot. And he knows it. Brice has made it his mission to know every part of my body and what I like. Let's give the boy a gold star for that one. He begins to move his kisses and licks up my body. Sweat coats my skin as my heart begins to race faster. His pupils are dilated as he looks up at me, all while laying more and more kisses up my body. I arch my back because the need for him is so great. He takes his time making his way up my body, the two of us savoring each moment, until he reaches my mouth and places one soft kiss on my lips.

"Oh, by the way. These lips belong to me as well," he says to me before he slams his mouth back onto mine. His kiss is frenzied with emotions, and I take because I'm greedy, and give because I need to.

Wrapping my legs around his waist, he lets out a groan. "I know I should be making love to you after a proposal, but I don't think I'll be able to go slow this time," he apologizes to me, and I feel as if I should be the one to apologize because that is exactly what I want from him right now. Our love isn't the slow burn. We are fast and frantic, needy and greedy, so why shouldn't our consummation be the same today, of all days?

Lifting himself with his arms, he positions his cock at my entrance and slowly glides his way into me. My walls instantly contract around him, pulling him in deeper until he can't fill me anymore. His pace begins agonizingly unhurried, and I instantly want more; that's the needy part of me. I squeeze my legs around him, signaling him to go faster; the greedy.

He gives me a lazy smile and playfully nips at my ear. I moan out loud and close my eyes. "I want to hear the words. Say it for me."

I scrunch my eyebrows in confusion and then it dawns on me. "Favor Walker." But because I'm moaning, it sounds more like 'Fawor Waaalker'. But he understands, because that was the brightest smile I've ever seen on his beautiful face.

Another deep thrust inside of me, this one I swear I feel in my stomach. "Again."

"Fav-" I'm unable to finish because he chose that time to pull out and push deep inside.

"Again."

I'm panting, and my heart is going to beat itself right out of my chest. Can he feel it?

Another thrust. "Again."

"Favor Walker." I manage to say this time.

"Again, Mrs." A bead of his sweat drops in my mouth, and I savor it like a person who was in the desert for months.

"Mrs.- Oh, my God." He swivels his hips, giving me the deeper penetration that I freaking love.

"Didn't know you were God, babe. Or were you calling me one?"

I try to buck my hips, but I can barely move him an inch. His chuckles feel like a vibrator on my clitoris.

"One more time, Mrs.," he teases.

I gulp in some air, as if this would help. "Mrs. Favor Walker." I'm finally able to complete my future name.

The love that shows in his eyes is overwhelming and consuming. He touches his forehead to mine, our bodies fused in so many different ways. But it's no longer just our bodies. It's us. We are one, our souls are one, our heartbeat is one.

He and I are us, and us is we, and we are one.

Chapter 24

Favor

The following day, Brice and I are up early. He has to go the stadium earlier than the rest of his team to talk with the coach about plays. Standing in front of the stadium with him before he goes in, we are locked in a kiss. I won't see or speak to him until after the game, so we are getting in our quality time now. Not that we didn't do that last night and then some.

"Good luck, baby," I murmur against his lips.

"Who needs luck when I have you?" He smiles at me, and I want to melt.

"I know it's just a few hours that I won't be able to talk to you or see you, but ugh, I hate that. I miss you already."

"Every touchdown I get, it's for you. Besides, look at the jumbotron. I have a surprise for you."

"What's the surprise?"

"It wouldn't be a surprise if I told you, nosy." He kisses the tip of my nose.

"You better go inside before Coach Vega has your ass on a platter."

"You're right. Gotta get to work, babe." He kisses me quick and releases me. My God, this man's kisses are swoonworthy.

I stand by my car, watching him walk inside the stadium. I won't be able to touch or kiss or feel him until later tonight. Hopefully, it'll be riding on the coattails of a win.

Getting back in my car, I head over to my dorm. I park my car in the lot and begin to head towards my room. I see Wayne standing in front of his car with the hood open.

"What's going on?" I ask him.

"My car would pick today, of all days, to conk out on me," he groans out.

"Fuck. You're supposed to be headed to the stadium for the team meeting, right?"

"Yeah, and Coach is going to have my ass for this if I'm late. Hell, I'm lucky that I got back on the team in the first place. Fuck *me*." He slaps the palm of his hand on his head.

"Come on. I'll drive you." I jingle my keys in front of him.

"Thanks. Greatly appreciated." He closes his car hood and grabs his gear out of the trunk. We walk over to my car.

On the drive to the stadium, I ask him, "How are you feeling? I know this is your first game since..." I'm unable to finish the words.

"I don't know how I feel. I'll miss playing with him. It won't be the same. But I promise you, with this second chance that I'm getting, I won't take it for granted. It is so easy to lose it all in the blink of an eye."

His mouth is downturned. I reach over and take his hand in mine, squeezing gently. "I think he is proud of you now. I know I am." I smile warmly at him.

"Thanks. You don't know how much that means to me."

I pull into the stadium's parking lot for the second time today. Wayne thanks me before grabbing his gear and getting out of the car. Sitting there, I watch him walk towards the stadium. My heart catches in my throat at the sight of my father. I haven't seen him since the Christmas Day fight, and I wonder for a moment why he's here. But then it dawns on me. He's here to stop Wayne from playing his first game. I jump out of my car and run towards what is about to become a collision course.

"I heard you were back on the team. I thought you would've had the decency to crawl back into the hole you came from, and died." My father's eyes are cold and harsh, I involuntarily shiver when I look at him.

Wayne's body goes rigid, his shoulder slumping.

"Dad. That's not fair." I scream out as I just reach them, panting.

My father looks at me, his lips curl and his nose wrinkle. "I'm no father of yours."

Now it is my turn to look stricken, though I don't know why. He said it to me before; you would think I should be used to it. But how, how do you get used to your father disowning you? My face drops, and a hand touches my arm. "Mr. Hollister, I understand why you hate me, sir. But don't take it out on Favor. She doesn't deserve that." Wayne's voice is pleading for compassion from a compassionless man.

"*Don't.*" Spittle shoots from his lips, and he angrily wipes at his mouth. "Don't speak to me about what she deserves. How could you possibly understand why I hate you? You don't understand. You couldn't possibly *understand*."

"But I *do*." Wayne lifts his hand and turns his index finger towards himself and stabs at his chest. "I may not understand on the level of a parent who has lost their only son, but I understand on the level of losing a loved one. He was my best friend, since we were little kids. He was like a brother to me. So yes, I do understand."

My father lifts an angry fist and shakes it at Wayne. "You're a disgrace to his memory. A disgrace to be in my presence, telling me you understand, when you can't possibly. I died that night when you killed Trevor." My father's body shakes with anger, and pain.

"I died that night, too. I tried everything to save him. But it was too late. Just too late." Wayne's voice cracks with emotion.

"Dad, we should move forward. That's what Trevor would want," I plead.

My father's eyes look haunted as he stares at us. He turns his head slightly and looks to the ground. "I can't forgive either of you for what you've done." He shakes his head as if he's in a daze. I take one step closer to him, but stop myself when he says, "I can't...I can't...forgive myself."

I feel as if the wind has been knocked out of me. Surprised, I look up at my father. "Forgive yourself?"

He's no longer aware of our presence; he's been transported somewhere we can't reach him. Perhaps he was always in that remote place, and we were the ones that were just passing by. "It's my fault." His words float through the air, as a strong wind picks up and spins the debris a few yards away in a circle.

I give that spinning debris my full concentration, as dirt and dead leaves turn in its own miniature version of a tornado. For a moment, I wonder if it's my brother making his presence known.

He lowers his head, and his shoulders collapse. "We argued that day. He told me he didn't want to play football anymore."

My mouth falls open at this confession. I've never heard Trevor and my father argue a day in my life. It was always me who argued with our parents, me who didn't understand them. Trevor was the good child in the family that obeyed every word our parents said.

He looks up with red-rimmed eyes. "I...I got angry at him. I threatened to disown him and stop paying for college if he left the team." He winces. "You see, he was supposed to be my legacy. He was supposed to be..." His words drift off.

I look at Wayne, and I can see in his face that he already knew about this. All this time, and he never said anything.

"He told me that he hated me and the game. Can you believe that? My son? The son of Kyne Hollister would never say such a thing. But he did. He told me he was tired of living his life for me. The last words he spoke to me were to tell me he hated me. And hours later, he was...he was dead. I will never get to make it up to him. I will never get that second chance just to earn his love again." He lifts his hand and points a finger at Wayne. "You took that from *me*. My second chance."

I think back to the eulogy on the day of Trevor's funeral. The Reverend made a point of saying the very last conversation Trevor had with our father that day ended with him saying 'I love you, Dad', and how that is all God's love the reverend preached about. Because nothing can break the bonds of a child's love of their parent. I remember how family and friends were able to find solace in the knowledge that Trevor said 'I love you, Dad' to our father. If our father had died that day, he would always have his son's love. But now, finding out that Trevor's parting words to our father weren't ones of love but of anger and hate, my legs become weak, and I stumble. Wayne catches and holds me up.

"Mr. Hollister, you have to work on forgiving yourself. I had to do that. Before I was able to move on, truly, I needed to forgive myself."

My father stares at him for a long moment. "I can't do that." He turns and heads back to his car.

I slowly push away from Wayne, needing for him to look me in the eyes when I ask. "You knew about the argument all this time?"

His face is crestfallen. "Yes." He says the word as if a burden has been lifted from him. "I didn't say anything because it wasn't my secret to share. Trevor has always hated football. But he did it so he could receive love from your father."

My mother's words from a few weeks ago haunt me as Wayne recounts the events of that day.

"Finally, he had the courage to tell your father he was done with it all. Your father, as you can imagine, didn't take it well."

I nod my head in agreement; I can only imagine how dad took the news. And 'not well' isn't even close.

"First time I ever heard Trevor raise his voice was on the phone that day." He pauses for a moment, as if gathering his thoughts. "After the argument, Trevor wanted to go to a party in the next town over. Something that he never would normally do. He was never into the party scene."

Trevor and I are both alike in that way. I never did understand, when we got the news, why Trevor was at a party to begin with; but now, now it all makes sense.

"He drove that night and got plastered. I was pretty lit too, but not half as bad as him. When we were leaving, he tried to get behind the wheel, and I stopped him." Tears fall down his cheeks, and he takes a few calming breaths before finishing.

"We fought." His voice chokes up, and he clears his throat. "In all our years of being best friends, that was the first time we ever fought." He places his hands on his hips and looks away, trying to regain his composure.

As Wayne takes a minute, alarm bells goes off in my head. Can I handle this? Am I ready to hear what happened that night? I just regained my friendship with Wayne. Will I lose him in the wake of the truth? My throat feels like it's closing, and I try to swallow down my despair.

"I got the keys away from him. But he insisted he wasn't staying." Wayne looks up at the sky. "What was I supposed to do? He was my best friend, and he was in pain. So I told him I would drive." He closes his eyes and inhales deeply. "I had no business behind the wheel. But I was young and stupid, and felt I was invincible. So, I drove." He turns and looks at me.

I open my mouth to tell him to stop, but I have no air in my lungs to form words. But somehow, I know - I just know - there is no stopping Wayne from this confession. A confession I should've heard years ago. So, he proceeds, his words becoming the motor driving me towards the wreckage. No brakes needed; this is a full-on collision.

"It happened so fast. Trevor asked me a question, and I turned to answer him. It felt like a second, but I guess that's all it takes. The other car came out of nowhere and struck us. We spun around a few times, and when it came to a stop, I saw Trevor wasn't moving. I was able to get out of the car and...I...I tried to get him out. When I finally got the door open, I laid him on the ground." He wipes the falling tears from his face. "And you know what he said?" He smiles as he looks up at the sky. "Typical Trevor, always worried about everyone else. He said, 'Don't worry. I'm just happy that you're okay.' Those were the last words he spoke." He falls to his knees, and I fall to mine and take him into my arms, crying into each other's shoulders.

I never asked for the details of my brother's death before because I always thought it would be too hard for me to hear. But now that I've heard them, I wish I'd had the courage to listen to it earlier. Perhaps I could've moved on and not wasted so much time being angry. My heart goes out to Wayne. He was a victim, just as much as my brother.

"Now that you have heard the story, do you still forgive me?" His voice is full of hesitation.

But my answer is instant. "Of course."

We both wipe tears from each other's faces, causing us to cry some more. We stay on the ground for minutes that seem like an eternity. Eventually, he smiles and kisses me on the cheek. "I better get inside."

We both stand up and give each other a hug. "Win this one in Trevor's name."

He winks at me. "You got it, little sis." He walks slowly towards the entrance, passing through a swirl of debris around his feet. As he walks through, a calmness settles, and I know in my heart that everything will be alright.

Chapter 25

Favor

I'm emotionally spent after an afternoon of truth discovery. I sit on the hood of my car, as the afternoon sun is swallowed up by the horizon. Slowly, the parking lot fills up with cars and people. I feel like a tiny ant in the middle of a bustling city of millions. A few people wave to me and ask if I want to join them at their tailgating parties, but I decline the invitations. I just need this moment, as my thoughts go back to Trevor on that night.

My heart feels like it weighs a thousand pounds and I don't have the strength to carry it. Wayne's confession cuts me deep that Trevor was in so much pain after his argument with Dad. I wish he had called me, or I, him. I don't know, perhaps I could've done something for him. He'd always been there for me, and I wasn't there when he needed someone. Mom said that I was the strong one, but I think it was more Trevor than myself. He was the stronger one, I see it now.

He always protected me from our father, and often tried to include me on things that my father would've otherwise left me out of. At the time, I was just rebellious and would do everything I could to make our parents miserable, but now I realize Trevor needed an ally.

Slowly it dawns on me that the game is about to begin. I stare at the stadium that has become my family's legacy, wishing it was torn down. Our legacy was built on lies, and this stadium represents what went wrong in my family.

But then there's Brice, and this is the beginning of his, no, *our* legacy. I make a decision that our legacy will not depend on this stadium, or this game, but on us and the foundation that we will build together.

I hop off my car's hood and walk towards the stadium.

Once inside, I head to the seat Brice had reserved for me. I say hello to a few people that I know and take my seat, and wait for the game to begin.

The Cougarettes are on the field doing their routine. I spot Jana instantly and wave, even though I know she can't see me. The cheerleaders form two parallel lines and wave their pom-poms as Coach Vega leads his team onto the field. The cameras zoom in on each of the players. On the Jumbotron, it flashes the player's name and position. Brice, because he is the quarterback, is the last to come out of the tunnel and onto the field. On his bicep is a black band sewn around the edge of his jersey sleeve, with the number twenty-two in white, and twenty-two painted on his cheek. Twenty-two was my brother's number.

For some reason, I didn't notice the entire team had this band sewn around their jersey, and the crowd erupts in applause. Everyone remembers my brother. Tears begin to stream down my face. Damn, today is such an emotional day. But at least right now they are tears of joy. A picture of my brother flashes on the Jumbotron, and the crowd applauds again as people around me begin to stare. But I don't pay them any attention because my eyes are now fixated on Wayne standing next to Brice. Wayne wipes tears away from his eyes, smudging the numbers painted on his cheek. I just know that Trevor is smiling from heaven as a sense of peace comes over me.

Brice jogs over to where I am sitting. I get out of my seat and run down the steps to meet him. I lean over the partition. He cups my face in his hands and kisses me. The crowd goes crazy over this, but our love for each other drowns out their noise.

"Happy?" he asks.

"Yes, thank you for this." I trace my fingers over my brother's number written on his cheek.

"It was Wayne's idea." He smiles bashfully.

"You better go, you have a game to win."

He kisses me one last time and jogs back over to his team.

By halftime, the Cougars are up by two points. Egon and his band give an incredible performance, and dedicate it to Trevor.

The final half of the game begins. A quick touchdown by the Timbers have the Cougars now trailing by five points. I'm down to one good fingernail because I've been biting them all throughout this game.

With just ten seconds left on the clock, Brice calls for a quick break and the team huddles. After a swift discussion, the huddle breaks and they take their positions on the field. Brice maneuvers around some players from the Timbers and looks for an opening. He finds one and throws the ball to Wayne. The stadium is quiet as we watch the ball go down the field in what feels like slow motion. Wayne rushes for the ball and easily sidesteps the opposing team member. The ball looks like it is about to fall short, but Wayne, with incredible strength and mobility, jumps in the air and connects with the ball, making the catch of a lifetime. He runs in for the touchdown, and the stadium erupts. The jumbotron replays the catch again in slow motion and flashes back to Brice and Wayne, celebrating with the rest of their team.

They did it. They won the Championship game.

Chapter 26
Brice

A week has passed since the Championship game, and I'm still riding on cloud nine. I have a kickass fiancée, and NFL recruiters have started talks with me. Thing is, I made a promise to my mother that I would graduate first, before signing any contracts. Even the awards ceremony, where Favor's dad was the speaker, went off without any drama. Kyne Hollister knows how to put on a public face when necessary.

Tonight, however, is a night of celebration. Jameson's father is hosting the championship party at their house. All is right in my universe, and I couldn't be happier.

"Babe, how many dresses are you going to try on?" I ask as I watch my fiancée try on what is probably the fifth dress of the evening. Since when did she get so picky about clothes?

"Sorry. It's just that tonight is very special. I want to make sure I look perfect for you."

"Babe you're always perfect. Besides, you think I care what other people think?"

"I know you don't." She smiles at me and places a kiss on my lips. Mmmm, she tastes like cinnamon. Which makes me hungry for something else. Just as I am about to pull her down on top of me, she moves away. "Oh no, you don't. Once you get started, we will be here until morning." She laughs as she smooths down her dress. Damn, she looks good in it. If I could just coax her over, I could probably get her out of it in less than a minute.

"Never heard you complain before." I give her my wicked grin. She usually falls for it.

"I am not complaining. But you are the quarterback, and we have to go to this party. Jameson's dad will expect you." Touching her hair with her left hand, the engagement ring I bought for her sparkles on her delicate finger.

"Okay, we'll go to this shindig, but we aren't staying long. There are better ways I can think of to celebrate." I sit up on the bed. "Now come here and give me a quick kiss so we can leave."

"Nothing is ever quick with you, and you know it. So, do you like this dress?"

"Babe, I fucking love that dress. You got me hard just looking at you." Oh wait. If I'm hard just looking at her, that means other men will be too. "Babe, on second thought, change that dress."

She looks into the mirror. "Huh? I thought you said you liked it?"

"Yeah, that's the problem. Other men will too."

She turns around and sticks her tongue out at me. "Just for that, I'm wearing it."

"Oh God."

"What?"

"I hope you have bail money."

"For?"

"I might need it because, babe, I swear if someone so much as sneezes in your direction, we are going to have a problem." I walk towards her and pull her into me. "Mine, babe. All mine," I say as I squeeze her ass. She giggles into my chest. I love that sound.

"Come on, Mr. MVP, let's go."

We drive over to Jameson's parents' house, and by time we arrive, the party is in full swing. Cal decided to come out, after Jana and Favor begged him the entire week to go. He is still not comfortable being around the team. I promised him that nothing will happen to him. Wayne, Egon, and I will look out for him tonight.

Jameson's parents' house is huge. Not quite as big as the Hollister house, but it's a close second. We are instantly greeted by some of my teammates and cheerleaders when we walk in. It feels good to have this much love in one room.

"Ah, the man of the hour has arrived," Jameson's father, Jim, announces. He walks over to us and shakes my hand, kissing Favor on the cheek.

"Thanks for having us over, Mr. Roth," I say to the very intoxicated man.

"Jim or Jimbo. You have earned the right to call me that. Welcome to the club of winners. Something my son will never know about," he tries to whisper, but fails miserably.

Ouch, those words have to hurt. I look over at Jameson sipping a beer, as he looks on from afar. "Umm well, thanks, Jim. It feels good to be a winner. But it was a team effort, after

271

all. If it weren't for my boys, including your son, we wouldn't be here celebrating."

Everyone does the Cougar chant.

"You see, not only is he talented on the field, but he is humble off the field. You have enough to brag about, but still won't take any credit. That is the making of a star quarterback. You mark my words. Big things to come for you."

"Thanks, sir," I say, while glancing around the room for an escape option.

"Make yourself a home. Enjoy." He steps closer to me and tries to whisper but again, fails miserably. "Too bad you have a girlfriend. A lot of good looking ass here tonight. I might have to have a taste." He gives me a punch in the arm, and I want to lay him out.

"Well, I wouldn't trade my fiancée for nothing out there," I say through gritted teeth. Now I know where Jameson gets his asshole nature from. It must run in the family.

I wrap my arm around my fiancée's waist. Damn, I never can get tired of saying those words: my fiancée. Wrapping my arm around her waist, we walk away from Jim, or Jimbo, or whatever it is he wants to be called.

"Babe, is he always an asshole?" I ask.

"Yes, actually. He can be a real tool at times."

"Slap me if I ever get like that."

She stops and looks at me. "You could never be like him, or my father. Your heart is too good."

"You forgot the most important thing."

"What's that?"

"I have you." I kiss her gently on the mouth.

"I swear, just once, can the two of you not be making out when I see you?" Egon says as he claps me on the shoulder and gives Favor a peck on the cheek.

"Bro. Did you get a load of Jimbo over there?"

"Dude, at least it explains Jameson," Egon replies with a toothy grin. A couple of music execs have been courting Egon's band since the Championship game. I think he is going to be offered a record deal any day now.

"Oh, so the party has finally arrived," Cal announces as he gives Favor and I a hug.

"Well, it looks like Jimbo over there is the party," I joke, and Favor elbows me in the stomach.

"Where is the rest of the gang?" my fiancée asks no one in particular.

"Jana is upset and drinking by herself in a corner somewhere. Wayne is also upset and is standing outside, trying to cool off," Cal explains.

"Why are they both upset?" Favor looks around the room.

"Honey, who knows? I still don't understand the two of them. It is obvious they like each other, so how come they're hiding it?" Cal places his hands on his hips.

Looking at me, she says, "I should go and check on Jana. "

"Okay, babe. I'll catch up with you later. I'll see if I can find Wayne to talk to him."

She gives me a kiss on the lips and goes off in search of Jana. I stare at her as she walks away. *Damn, how did I get so lucky?*

Egon slaps me on the shoulder. "You got it bad, bro." He laughs.

I guess he's right. I do have it bad. "That's going to be you one day, my man." I slap him on the back as I laugh at him.

He shakes his head. "Never, man. Too many ladies out there will be missing out on the love machine."

"Did you just say that?"

"Yep." He grins from ear to ear.

We are about to look for Wayne when we hear raised voices coming from another room. The three of us walk in the direction of the voices.

"You're embarrassing yourself. Just go upstairs already," Jameson snarls at his father.

"Embarrassing? You wouldn't know the first thing about embarrassment. Every day I look at you is an embarrassment. You couldn't hang on to the top spot, could you? Hell, you couldn't even land the girl, could you? You're just a bottom feeder. Second rate. That's all you'll ever be," his father yells at him as the room quiets.

Jameson looks around the room and sees all the staring faces. He throws his hand up in the air. "I don't need this shit." He pushes past his father and walks out of the room.

For the first time since knowing Jameson, I feel sorry for him. Jim looks around the room, raising his glass in the air. "Let the party go on. The loser has left the room." He takes a sip of his drink as he tries to stand up straight.

No one says anything as they look at the trainwreck standing before them. I shake my head and turn to leave the room, with Cal and Egon behind me. I start looking for Favor so we can leave, but as we walk down the hall, we see Kevin Shore talking to some girls. Why is Kevin Shore here? He's no longer a part of the team. Cal tenses when he sees Kevin.

"Hey, what's going on?" I ask Cal.

"I knew I shouldn't have come here tonight," Cal says in a low voice.

"No one is going to mess with you. Besides, as soon as I locate Favor, we are out of here."

"Yeah don't sweat it, man," Egon says, as he keeps an eye on Kevin.

Egon and I place Cal in the middle as we walk past Kevin, who instantly notices us and glares.

"Well well, if it isn't the pretty boy, the fag, and the wannabe musician."

Cal tries to turn and go in the opposite direction, but I hold him in place. "Really? Only thing I see is a wannabe bad boy." I take a step closer to him. "You're a spoiled rich brat, who has probably never had to have a real fight in his life. I grew up on the rough side of Philly, where I had to fight five times a day to prove myself. You think you can handle me?" I beckon for him to take a step towards me. Guys like him come to a dime a dozen. They pick on weaker people just to make themselves feel better.

Kevin stares at me for a moment before walking away. Just what I thought he would do. We stay in place, making sure he wasn't coming back.

I look at Cal. "You okay?"

He nods his head. "Yeah. Thanks."

"Was he the one that did that to you that night?" Egon asks.

Fear comes across Cal's face. His lips draw into a fine line.

"You know, protecting him is not doing anyone any good. He should be in jail for what he did to you," I press.

"Let's just switch the subject," Cal says, looking down.

"Alright. I'll drop it for now," I reply as I look at Egon, who just shakes his head.

We finally find Favor and Jana. Jana is shitfaced, and can barely stand. She takes a step forward and trips, but Egon catches her in time before she faceplants. Oh, this night just keeps getting better and better.

Tipping my chin in the direction of Jana, I ask, "What's with her?"

"She won't tell me," Favor says as she wraps her hands around my waist.

"Babe I think it is time for us to blow this popsicle stand.
"

She laughs at my words and looks at Jana with concern. "Can she ride with us?"

"Of course. No questions asked."

"Did you find Wayne?" she asks me.

"Oh shit. I got caught up in Jameson's family drama, I forgot. Let's all look for him, so we can all leave at the same time."

Everyone agrees, except for Jana. "Wayne shmayne. I won't ride with him," Jana announces in a slurred voice.

"Alright, baby cakes, you'll ride with me," Egon says as he holds her up. She gives him a smile then belches. Oh yeah, that's sexy.

How did I become the gatekeeper tonight? I rally the troops so we can find Wayne and eighty-six th s place. After searching several rooms, we find Wayne standing by himself in a corner.

"Bro we're outta here," Egon says.

Wayne looks up and takes in Jana's condition, and then shakes his head. "She's drunk again?"

"I'm not drunk," Jana yells at him. She tries to walk over to him but stumbles again. Wayne moves quickly and catches her.

"Sure, you're not drunk," he says sarcastically as he lifts her into his arms.

Can this night get any more interesting? Now that we have our full group, we begin to weave through the throngs of people so we can leave. A few people stop us to talk in their drunken banter. As I am talking to one of my teammates, I notice Jimbo pushing up on one of the cheerleaders. She is trying to avoid his advances, but he is insistent. I begin to wonder if I should intervene or not, so I just look on, ready to step in if things escalate.

"She said *no*. So, leave her alone." Jameson's voice carries across the room.

Jimbo doesn't pay his son any attention as he tries again to grope the cheerleader. Jameson rushes over to his father and pushes him, causing him to stumble and fall to the floor. Jimbo tries to stand up, but Jameson kicks him. A crowd gathers around them, watching in horror. Jimbo is too intoxicated to stand up and Jameson takes full advantage of it. He begins punching and kicking his father repeatedly as people scream.

Everything happens so fast after that. Someone calls the cops. Jimbo lays unconscious on the floor, as the cops remove Jameson from the premises in handcuffs. Jimbo is taken to the hospital. What the fuck just happened?

Chapter 27

Favor

The following day after the party, campus gossip is swarming with the news of Jameson and his father, and Jameson's arrest. Jameson's father decided not to press charges against his son, so we expect Jameson to be released sometime today. I always knew Jameson's father was a jerk, but I never knew it was that bad. Jim is starting to make my father look like a saint.

I'm getting ready to meet Brice for breakfast, and he should be here any minute. Looking over at my very hungover friend, I ask, "So what happened with you and Wayne last night?"

"I don't know what you mean," Jana pouts. Not the pout that she practices to get her own way; this one is genuine.

Alright, so we are going to play it that way, are we? "Jana, it's pretty obvious that the two of you are dating. Did you guys have an argument yesterday?"

She looks at her fingers, obviously trying to avoid my question. "We aren't dating."

I give her a look, letting her know I know she's bullshitting me.

Her eyes open wide. "No, seriously we aren't dating. That's the problem. I like him a lot."

Sitting on my bed, I ask, "I can tell he likes you also. So…what's the problem?"

"He seems to think he doesn't deserve to be happy."

"What? Why?"

She gives me a stupid look.

"Oh."

"Exactly. Favor, I don't know what to do. I care for him."

"Would you like for me or Brice to talk to him?"

"No. His mind is made up. I'll get over it."

"Well, I am here for you if you need me."

"I know. He was pissed at me for getting so drunk last night. That didn't help our situation either."

"Come on. I know just the thing to make you feel better. Waffles."

She turns green and bolts out the door. I just hope she makes it to the bathroom in time. After a few minutes, I check on her and she tells me she is too hungover to go out. I promise to bring something back for her to eat. When Brice and I arrive in town to have breakfast, we see Kevin talking to Cal outside the diner. I squeeze Brice's hand, and he nods his head, acknowledging he sees what's going on. We walk within earshot.

"You better not tell anybody about what happened." Kevin leans in closer to Cal.

Cal grimaces at the closeness of Kevin. "I...I won't."

"Tell anybody what?" Brice asks, releasing my hand and taking a step forward.

"None of your fucking business. This conversation is between me and him," Kevin says in a menacing tone.

"Cal, are you alright?" Brice turns his attention to our friend.

Cal looks at him with an ashen face and trembling lips. Kevin decides to answer for him. "Yeah, he's fine. I was just leaving anyway." He slaps Cal hard on the shoulder and begins walking in the opposite direction.

"Cal, what was that about?" I ask, stepping closer to him. "We're your friends, you can tell us."

"I can't talk about it."

"Listen, we already have a sneaky suspicion that Kevin is the one who beat you up at the club that night. What we don't understand is, why protect him?" Brice questions, crossing his arms.

Cal looks around to make sure no one is listening. "Yes, it was him that beat me up," he whispers.

"So, tell the police," I say in a sharp tone.

"You don't get it, do you? You could never understand what it's like being a gay man in society. I only recently came out, just before I started coming to this school. That's why I ended up here, because my parents are ashamed of me. Then I get beat up because I'm gay? Next thing you know, I'm the gay poster child. I just want to live my life without worry. Why can't people just accept me for being me?" he cries out, and my heart breaks for him. I guess I never thought of it that way before.

"Cal I'm sorry. I truly am. But you can't let him get away with this," I tell him.

"And then what? I'm ridiculed at school even more than I am now?"

"No, you get to put a scumbag in jail before he does it to someone else. He could've killed you that night," I explain.

"Cal, we are here for you. We will go to the police station with you if you want," Brice tells him.

"No. My parents are already ashamed of me. Just back off, please."

Brice gives me a look to let the subject go. "We are about to grab some breakfast. Why don't you join us?" I ask.

"Thanks, but no. I'll just head back to campus." He gives me a hug, and walks off.

"We have to do something," I tell Brice.

"Yeah, I know, but what? We can't make a confession on his behalf."

"I know, but we can't let Kevin get off that easy."

"We won't. We'll think of something. I promise." He kisses me on my forehead.

**** ****

A few days later, Jana and I are walking in town together, window shopping. It's the perfect girls' day out. Jana is still semi-sulking about her relationship, or lack of one, with Wayne, but a double shot macchiato latte helps to put a smile on her face.

"So, when are you setting a date for the wedding?" she asks me.

"Umm, we want to graduate college first. After graduation, that's when I'll start planning. Also, a major part depends on which team he signs with."

Jana bounces up and down in her typical happy-go-lucky way. "I'm so excited."

"Well, we still have over a year to go."

"What are you two going to do for the summer?"

"We haven't discussed it yet. I know I don't want to be away from him for that long."

"At least his mother likes you."

"Yeah, that helps a lot." I smile.

"Hey, let's stop in the Wreck Room. I'm tired of walking and could use a drink."

"Sure." We go inside the Wreck Room, a local bar where most students from our college hang out. It has video games and sports channels, among other things; it's like an adult version of an arcade.

Taking a seat at a booth, we give the waitress our orders. Jana shoots out a text to Cal, who is in town running errands, letting him know to meet us here.

"Cal said he will be here in ten minutes," Jana says, placing her phone down on the table.

When Cal arrives, he and Jana begin doing rounds of shots. Two hours later, I'm starting to wonder if I'm going to have to carry these two out of the bar.

"I feel like dancing," Jana announces, as she stands on top of her seat and starts to wiggle her butt.

"Come on girlfriend, let's dance." Cal holds his hand out for Jana to take. They both head to the dance floor, leaving me at the table, shaking my head.

A few guys approach Jana as she dances seductively with Cal. Jana is playing it up to the crowd as men whistle at her. I roll my eyes because I hate it when she gets like this. She never really knows her limits when she drinks. Jana closes her eyes as she dances to the music and that's when I see him. Kevin. He comes up behind her, placing his hands around her waist. Jana is too inebriated to notice at first. She keeps gyrating to the music, and Kevin is rubbing against her from behind. I stand up to go get her, but she opens her eyes and turns around. Seeing that it's Kevin who is holding her, she pushes him away. Anger flashes in his eyes and he moves towards her. I run to the dance floor and grab Jana's hand, pulling her out of the way. We go back to our table to settle our tab. Sensing it is time to go, I grab Cal and usher them both out of the bar.

Once inside of my car, my hands are shaking so bad I can barely hold my phone to send Brice a text. He was supposed to meet us at the bar later, with Wayne and Egon. I place the phone down and decide to text him when we get back to my dorm.

"He is a madman," Jana says in a shaky voice, the situation having completely sobered her up.

"Let's get out of here," Cal says from the backseat.

I start the car and begin driving through town. The roads leading to our school are pitch black, and the only lights to be seen are the ones from our tail lights. I maneuver through the winding roads, my hands still shaking from the bar incident. A car comes up behind us with their high beams on. The light is so bright I can't see where I am going. The car begins honking its horn repeatedly while shining its high beams directly in my rearview mirror.

"Who is that?" Jana cries out.

"One guess," Cal replies.

"He wouldn't?" The words leave my mouth but it quickly dawns on me that yes, Kevin would. He is known to be a ruthless player, both on and off the field. My mind begins to race as I try to figure out how to get out of the situation.

The car pulls up to the side of us as someone throws a bottle at the driver's side window. The bottle crashes into my window, and I scream out, swerving the car to the side before regaining control. I feel my heart thumping in my chest as adrenaline flows through my body. *Think.* Pushing my foot on the accelerator, we shoot forward, ahead of the car. If I can outrun him until there is a turnoff, perhaps I can lose him. The car speeds up behind us, hitting us. The three of us jerk forward, and Jana begins screaming. My mind is going a million miles a minute as I try to figure out what to do.

WHAM. It's the sound of metal on metal hitting, and the noise is deafening.

"Oh, my God. What are we going to do?" Jana cries.

"I don't..." WHAM. WHAM. WHAM. I try to regain control, but the car veers off to the right, and we fly into a ditch, coming to a stop only when we hit a tree.

Chapter 28
Brice

Wayne and I are sitting in my car as Egon gets a number from a girl he saw walking by. I sure don't miss those days of picking up girls for one-night stands. I shake my head as I watch him use all his classic moves on her. She is obviously feeding into his bullshit. Glancing at the time, I see that we are running late. Favor sent me a text earlier, and asked if we wanted to join her and the gang at the Wreck Room. I wasn't really up for hanging out, but decided to go since Egon and Wayne said they were going. I honk my horn at him, and he holds up his hand to give him a second. Shaking my head, I have to laugh.

"We should text the girls and let them know we're running late," Wayne says from the backseat.

"Yeah. Shoot out a text to them while I keep an eye on jerkoff there."

Wayne types on his phone, while Egon slides into the passenger seat.

"Homerun, my man," he smiles, holding up his phone.

"I don't know why you bother storing their numbers in there. You never stick around long enough for it even to save in the cloud." I start the car.

"Hey, just because you're an old, basically married man now..."

"Yeah, whatever. Ready?"

"Let's roll, bro," Egon says, slapping me on the shoulder.

It's already dark as I make the drive towards town. Egon and Wayne are in the middle of a debate about who is the best guitarist, when I notice something peculiar. Kevin Shore's car speeds by us, the front a mangled mess.

"That was Kevin's car, wasn't it?" Egon asks, as he turns to look at the tail lights of the car.

"Sure looked like it," Wayne says, his head facing the same direction.

"Wonder if they hit a deer or something," I muse, keeping my eyes on the road.

"Must have. The front end of his car was wrecked, bro." Egon sits back in his seat and plays air guitar to a song on the radio.

We continue to drive in the dark, down the winding road. Up ahead, I see what appears to be a figure standing in the middle of the road.

"You see that?" I ask no one in particular.

"Yeah. Someone is flagging us down." Egon sits forward to get a closer look.

I slow the car to a crawl as we pull up closer, and I see it's Cal. Stopping the car in front of him, the three of us jump out of the car.

"What happened? Where is Favor?" I ask, as I take in Cal's condition. He has bruising on his face and cuts on his arms.

"That *maniac* Kevin ran us off the road," Cal tells us, as he points in the direction of where it happened.

"*What?* He just drove past *us*." Wayne yells out and looks back in the direction of where we last saw Kevin.

I grab Cal. "Where's Favor?"

"The car fell down the ravine. She and Jana are trapped. I tried to get them out." Cal is already headed toward the car, and we follow behind.

We make our way down the ravine slowly, as we maneuver around rocks and soft patches of ground, until we reach a drop that has to be about four feet. I make the first jump down and help the others. Turning around in search of the car, we find it partially hidden behind some bushes. Egon hangs back to call 9-1-1 while Wayne, Cal, and I run to the car. It's on a weird ninety-degree angle, held in place by what seems to be some tree branches. The tree looks sturdy enough, and I hope it can hold up until we can free them.

Wayne tries the doors but is unable to open them. Jana is awake and hitting on the passenger window. Wayne attempts to reassure her, as I look in the driver side window to see Favor, who is knocked out, a long gash on the side of her left temple. The impact from the hit, along with the air bags, must have rendered her unconscious.

Thoughts of the possibility that I could lose her go through my head. I can't let that happen.

"I got out through the back window." Cal points, and we all run to the back of the car.

"I'll climb in and see if I can get them out," I say immediately, taking off my coat.

"Jana's legs are pinned," Cal explains.

I look at Wayne and fear seems to have gripped him.

"Eg...what's the ETA of the ambulance?" I yell out.

Egon walks towards us, his phone still to his ear. "Twenty minutes. I'll have to climb back to the top and wait for them," he says as he takes in the whole situation and communicates it back to the operator on the phone.

"*Fuck.*" Wayne yells out as he runs his hands through his hair in frustration.

"We might have to wait for 9-1-1 to get here," Cal announces.

Before either of us get a chance to agree or disagree, we hear a loud popping sound. The sound of tree branches breaking. The car makes a downward shift, and then suddenly stops. So much for waiting for 9-1-1.

"We gotta get them out *now*," I say, as I search frantically for something to break the windows with. Wayne immediately catches on to what I am doing, and he begins to search as well, while Cal tries to keep Jana calm.

Finally finding a broken log, I lift it and try to hit the window. The car shifts again...*fuck.* Looking over at Wayne, we both know there is only one other way.

"I'll go in through the back window," I tell him. I have to get her out. We have so much to live for together, and I can't lose her.

"Bro, let me go in. I owe it to her and her family, and my girl is in there too," Wayne says.

"No time to argue, man. I'm going in." I shake my head at him.

"No one should go in. We should wait." Cal tries to be the voice of reason.

We both ignore him and walk to the back of the car where Wayne gives me a lift up. I place half of my weight on the back of the car, and the car seems to hold. Climbing through the back window, I now have to see how to get the girls out.

"Oh, my God, Brice. We're going to die." Jana cries out.

"No one is going to die today." I refuse to let my mind go there.

"She hasn't moved since we hit. I checked for a pulse, but…" Jana's voice drifts off.

I can't think about that now. She isn't dead. "I'll have to get you out first, 'kay?"

Jana nods at me frantically. "My legs are pinned."

I try to angle my body towards the front to get a better look at what is pinning her. The front of the car is smashed in. *Double fuck.* "See if you can recline your seat backward," I tell her, hoping that it will work. She reaches to the side of her seat and the seat starts moving back. Thank goodness, something might just go right. I reach over and unsnap her seatbelt. "Okay. Do you feel any pain anywhere?"

"My head and my legs are sore."

291

"Okay, good." If she can feel pain, then she isn't paralyzed. "I'll try to be careful with you." Pulling her out of her seat, I call out to Wayne to catch her. Lifting her up, I push her as gently as possible out the back window. Wayne catches her just as the car shifts again. The car slides downward slightly and stops. My heart drops to the pit of my stomach.

"Bro, all good?" Wayne yells out.

"Yeah, all good," I lie. Fuck no, it's not all good. "Gotta make this quick. Not sure how much time we have left," I continue honestly. I climb to the front as smoothly as a guy my height can. I do the same thing that I had Jana do. I release Favor's seatbelt and recline her seat back. Climbing to the back again, I slide her out of her seat. In her unconscious state, she is dead weight. Calling out to Wayne to make sure he is ready to grab her, I lift her towards the opening of the back window. Wayne and Cal slide her out as I climb out behind her. I make sure she is safely clear of the car before I climb completely out. Feeling it shift downward again, I jump, just as the car goes crashing down to the bottom of the ravine. I land awkwardly on the ground and feel a jolt of pain go through my knee.

Wayne has Favor spread out on the ground, still unconscious. Ignoring the pain, I crawl my way over and check her pulse. It's there, albeit a faint one. Letting out a breath I didn't realize I was holding, I hear the distant sirens coming closer. Kissing the love of my life on her forehead, I say, "Help is coming, baby. Hang in there for me. Help is coming."

Chapter 29

Brice

The day after the accident, we are all at the hospital. Favor regained consciousness in the ambulance, and the doctors are keeping her for further observation. Jana and Cal were released earlier this morning, but stayed to wait for further updates on Favor's condition. Kyne and Birdie Hollister came up immediately after hearing the news of the accident.

They are both taking this hard, considering how Trevor died. Neither one of them has left her side since their arrival.

"Mom, I'm okay, really," Favor says, as she tries to elevate her bed. Her mother instantly stands to help her daughter sit up, and fluffs her pillows for her.

"Please, I need you to take it easy." Birdie kisses her daughter's forehead. "You don't know how much I was worried when we received that phone call last night."

"Both of us." Kyne stands up and squeezes his daughter's hand. Tears fall down his face as he gives his daughter a faint smile. "I-I have to tell you something."

"Dad, its not necessary. We both said a lot to each other through the years. I'm just happy to have a father, that's all."

"I wasted so many years," he says under his breath.

"We all did." Birdie smiles warmly at her husband and daughter.

"Thanks to Brice, I'm alive." My fiancée smiles at me as I stand at the foot of her bed.

"Brice, I can't thank you enough for risking your life for our little girl." Birdie gives me a hug.

Kyne extends his hand for me to shake. I pause for a second and look at it. Deciding, if Favor can push the past aside, so can I, so I take his hand.

"I didn't do anything." What they don't seem to understand is she is my life, my reason to live.

There's a knock on the door and the same police officers who were on Cal's case walk in. Instantly recognizing me and Favor, they nod at us. Cop number one seems to be a Kyne Hollister fan, and instantly falls all over himself at seeing him.

"We are here to ask some questions about the accident last night," Cop number two says, taking out his notepad and pen.

"That was no accident. That son of a bitch, Kevin Shore, ran my fiancée's car over."

"Are you sure?" Cop number one says.

"Yes, I am. Cal, Jana, and I saw him and his friends in the car."

"Cal? As in Calson Deysine? The one that was attacked a few months ago in the club?" Cop number two asks.

"Yes, the very one," I say, through gritted teeth.

"Is Mr. Deysine still here for questioning?" Cop number one asks.

"In the waiting room," I reply, as I walk over to Favor's side, holding her hand.

"And where were you, Mr. Walker?" Cop number two asks.

"I was driving into town with Wayne and Egon, to meet my fiancée and friends at the Wreck Room. On our way into town, Kevin's car drove past us. The front of his car was badly damaged, but we didn't think anything of it. We thought it was a deer or something. Anyway, we kept driving until we saw Cal standing in the middle of the road, waving us down."

"Did you have an altercation with Mr. Shore earlier yesterday, Miss Hollister?" Cop number one asks.

"Not myself, but my friend Jana did. She was dancing, and Kevin wanted to dance. She pushed him away, and he got upset. We left right after."

"And soon after that, he ran you off the road?" Cop number one presses.

"Correct."

"Listen, officers, I want this madman placed behind bars. As you know, my wife and I have already lost a son to a car accident, and we almost lost a daughter. A person like this clearly should not be walking the streets."

"We will do everything in our power to do so, sir. We'll have to question the other witnesses," Cop number two says, as Cop number one heads towards the door.

Both officers exit the room to question Cal and Jana, and I step out to see what I can overhear.

"Mr. Deysine, it is nice to see that you are up and about," Cop number one says.

Cal looks down at his feet, and Jana gives him a hard look. "Are you here to question us about the maniac, Kevin Shore?" Jana asks, while Wayne holds her from behind in his arms.

"Yes. Miss Hollister and Mr. Walker have advised us that Kevin is the one who ran the car, that you were a passenger in, off the road."

"Yes, he did. He is also the one that beat up Cal," Jana cries out. "He could have killed us all."

"Is that true, Mr. Deysine? Is Mr. Shore the person who beat you up that night?"

Cal looks at Jana and back at his feet again. He seems to not know what to do.

"I swear Cal, if you don't tell them the truth, I'll never speak to you again. He almost killed us. And Favor, who has always been there for you." Jana tries to go over to Cal, but Wayne holds her in place.

Cal's chin trembles before turning his attention back to the cops. "Yes. Yes, he is the one that beat me up that night. He is also the one that ran us off the road last night." He whispers out the words.

Relief settles over me that Cal has finally admitted the truth. Egon walks over to me and claps a hand on my shoulder. "How is my future sister-in-law?"

Looking away from the cops talking with Cal, I focus on Egon. "Good. Anxious to get out of here."

"When can we break her out of this joint?"

"Doctor said he would clear her to leave later today. She is going to go home to recuperate. Her parents are beside themselves."

"Going with?"

"Yeah. I can't let her out of my sight, especially after what happened last night." A lump forms in my throat. "I can't believe that I almost lost her." The emotions from last night overwhelm me, and I can't talk as I hang my head.

"Bro, you saved her. Don't focus on the 'would of, could of' bullshit. Focus on the here and now. She is alive because of you. Now, if that don't earn you a lifetime of blowjobs, then I don't know what will," he says with a laugh.

Leave it to Egon to turn this moment into sex. I have to laugh at his comments, as somewhere in the back of my head, I wonder, *Has it earned me that privilege?*

Epilogue
Favor

Spending the past two weeks at my parents' house while I recuperate has been great. My parents have shown me the love I'd always hoped for, and Brice has become completely overprotective. I swear, if I so much as act like I am about to trip, he is running to catch me. That accident shook him to his core, and it has made me realize just how much we are meant to be together. I still can't believe he risked his life to go into the car to rescue Jana and me. He sprained his knee in the process, but the doctors said he would be fine and back to one hundred percent in no time at all. Thank goodness for that, as discussions with pro teams are just beginning for him, and an injury could've put a stop to it all.

It's wonderful to see how my parents have completely welcomed Brice into our family. Brice's mom offered to fly out to see me, but I didn't want her to take off work on my account, so I thanked her, but told her not to worry. She has called me every single day to check on me, and I love her even more for it.

Kevin Shore and his friends were arrested soon after my release from the hospital. Kevin was arrested on two criminal charges; the first being a hate crime, and the second, for purposefully running someone off the road. Kevin's father, who is a well-known attorney in the state, will represent him in court. I'm afraid the court of public opinion has already condemned Kevin, with me being Kyne Hollister's daughter. My father has placed a lot of pressure on the District Attorney to pursue this to the fullest extent of the law.

Walking outside on my family's property, Brice and I are enjoying some alone time together.

"Ready to get back to campus?" he asks me, while holding my hand as we walk down a pathway leading to the woods.

"Yes, I guess. I'll miss having my big bed, and you in it." I stop to give him a quick kiss.

"Not like that big bed of yours has seen any action." He winks at me. The doctor gave me the 'all clear' a week ago. Brice, being so damn overprotective, has resisted the urge, as well as my nightly pleadings.

"By no fault, or lack of trying on my part," I retort.

"I just want to make sure you're healthy."

"The doctor said I was good to go." I put on a pouty face.

He smiles at me and kisses my lips. "Babe, you don't know what it was like seeing you like that. I thought I might lose you."

"I'm okay. Especially when I'm in your arms. Besides, I'm made from tougher stuff. I'm Kyne Hollister's daughter, after all." I give him a sheepish grin.

"I know. Just be patient with me, 'kay?"

"Okay. I get it." And I do. It would've torn my heart out if I'd seen him that way, so I can give him this.

"Hey, I got a call from Egon earlier."

"What is he up to?"

"His band got an offer. It's not the best offer, but it's something. They get to record one album, and the record company will send them out on tour with one of their bigger acts, to promote State of Mind's debut album."

I stop in my tracks, and begin jumping up and down. *Wait, did I just become Jana?* "That is great. We have to celebrate when we get back."

"Jana and Cal have already started planning the party," he says, holding me in place, fearful I might hurt myself with my jumping.

"When do they start recording?"

"Over the summer. They'll be heading to New York to cut the album."

"Will he be dropping out of school?"

"Not sure. Probably. I just don't see how he will be able to work on the album, and then promote it while in school."

"Is that what he said?"

He shrugs his shoulders. "Nah. It's what he *didn't* say over the phone. I think he is waiting for us to get back to talk to me. We're like brothers, and have always been together, since we were kids. It's going to be strange, now that one of us is leaving. I'm happy for him, though."

"The distance won't matter. Your friendship is strong."

"I know. It's just going to suck not being able to hang with my boy whenever. But hey, I still have you." He smiles down at me.

"Yes, you do, and don't you forget it." We kiss before intertwining our fingers, and begin walking again. "Hey, I have an idea. Why don't *we* go to New York this summer? You and I haven't figured out what to do, anyway."

He stops to give it some further thought. "You know, that might work."

"Exactly. After we break for summer, we can spend a week with my parents, and then a week with your mom, before we head to New York for the summer. It will give us two months with Egon before you have to be back in time for football practice."

He cups my chin with his fingers. "You wouldn't mind?"

"As long as I'm with you, it doesn't matter."

"I knew there was a reason why I love you." He leans in for a kiss.

"Ditto," I tell him as I gently grab his collar, pulling him closer to my lips.

The pieces of my life have finally fallen into place. I have my parents back, and our relationship has never been stronger. I have my best friends, and Wayne, the "brother" I can always count on to be there for me. And I have Brice, the football player I never wanted to date but always knew I needed. Life is perfect.

THE END

A Letter From the Author

Dear Reader,

As always I thank you for taking the time to read my book and making this journey with me. I hope that you enjoyed Favor and Brice's story as much as I enjoyed writing it. In some ways Brice is currently my new favorite book boyfriend, shhh, don't tell Tick that (smile).

As usual I took on some hard topics and I try to show there is a path to happiness. In some ways writing this book has helped me to grow as an individual as I did my research on the hard topics of Drunk Driving, and Hate Crimes. I do not condone any of this in any form whatsoever.

If you or someone you know is a victim of a hate crime, I urge you to call the police and never take matters into your own hands.

I also urge you to never drink and drive. It's not just your life that is on the line.

Be Healthy, Be Safe, and most importantly Be Blessed,

Autumn Sand

Acknowledgements

I can't believe this is my third book! Boy does time fly. I have enjoyed each and every moment of my writing journey and I am so happy that you have come along for the ride.

Now for the favorite part of my journey, acknowledgements. I could never thank these people enough who have helped me make this happen. First, I want to thank the reader for reading. I appreciate each and everyone one of you, thank you. Next, my incredible friend and P.A. Britta Neal who always manages to get me back on track. Jennifer Reynolds, my wonderful publicist, who is constantly promoting my work. Tracy Willoughby and Kelley Benson, who started out as readers but I now consider my friends.

Of course, I have to thank my street team, Autumn's Twisted Sisters! What an incredible group these ladies are. They are very supportive and I love them to pieces. Shout-outs t Carl, Richard, Chucky, and Melanie for being there every step of the way.

There are a host of other's that help to make my world better and they know I love them all.

About the Author

Autumn Sand was born and raised in New York City. Considering herself a true New Yorker in every way from the restaurants that she eats to the shoe fetish she has. Oh yes at one-time Autumn has had a shoe collection of 300 and has the credit card statements to prove it. Other than shoe shopping she has various interests such as reading, writing, and traveling. Autumn has worked in the fashion industry for most of her adult life before pursuing writing. She is reluctant to call herself an author but considers herself a person who writes words that people just so happen to like to read. As you can tell Autumn has a sarcastic sense of humor and loves to make her friends laugh in all occasions. She enjoys a good glass of wine but her go to drink of choice is a Jack Daniels and coke with a twist of lime.

I would love to hear from you. Please email me if you would like to join my mailing list for future updates on upcoming books or just to tell me your favorite part of the book. Don't forget if you loved the book to rate it and leave a comment on your eBook forum.

Email: contact@autumnsandauthor.com

Facebook: https://www.facebook.com/autumn.sandsauthor

Twitter: https://twitter.com/autumn_sand

Goodreads: https://www.goodreads.com/autumn_sand_author

Website: http://www.autumnsandauthor.com/

www.ingramcontent.com/pod-product-compliance
Lightning Source LLC
Chambersburg PA
CBHW062123170626
46813CB00002B/555